A MIDNIGHT CLEAR

By Kristi Astor

A Midnight Clear

"Swept Away" in *Lords of Desire*

By Kristi Astor writing as Kristina Cook

To Love a Scoundrel

Undressed

Unveiled

Unlaced

A MIDNIGHT CLEAR

KRISTI ASTOR

ZEBRA BOOKS
KENSINGTON PUBLISHING CORP.

http://www.kensingtonbooks.com

ZEBRA BOOKS are published by

Kensington Publishing Corp.
119 West 40th Street
New York, NY 10018

All Kensington titles, imprints, and distributed lines are available at special quantity discounts for bulk purchases for sales promotion, premiums, fund-raising, educational, or institutional use.

Special book excerpts or customized printings can also be created to fit specific needs. For details, write or phone the office of the Kensington Special Sales Manager: Attn. Special Sales Department. Kensington Publishing Corp., 119 West 40th Street, New York, NY 10018. Phone: 1-800-221-2647.

Zebra and the Z logo Reg. U.S. Pat. & TM Off.

ISBN-13: 978-1-4201-0547-6
ISBN-10: 1-4201-0547-7

First Printing: November 2010

10 9 8 7 6 5 4 3 2 1

Printed in the United States of America

Chapter 1

December 1908
London

"What's this, the society page?" Troy asked, lifting the newssheet from the chair's rolled arm and turning toward his aunt with a smile. "Do you really read this rubbish?"

"And why not?" she replied indignantly, dropping her lorgnette between her ample breasts. "Far more interesting than the financial page." Her faded eyes narrowed as she studied him closely. "Is that paint there in your whiskers?"

"Hmm, what?" Absently, Troy stroked his chin.

She scowled at him as if he were a naughty child. "I said 'paint.' In your whiskers."

"Ah, yes. Likely so." He sat, resting one ankle on the opposite knee. "But don't fret, my dear aunt. I'll make myself presentable before tea. Now, let me see . . ." He snapped the paper before settling it in his lap, his eyes scanning the page. "I can't for the life of me . . ."

His gaze skimmed across a photo of a woman, one cheek slightly turned, her dark eyes staring straight into the camera's lens, the barest hint of a smile tipping the corners of her mouth. Troy's breath caught in his throat as the thrill of recognition washed over him. It was *her*. Dear God, but it was. A name. There must be a name—

"For the life of you, what?"

He nodded, his hands suddenly shaking. "I'm sorry. What?"

"You said, 'I can't for the life of me,' and then naught else. Troy? Dearest?"

Her words barely registered in his brain. Instead, his eyes roamed the text beneath the picture, looking for the name he knew he would never forget, once learned.

> *Sir William Granger and his lovely daughter, Miss Miranda Granger, have lately retired to their country estate in Surrey, having returned from New York but a fortnight ago aboard the* RMS *Mauretania. It is rumored that they will be among the guests of distinction at the Christmastime opening of the new seaside resort, the Grandview Hotel in Eastbourne. As one of the hotel's principal investors, Sir William . . .*

Miss Miranda Granger. He let out his breath in a rush, his gaze involuntarily drawn back to the woman's face, immortalized in newsprint. His muse. He had to paint her—*had* to. He'd thought of nothing else since that night so many months ago, the mysterious woman standing on the ocean liner's deck with eyes that hinted of sorrow and despair even while she smiled shyly at him, her face illuminated by the silvery light of the moon. He'd asked for her name then, but she had refused to give it. At the time, it hadn't mattered overmuch.

He had only sought to remember the exact curve of her neck, the tilt of her lashes, the rose-colored hue of her lips, the gentle swell of her breasts beneath her bodice. She had been delicate—so very delicate, so fragile. Though he could not fathom why, her face and form had captivated him beyond reason.

"Troy, darling, whatever is the matter with you? You're positively trembling!"

He shook his head, attempting desperately to clear it. "Am I? How very odd." It took every ounce of his reserve to keep his voice steady. "I say, what do you know of Sir William Granger? Of Surrey?"

"Obviously we are not acquainted, though I do hear an *on dit* about him now and then. Why ever do you ask?"

"And what of this Grandview Hotel in East-bourne?"

"Simply stunning, they say, with a grand lawn sloping down to the sea and excellent views of Beachy Head. Opening in a fortnight, I believe. All the papers are carrying reports. A grand fete being planned for Christmas Day, the actress Simone DuBois engaged to perform. Didn't the paper say that Sir William Granger would be in attendance? With his daughter Miss Granger, the poor girl." His aunt brushed crumbs from her voluminous skirts.

Instantly, his attention snapped into focus. "What do you know of Miss Granger?"

"Only that her father is a widower twice over, and she has two half sisters to raise—hellions both, from what I hear. His last wife died nearly a decade ago, and still the man hasn't remarried." His aunt shook her head, clucking her tongue against her teeth in disapproval. "The poor girl's a spinster now."

"Is she?" She'd seemed too young for that distinction.

"Indeed." His aunt nodded. "And so unfair. A daughter should not be forced to sacrifice her own happiness in order to raise her siblings. Wherever will that leave her when her father's gone?"

Troy swallowed hard, his gaze fixed upon Miss Granger's photograph. "A fine question."

"Well, his fortune is rumored to be enormous. Even split three ways it will leave her a very rich woman, if nothing else. That should bring her some comfort, eh?"

"I must go," Troy said, carefully folding the page in two and tucking it inside his waistcoat.

His aunt leaned forward in her seat, her eyes regarding him sharply. "Go? Where?"

He rose on shaking legs. "To the Grandview Hotel. The opening. I must see to the arrangements straightaway."

His aunt just shook her head. "Don't be daft, Troy. It's by invitation only, my dear boy. Whatever has come over you? Besides, what about Christmas?"

He took out his watch and flipped open the case. Half past four. Damn, he couldn't ring François now—not with his aunt listening in. He'd have to hurry to François' office, instead, before he left for the day. No time to waste. "If you'll excuse me," he said with a bow, then hastened toward the door.

"My paper!" he heard his aunt sputter indignantly as he stepped out into the foyer.

There must be a way, he thought, his heels clicking against the floorboards. Now that he had identified his muse, he could not let her slip through his fingers, not this time. After all, he'd only seen her thus far in the light of the moon. Why, there was still the light of the sun, the false light of the electric lamps to paint her by. And paint her he must.

The three half-finished canvases in his room were testament to his obsession with the heretofore-nameless woman, and he knew enough of his own talents to know that his obsession was the key to his success. Hadn't his masters in France said as much?

He must somehow secure an invitation to the opening of the Grandview Hotel, and he must find her—the mysterious Miss Granger. His paintbrush would unlock her secrets; of that he was sure.

Two weeks later . . .
The Grandview Hotel, Eastbourne

"They say, miss, that on a clear day you can see the chalk cliffs at Beachy Head." Sullivan bustled about the room, unpacking trunks and hatboxes and settling toiletries on the wide marble vanity.

"Is that so? How lovely," Miranda murmured, peering out the window as the sun began its slow descent toward the sea.

"Will you be going down to tea?" Sullivan asked, stopping to stare at her with a furrowed brow.

Her father would expect it, of course. Miranda had claimed a headache and made her excuses upon their arrival at the lavish resort, leaving her father to his many associates—his fellow investors in this new, grand establishment. She only wished to be alone. Had her father no idea of the significance of the date? Perhaps not, but Miranda would never forget. *Never.*

"I don't believe I will. I'm still feeling poorly," she said at last, the lie slipping effortlessly from her tongue. "I'll send a message to my father."

"Very well. Shall I help you undress?"

Sullivan's displeasure was evident, but as Miranda's lady's maid, she had no right to openly criticize, nor would she presume to do so.

As the maid began to remove the pins from Miranda's enormous silk-covered hat, a knock sounded on the door, startling them both. A hat pin clattered loudly to the vanity, then rolled onto the thick carpet below.

"Likely the chambermaid," Sullivan said, striding out toward the room's antechamber. "I'll ask her to return later."

Miranda turned toward the vanity and sat on the chair before the looking glass. The face that stared back at her was a stranger's face, one she barely recognized as her own. Lately she'd taken to avoiding mirrors. She did not want to see this new Miranda, this foreign person inhabiting the shell of a body her old self had left behind.

Turning her face from the glass, she sighed heavily. The high, lace collar of her blouse was itchy and constricting, as if daring her to take a deep, restorative breath. Voices rumbled in the antechamber, and then she heard the door shut. Miranda sighed again. Sullivan would return any moment now; time to school her features into a placid mask.

"Who was it?" she asked when the maid reappeared.

"A man, Miss Granger. An American. Wishing to speak with you. I told him no, of course, but he was quite insistent."

Miranda frowned. "How odd. A gentleman? Did he give his name?"

"Yes, but it is not one I recognize. A Mr. Troy Davenport, miss. He's clearly not a gentleman or he would never have made such an inappropriate request."

"He didn't expect to converse with me in my rooms, did he?"

"He was bold, but not that brassy. No, he said you should meet him in the Rose Salon, at half past five. I told him you would not consider it."

Miranda couldn't help but smile. "And what did he say to that?"

"Just one word, miss. *Maury.* Has it any meaning to you?"

Maury? Miranda clutched at her skirts in confusion as she pondered the cryptic message. Could he mean the *Mauretania?* The RMS *Mauretania* was the passenger liner on which they had traveled to New York early in the fall, and then back again just last month. Had this Mr. Davenport been a fellow passenger on one of the voyages? Whatever other explanation was there? And if so, what was his purpose in calling on her now?

"The ocean liner," Miranda said, shaking her head in bewilderment. "I think he means the ship."

"Yes, of course. I'm sure you're right—I've often heard it called 'the *Maury,*' though it didn't occur to me. Well, no matter. I sent him away and told him to stay away, lest I'd notify the authorities."

"Thank you." Miranda nodded, glad to be rid of any intrusion. "I think I'd like to lie down, if you don't mind. I can manage my clothes, if you'll only help me dislodge this ridiculous hat without ruining my hair. Perhaps I will change and join my father later, after tea."

"Very well, miss," Sullivan said, then set to work. "Shall I go check on Miss Grace and Miss Gertrude, then?"

Miranda nearly groaned aloud at the mention of her sisters. She'd seen them settled into their own chamber, just next door, where they were no doubt still chattering happily as their own lady's maid bustled about, unpacking their things. Lord knows the two of them hadn't paused for a breath since they'd set off from home that morning in their father's enormous Mercedes touring motorcar.

"There's no need for you to check on Grace and Gertie," she said at last. "Let Bridget deal with them. It *is* her job, as disagreeable as it might be. Go and have your own tea, Sullivan. It's been a long day, hasn't it?"

She nodded her head, her steel-gray hair entirely immobile beneath the old-fashioned lace cap she wore. "Indeed, miss. I'll leave you to your rest."

Minutes later, Miranda found herself mercifully alone, sitting on the edge of her bed, contemplating taking a nap. How she'd hoped that spending Christmas at the Grandview would be just the tonic she needed to make her forget her past, to get her through the always-painful holidays without thinking of things best forgotten. A change of scenery would surely provide a much-needed distraction, and she'd readily agreed to spend a fortnight there, enjoying the season's festivities. And yet, even now, dark thoughts began to crowd her mind, making a nap impossible. She rose and went to the window, instead. Pulling back the crisp, white curtains, she peered out, able to make out the chalky cliffs of Beachy Head in the distance, as promised.

They were beautiful, yes—but horribly treacherous, a popular site for ending one's life. What a horrible way to die, she thought—falling into the cold, rocky sea from such a height. Still, she could relate to such depths of despair. She'd been there. A shiver worked its way down her spine, and she let the curtain drop back against the glass.

Her gaze was drawn toward the antechamber, toward the room's door that led out into the wood-paneled corridor. Who was this mysterious Mr. Davenport, and what did he want with her? What would possess the man to bypass her father's protection, and boldly rap on her chamber's door? As Sullivan suggested, no gentleman of her acquaintance would do such a thing. Of course, Sullivan *had* said he was an American, and the rules of propriety were a bit more relaxed across the Atlantic. Still, this went beyond the pale. She'd never heard the likes of it.

Clasping her hands into fists, she searched her memory—if nothing else, then to escape other, more painful memories. Had she met an American on board the *Mauretania*? One with whom she had become well enough acquainted to warrant such an intrusion?

No. She had mostly kept to herself. Except that one night, the night she'd escaped from Grace and Gertie's silly prattle and found herself on the second-class deck, a place where no one would dream to look for her. She'd stood at the rail and stared down at the black water, the image of the moon reflected off its surface, and she'd spoken to no one. Except . . .

The painter. A beautiful man with hair the color of bronze, his pale eyes piercing and arresting, even in the moonlight. He'd been an American, but she hadn't dared to give him her name. How could he possibly have learned her identity? And even if he had, what would he be doing there at the Grandview Hotel?

She raised the back of one hand to her mouth, refusing to recognize the swell of hope that rose in her breast. How she'd longed to see him once more, to speak with him at length, to learn what moved him to put his brush to canvas. Had her deepest wish, her most secret desire come true?

No. It was impossible. Besides, she should have forgotten him the moment she left his company, as he had no doubt forgotten her. As it should be. Hadn't she learned her lesson, in the most painful way imaginable?

She forced herself to turn from the door, to walk back toward the vanity. Her gaze landed on her watch, a Chinoiserie-enameled oval hanging from a delicate gold chain. With shaking hands, she turned it over. Half past five. Turning back toward the door, she considered her options. Dare she?

Sullivan would not approve, and her father would be livid. They were her keepers, the two of them. Yet she had a mind of her own—she was a grown woman of twenty-eight, not a child.

Besides, roaming about the hotel was preferable to sitting in her room thinking dark thoughts, wasn't it? She would go—if only to satisfy her curiosity. She need not speak to him; she would simply walk by and see if, by chance, it *was* him.

And if it was . . . well, she need not worry until it proved to be so. With a steadying breath, she slipped the watch chain over her head, then went to the wardrobe and retrieved her woolen coat. Why, she couldn't say, except that she wanted to be prepared for any eventuality, including escaping out-of-doors if need be.

She slipped into the coat and reached for her reticule, stuffing her gloves inside before hurrying through the antechamber and out the door, closing it softly behind herself before she had the chance to reconsider. Her palms damp, she reached into her bag for the key. After glancing around to make certain that no one was observing her, she slid the key into the lock and turned it, then slipped the key back into her bag and hurried away.

Slightly breathless, she found the Rose Salon only minutes later, after inquiring with a bellman.

The door was ajar, the room empty. But as she stepped closer, she saw that the room wasn't empty, after all—a lone man stood in the corner, gazing up at a painting on the pale rose-colored wall, his hands clasped behind his back.

Miranda reached for the doorjamb, trying to steady herself as she searched for something familiar in the man's stance. And then, as if he sensed her presence there in the doorway, he turned.

And there it was, the face that had teased her dreams for so many nights. Vivid green eyes startling in a sun-browned face, deep bronze hair falling carelessly across his forehead. It was *him*, no doubt about it, though she could not fathom how or why.

Nor did she want to know—couldn't afford to know. With a sharp intake of breath, Miranda turned and fled.

Chapter 2

Troy spun toward the door, just in time to see a blur of gray disappear down the corridor. *Could it be?* His heart hammered against his rib cage, and for a moment he found himself unable to move a muscle. Instead he stood there like a damned fool, staring at the empty doorway for what seemed an interminable time before he came to his senses and went after her.

As clumsy as a schoolboy, he hurried out into the corridor, nearly colliding with a bellman pushing a cart laden with trunks.

"Pardon me, sir," the boy called out as Troy righted himself and looked wildly about. *Where had she gone?*

There, a flash of gray, at the end of the corridor. Off he went, forcing his gait to maintain an air of dignity, groaning each time a hotel guest stepped into his path, keeping him from his quarry. He dared not call out to her; he wasn't even entirely certain it *was* her, as he'd gotten little more than a glimpse of the back of her coat, of her long neck, of dark hair piled high upon her crown. Whoever she was, she wore no hat and she was decidedly alone, unchaperoned.

He hurried his step as she made yet another turn and disappeared from view.

"Where's the fire, young man?" A very round, very dour woman stood in his path, a walking cane gripped in one gloved hand.

"If you'll pardon me, ma'am," he said, tipping his hat as he made to go around her.

Her eyes narrowed at once. "Aren't you Agnes Davenport's nephew? The painter, from New York?"

Bloody hell. It figured; hundreds of people there at the hotel, and who does he run into at a time like this but the *one* guest acquainted with his aunt. Gritting his teeth, he forced himself to remove his hat and nod.

"I am, indeed. Troy Davenport at your service, madam."

Her frown gave way to a jowly smile, her faded blue eyes dancing merrily. "Why, I've a painting of yours, a landscape, hanging in my front parlor. A gift from your aunt. Lovely, just lovely."

Ah, so dear old Aunt Aggie was now giving them away. To curry favor with the aristocracy, no doubt.

"Are you on your way to tea, then?" she asked, clutching her cane more tightly. "I'm to meet my granddaughter in the dining room, but I'm sure she wouldn't mind—"

"I'm afraid I cannot," Troy interrupted, "but perhaps another day?"

Her eyes narrowed a fraction at the slight. "Tomorrow, then? For breakfast."

Damn, but she was persistent. "Very well, madam. I'd be honored." He needed to end this discourse and find Miss Granger, and fast.

"Go, then." She waved her cane in the air. "Off to wherever you were headed in such a hurry. I shall see you tomorrow, at half past eight. Oh, I nearly forgot!" Troy watched in carefully concealed exasperation as she fished in her bag and produced a crisp, white calling card, then pressed it into his hand. "Ask to be shown to my table. Good day, Mr. Davenport."

At last, she dismissed him with a nod. *Thank God.*

He nearly ran to the end of the corridor and turned right, finding himself in a large, glass-domed atrium. He looked about wildly, but Miss Granger was nowhere to be seen. *Damn it to hell.* He'd lost her. Unless . . .

Several pairs of French doors opened up to a patio, and beyond that lay the hotel's great lawn. A wooden boardwalk edged the far side of the lawn, and past that stretched the wide, sandy shore.

In seconds, he was striding purposefully across the grass, his eyes scanning the clumps of guests that gathered here and there, enjoying the unseasonably warm, sea-scented air.

And there she was, at the far end of the boardwalk. Alone. The hem of her rose-and-white striped skirt flapped against her gray coat; a silk sash danced on the breeze. For a moment Troy simply stood there and watched her, noting the way the waning sun cast golden shadows across her hair. One dark lock escaped its binding and fell carelessly across her shoulder.

Reaching up to rub his chin with his palm, he took a step toward her, then stopped. As if sensing his approach, she began to glide away, off toward a sandy path at the edge of the boardwalk that wound through low, wind-gnarled trees.

On silent feet, Troy followed. Like a hunter closing in on its prey, his heart accelerated, the steady pounding discernible over the din of the incoming tide. A pair of gulls dipped past his head, calling loudly to one another as he closed the distance between himself and the woman, the anticipation hurrying his step.

When he was no more than ten feet from her, she turned, her eyes widening with surprise.

Troy froze, then reached up to remove his hat.

"Dear God, it really *is* you," she said, her voice a mere whisper. "But how . . ." She shook her head, looking slightly dazed.

"Troy Davenport, ma'am. We met aboard the *Mauretania*. And you are Miss Miranda Granger, I presume?"

"What do you want?" she asked, her voice now steady and firm.

"Only to speak with you. May I join you?" Without waiting for her reply, he hurried to her side and offered his arm.

"I . . . I haven't a chaperone." She shook her head, taking a step back from him.

"I mean you no harm, Miss Granger. Just a simple stroll, nothing more."

"Well . . . perhaps," she faltered, taking his arm at last and falling into step beside him. "I . . . this is quite irregular."

"And I sincerely apologize for that. But as I had no one to make the introduction, there was no other way."

In the distance, Troy could make out a line of carriages and the occasional motorcar. Filled with fancily dressed ladies and gentlemen, no doubt, out for a late-afternoon drive up and down the promenade.

"How did you learn my name?" Miss Granger asked, drawing his attention away from the sounds of jingling reins and sputtering engines in the distance.

"The society page, of all places. I was in London, visiting my aunt, and there you were. In the *Daily Mirror*."

A faint smile tipped the corners of her mouth. "That photograph was taken several years ago. I'm surprised you recognized me."

"You've not changed at all. Except, perhaps, grown more lovely."

He saw her blush, her eyes trained on the path ahead. "And what connection have you to the hotel?"

"None at all, I'm afraid. Finagling an invitation took a bit of creativity on my part."

She shook her head. "But why?"

No reason to beat around the bush. "I came because I had to see you," he said.

She stopped abruptly and released his arm. "I'm flattered," she said, obviously choosing her words carefully. "But I cannot see why you would presume that I would wish to see *you*, Mr. Davenport."

Troy silently cursed. This was going to be far trickier than he'd imagined. How in God's name was he going to get her to agree to let him paint her? *But I must,* he reminded himself. Somehow.

Inwardly, Miranda winced as her words hit their mark. She saw the indecision darken his features. It took every ounce of fortitude she possessed to remain so calm, so dispassionate, when her emotions were in such turmoil. All these months he'd been nothing but a fantasy—a handsome, mysterious face to envision as she touched herself in places she knew she should not dare. But she did; oh, how she did—wicked, wanton woman that she was.

Could he read her thoughts? Did he know just what she imagined those hands of his did to her, those rough, calloused hands that were nothing like the hands of the gentlemen of her acquaintance? A flush stole up her neck, warming her skin beneath the high, lace collar of her blouse.

A man like Troy Davenport could never be anything but a fantasy to her, one who lived across the vast ocean—and yet here he stood, in the flesh.

And dear Lord, but he was handsome, somehow

boyish and virile all at once. Just as Paul had been, she realized. Did that explain the attraction? Feeling crushed by the weight of his stare, she dropped her gaze, forcing aside all thoughts of Paul, of his betrayal.

With a heavy sigh, she glanced back up at Mr. Davenport, allowing herself to study him more closely. He was tall, nearly six feet to be sure, and far broader in the shoulders than she'd remembered. His suit of clothes was well made if only slightly out of fashion, and the bowler hat he carried was noticeably shabby around the brim.

He was likely several years her junior, she realized with a start. On the ocean liner's deck, lit only by the moon, there had been no hint of his youth, but now . . . now it was plainly evident in his features. She swallowed hard, suddenly wishing he would say something—anything—to break the tense silence.

At last, he did. "Indeed, Miss Granger, I apologize for my presumptuousness. Still, it could not be helped. We have business to discuss, you and I."

Miranda shook her head in frustration. "I cannot understand what business we might have, Mr. Davenport. We are barely acquainted, having only conversed for a half hour—no more—and many months ago, at that."

He stroked his chin, drawing Miranda's attention back to his hands. They were the hands of an artist, the fingers long and elegant, the nails stained with traces of pigment.

"I'd say it was at least an hour, our conversation," he answered, and Miranda could only hope that he hadn't noticed her fascination with his fingers.

"And what if it was? Surely by now you realize that I had escaped from the first-class deck on the night in question, seeking solitude and anonymity. You were simply a nameless man with whom I gazed at the moon, nothing more." She let out her breath in a huff. "I really must go. If my father were to find me here, alone with you—"

"What would he do? You're a grown woman, are you not?"

Miranda bristled at the insinuation. "I am an unmarried woman, sir, and under my father's protection. And you are an interloper here, from what I can tell. However did you manage an invitation?"

"Oh, I have my ways," he said cryptically. "And look"—he produced a white card from his waistcoat—"I even have an invitation to take breakfast tomorrow with"—his eyes scanned the card—"Lady Philomena Barclay and her granddaughter."

Miranda spoke before she thought better of it. "Oh, good heavens, Lady Barclay will have you married off to her granddaughter by teatime. After all, no one else will have her."

A smile spread across his face, crinkling the corners of his eyes. "Is that so? Well, then, I suppose I should thank you for the warning."

"What do you want from me, Mr. Davenport?" she asked, abandoning all pretense of cordiality now. There was no more time for games. She must know at once why he was pursuing her so she could nip it in the bud. "If it's money, then—"

"I don't want your money." He folded his arms across his chest and met her gaze with his own unflinching one.

Her cheeks burned in response. "Well, then, I don't know what you might have heard, but I am a lady, and—"

"I don't want your virtue, either."

She hadn't thought it possible, but her cheeks burned hotter still. He was a stranger. If he didn't want her money, didn't want her virtue, as he so casually phrased it, what else could he possibly want? What else was there?

"I only want to paint you," he said softly, as if he'd read her mind.

Miranda thought she must have misheard. "To *what*?"

"Paint you. I must paint you."

For a moment, she simply stared at him in disbelief. *Paint me?* "Have you lost your mind, Mr. Davenport? You can't paint me."

"Why ever not? Anyway, I *have* begun to paint you. Several times, in fact, from memory alone. But I must have you sit for me. Here, at the Grandview. Now."

"You mean sit . . . sit for a portrait?" she stuttered.

"No, nothing as pedestrian as that. A study of light, perhaps. A series of paintings, here by the sea at different times of day. Yet another series indoors, studying the effects of different lighting upon your skin."

Miranda could not conceal her shock; she simply gaped at the man as if he'd grown two heads. "I'll see that my father has you removed from the hotel at once," she snapped, then turned on her heel and began walking briskly back toward the boardwalk.

Troy watched her retreat in stunned silence. *No, it cannot end this way.* "Don't go, Miss Granger," he called out, catching up to her and matching her stride for stride. "You must hear me out."

She stopped and turned to face him once more. "You're mistaken, Mr. Davenport. I needn't do anything I don't want to do."

"If I were a rich man, you would hear me out, wouldn't you?"

"If you were a rich man, Mr. Davenport, we would not be having this conversation."

The irony almost made him laugh aloud. Still, he could not help himself; he reached for her slender wrist and captured it in his grasp. "Is that what you think of me?"

She tugged her wrist from his hand, but not before he felt the bounding of her pulse beneath his fingers. "You've suggested that I do something indecent, sir. What else am I to think of you?"

Troy raked one hand through his hair, groaning inwardly in frustration. A lady needed to be wooed, he realized—a bit too late, it would seem. He'd been far too abrupt in his approach, and far too out of practice where ladies were concerned. "I've gone about this badly," he said, maintaining a respectful distance so as not to frighten her away. "Pray, forgive me, Miss Granger. I admit I can be a bit"—what was the word?— "*overzealous* at times," he finished. "It is perhaps my greatest weakness and yet my greatest strength, all at once."

"I'm afraid I don't—"

"But I am an artist," he interrupted, "and I must tell you that you captivated my imagination that night aboard the *Mauretania*. You've become my muse, one might say. I do not wish to convince you to do anything that makes you uncomfortable, but I must paint you; I haven't a choice. It's simply something I must do, as surely as I must breathe. Can you possibly understand that?"

"No," she murmured. "No, I cannot. Though I suppose I should be flattered."

"I realize that I am a stranger to you, and that I take great liberties in addressing you as I have. We must rectify that at once; before you refuse me, you must get to know me. You must allow me to make your acquaintance."

"Then I must insist you do it properly, sir. Through my father." She shrugged, and Troy almost swore he saw the hint of a smile playing upon her lips.

"Hmm. Very well. Any suggestions on how I might accomplish that?"

"Do you enjoy playing hazard, Mr. Davenport?" she asked, readjusting her gloves.

"I'm particularly fond of dice games," he answered.

She nodded approvingly. "I believe my father is scheduled to participate in a tournament this very evening, in the Oak Room. After dinner."

"Interesting."

"Indeed. You might like to know that he favors young men who play it safe over those who take foolish risks when placing bets, and he enjoys a good Malaga wine while he plays. Oh, and he thinks motorcars are unnecessary and frivolous. And you might consider complimenting his cravat, no matter how silly it looks."

Troy couldn't help but laugh. "Is that all?"

She only nodded in reply.

"You're a fascinating woman, Miss Miranda Granger."

"And you're full of flattery, Mr. Davenport."

"Something I'm sure you're well accustomed to," he shot back.

A shadow flitted across her eyes, and the mood shifted at once. "I must go," she said softly, her gaze drawn back to the hotel. "It's getting cold, and Sullivan is going to be beside herself with worry."

"Sullivan?" Troy asked.

"My maid." She lifted a watch pendant from a chain around her neck and peered down at it with drawn brows. "Goodness! However did the hour grow so late? I must go at once."

"Let me escort—"

"Heavens, no!" She sidestepped his proffered arm, smiling up at him apologetically. "I'm afraid, sir, that until we are properly introduced, we must act as if we've never met. Have I your word?"

"Of course," Troy answered, though he wasn't entirely certain he meant it.

"Good-bye, then."

And with that she was gone, leaving Troy there, staring at the foamy sea, a smile of self-satisfaction spreading slowly across his face.

At last . . . he'd found his muse.

Chapter 3

The little minx had lied, damn it. About *every-thing*. Troy untied his necktie with a groan of frustration, then pulled it free from his collar and tossed the length of black silk onto the chair beside the hearth. He should have known, of course. Her encouragement had been far too easily given.

The evening had been a disaster. He might as well forget obtaining a legitimate introduction to Miss Granger now—her father despised him. Everything he'd said, from the moment he'd walked into the Oak Room and taken a seat at the gaming table, had been wrong.

Troy had complimented the man's old-fashioned cravat, only to earn a scathing glare. "Damned valet must go," Sir William had muttered under his breath in reply. As they'd begun to play, Troy had ordered him a Malaga wine, hoping to earn his favor. Instead, the curmudgeonly Sir William had launched into a tirade about filthy Spaniards and how they could keep their spirits to themselves. 'He favors young men who play it safe,' Miss Granger had said. To the contrary, Sir William scoffed at Troy's hesitancy, all but calling him a coward. "Have you no ballocks at all?" the man had asked him while casting him a scornful glare. Indeed, every opinion he'd put forth—from drink to clothing to motorcars—had earned Sir William's contempt.

By the time Troy had caught on to Miss Granger's deception, it was entirely too late. The die had already been cast, and what recourse had he? It wasn't as if he could simply tell the man that he hadn't meant anything he'd said or done, that he'd simply been following Miss Granger's advice. No, he couldn't even admit to having conversed with her.

What now? He unbuttoned his coat and tossed it to the chair, his mind completely devoid of answers. He couldn't think of a single way to wrest an introduction, and without an introduction, he'd never be allowed to speak with her again, much less paint her.

He eyed the stack of blank canvases in the room's corner, his box of paints and brushes beside them. *No.* He could not fail; not this time. There had to be a way. He would not give up so easily.

He flipped open his watch, surprised to see that it was nearly three in the morning. Blast it, but he'd promised Lady Barclay that he'd join her for breakfast—in little more than five hours, he realized. Tossing the watch to the dressing table, he groaned aloud. Perhaps he'd be able to think more clearly after a few hours' sleep. With that, he turned out the light and collapsed onto the bed, still half-clothed.

Exactly five hours later, he glanced into the mirror above the commode to straighten his necktie. He'd had a bath and a shave, and though his head throbbed from too much drink and not enough sleep, he felt somewhat hopeful. He hadn't a plan, not yet. Still, he was confident that an answer would present itself in due course. It had to; failure was not to be countenanced. Now that he'd found her, he could not take "no" for an answer.

But first, he had to see to his morning's social obligation. After all, it would do no good to insult Lady Barclay. For all he knew, she was well acquainted with Miss Granger. At the very least, he might be able to extract information about her. Subtly, of course. No use tipping his hand.

Minutes later, he entered the dining room, reining in the urge to crane his neck this way and that in hopes of spying Miss Granger amongst the diners. Instead, he gave his hostess's name and followed the maitre d' to a table on the far side of the room, tucked into a corner beside a wall of windows.

"There he is," Lady Barclay called out in greeting. "Mr. Davenport, I'm so glad you could join us. Allow me to present my granddaughter, Miss Margaret Soames."

Troy removed his hat and turned to bow to Miss Soames, a curvaceous blond girl with pale ivory skin and eyes that were a bit too large for her face. Still, it was an attractive face—interesting, even. Perhaps the meal wouldn't be as unpleasant as he'd supposed.

And then she spoke. "Goodness, Grandmama, you said he was handsome, but not as handsome as this," she said with a giggle, her voice a nasal whine. "I think I'd like to sit for a portrait, after all."

"Portrait?" Troy asked, taking his seat across from the two women.

Lady Barclay laid a hand over her granddaughter's. "Shush, Margaret, let the man have his breakfast first. La, we can do business later. Oh, waiter?" She tapped a spoon against her water goblet.

Miss Soames changed her mind about her order several times as the harried-looking waiter bent over their table. "No, never mind the sausages. Not good for my complexion." She glanced up at him with a coy smile before turning her attention back to the waiter. "And make that three-minute eggs, instead of four-minute. Two eggs. No, three. Can you read that back to me? I don't suppose you'll get it right," she said with a dramatic sigh.

"Have anything you'd like, Mr. Davenport," Lady Barclay offered once she'd placed her own order. "Though these prices are outlandish, aren't they?"

Troy settled on coffee and toast.

He was relieved when the food was delivered, as eating would no doubt curtail the banal conversation he was painfully engaged in. As it was, he hadn't a clue what they were talking about, chattering away about this and that. He simply nodded at appropriate intervals, grunting a reply now and then. As he spread marmalade on his toast, he searched his mind for a way to extricate himself from the table as soon as he was finished eating.

"So, Mr. Davenport," Lady Barclay said, interrupting his plotting and planning, "I've told my granddaughter that she must allow you to paint her. A portrait, to go above the mantel in the drawing room. Might you begin this afternoon?"

"This afternoon?" he sputtered, dropping his marmalade-covered spoon to the crisp white table linen beside his plate. "You must excuse me, Lady Barclay, but I'm not a portraitist," he said once he'd regained his composure.

"Well, you're an artist, aren't you?" Lady Barclay regarded him across the table with drawn brows, her jowly mouth pursed into a frown. "How hard can it be to paint a simple portrait?"

Troy chose his words carefully. "I am an artist, but I don't work on commission. Nor do I specialize in portraits, Lady Barclay. I generally paint what I am inspired to paint, and nothing more.

I'm sure you can find a willing portraitist in London who—"

"But I want *you* to paint my granddaughter, Mr. Davenport, not some trained monkey in London. Your aunt says you're a man of the world, trained in France by some of the best masters. Only you will do, where my granddaughter is concerned. Surely you can find inspiration in a face like hers. She's lovely, isn't she?"

"Indeed," a stunned Troy managed to mutter, though he could say no more in reply. The ensuing silence was uncomfortable. Miss Soames simply stared at her plate, pushing around bits of egg with her fork. Troy cast about anxiously for a way to refuse them without causing too much offense. Why he should care if they were offended, he did not know. Still—

"Lady Barclay, Miss Soames," a now-familiar voice called out, as soft and sweet as honey. *Miss Granger.*

Troy half turned in his chair, rendered entirely mute.

By God, but she looked like an angel, a delicate angel crafted from the finest porcelain. And her face . . . well, there was something extraordinary about the ordinariness of her features. A contradiction, of course. Everything about the woman was a contradiction. He had to fight the urge to bolt from the table and find his paints at once, to capture the exact smile on her rosy lips as she smiled down at Lady Barclay and Miss Soames.

"Good morning, Miss Granger," Lady Barclay trilled in reply, tipping her head in her direction. Miss Soames said nothing, her lips drawn into a tight line.

"Maggie, don't be rude," Lady Barclay murmured as soon as Miss Granger had moved on, out of earshot. "She *is* Sir William's daughter, after all."

Miss Soames wrinkled her nose. "She's always putting on airs, when everyone knows—"

"Enough, dearest," Lady Barclay interrupted, elbowing her granddaughter in the ribs. "We have a guest, remember?"

"Are you well acquainted with Miss Granger?" Troy had spoken the words aloud before he had thought better of it.

"As well as I'd like to be," Miss Soames said, rather uncharitably. At once, her pale blue eyes narrowed suspiciously. "Why do you ask?"

Troy shrugged. "No reason. I played dice with her father last night. Rather unpleasant man, if you ask me."

Lady Barclay fixed her granddaughter with an angry stare before returning her gaze to his. "Sir William is a fine man. I knew his first wife well, a lovely woman. I should ask him to dinner," she said, tapping her finger to her cheek. "And Miss Granger, too. I suppose I should include the other two, as well—frightful girls, but there's no helping that. Anyway, what were we discussing? Oh, yes. The portrait of my Margaret here. You simply must say yes, Mr. Davenport."

Troy's mind began to work feverishly. Lady Barclay and Miss Soames were acquainted with Miss Granger; they might, in fact, dine with her tomorrow. Right now they were the only link he had, the only possible means of an introduction. As unpalatable as the idea of spending any more time in Miss Soames's company was, that tenuous connection was too dear to give up.

"Yes, then," he said, silently cursing himself even as he agreed. "We must get started right away."

Troy could only wince inwardly as Miss Soames squealed her delight, her cold, hard eyes glittering as if she'd just been handed a favorite toy.

Lady Barclay smiled triumphantly. "In our chambers, then? This afternoon?"

He raked his hand through his hair with a groan of frustration. God save him from women like Margaret Soames. If Lady Barclay thought she was purchasing a plaything for her granddaughter, she was sadly mistaken. He would paint her portrait—in public—and nothing more.

He rose from his chair, laying his napkin on the table beside his plate. "A beauty like Miss Soames needs a far more dramatic background than that. The weather is mild for December, the sun strong in the afternoon. I'll see you on the far end of the boardwalk at half past two. Wear something warm, and be sure to bring a parasol. Now if you'll both excuse me."

Without waiting for their response, he strode out.

* * *

He was painting Miss Soames. For two days now, she'd watched him. From a distance, of course. He'd set up an easel at the far edge of the boardwalk at half past two each day, and Miss Soames had leaned prettily against the wooden railing, a parasol held over her head, till teatime.

Miranda would never admit it, but she was jealous. After all, he'd said he wanted to paint *her*, not just anyone. But apparently Miss Soames would do just as well. Of course, her father would never have allowed it, whereas Lady Barclay stood by watching the painting's progress, a beaming smile upon her face.

Even from across the lawn, Miranda could see that the pretty, doll-like Miss Soames simpered and batted her lashes all the while Mr. Davenport toiled away at the easel. How did he react? she wondered. She couldn't say, for she could not see his face. Even so, Miss Soames's invitation was unmistakable. Was he already warming her bed?

It's none of my business, Miranda told herself sharply. Exhaling slowly and deliberately, she set aside the leather-bound book she'd gripped in her hand, though she had not read a single word. Her stomach grumbled noisily, indicating that it was nearly time for tea. The afternoon sun had moved out toward the sea, painting wide orange swaths against the clear blue sky. A lovely winter's day, and yet she felt no more at peace here than she did at home. No, there was no escape from her own mind, from her own melancholy.

Any moment now, Grace and Gertie would return from strolling the grand pier by the sea, and she'd be forced to listen to their nonstop talk of who wore what and who flirted with whom. That, at least, would provide a brief distraction. Small consolation.

When she finally glanced back toward the boardwalk, she saw that Miss Soames had moved away from her position against the railing, and Mr. Davenport was packing up his easel and supplies. She knew she should go, before he saw her there.

Yet she could not force herself to rise from the cushioned lawn chair where she sat, a blanket draped across her lap for warmth. Instead, she felt compelled to stay, to watch as he made his way back toward the hotel, both a shivering Miss Soames and Lady Barclay in tow. After all, he wouldn't dare to stop and converse with her. He couldn't; they had not yet been introduced. At least, not formally.

She placed her book in her lap, opened randomly, and resumed the pretense of reading. Now and then, she glanced up, watching their approach. Inexplicably, her heart began to beat a wild rhythm as Mr. Davenport moved toward her. Every few feet, someone rushed up to him, speaking words that Miranda could not hear, then pressed a card into his hand. Beside him,

Miss Soames's and Lady Barclay's lips were moving, their faces animated.

Miranda held her breath as their party reached her side, not two yards from where she sat. She saw the light of recognition in Mr. Davenport's eyes as he spied her there and stopped dead in his tracks. For one horrified moment, he looked as if he were going to speak to her. His mouth opened ever so slightly, then closed again, his eyes never leaving her face.

"Miss Granger!" Lady Barclay called out, hurrying over. Miss Soames stayed rooted to Mr. Davenport's side, eyeing her warily, as she always did. "How good to see you out taking some air. It's quite restorative, isn't it? I've asked your father to join us for dinner tomorrow, but I haven't yet received a reply. You must tell him to accept; I'd love to have you and your darling sisters, too."

Miranda rose, setting aside her book and blanket. "I . . . I'm not certain of his schedule, but I'll be sure to mention it to him." She cleared her throat uncomfortably, feeling the weight of Mr. Davenport's stare upon her. "It's very . . . very kind of you," she stuttered, feeling entirely disconcerted.

Lady Barclay looked back over her shoulder to where Mr. Davenport stood with her granddaughter. "Oh, you must pardon me," she said, glancing back at her with a scowl. "Have you been introduced to Mr. Davenport?"

Miranda felt a sudden heat flood her cheeks. "No, I . . . um, I've not yet made his acquaintance."

"Well, then, Miss Granger, I present Mr. Troy Davenport of New York. Mr. Davenport, Miss Miranda Granger of Surrey. Mr. Davenport is an artist, you see. Trained in France," she added.

"Is that so?" Miranda asked, putting off the inevitable. "How fascinating."

"Indeed. Come, Mr. Davenport. Don't just stand there like a dumb ox."

Summoned into action, Mr. Davenport laid aside his easel and supplies and closed the distance between them, reaching for her hand. "I'm pleased to make your acquaintance, Miss Granger," he murmured before pressing his lips against her knuckles.

Miranda swallowed hard before replying. "Likewise." She tugged her hand from his grasp, hoping he did not notice the way it trembled.

"Mr. Davenport is painting my portrait," Miss Soames offered, stepping up to tuck her hand into the crook of Mr. Davenport's arm.

"That's quite an honor," Miranda said, wishing that they would hurry off. The tension in the air positively crackled. She reached for her book, tucking it beneath her arm. "It was so good to see you, but if you'll excuse me, I must go find my sisters."

Lady Barclay nodded. "Of course. Don't forget to speak to your father about my invitation. Come now, Margaret. We're to meet Lady Bamber-Scott in a quarter hour. We must hurry."

"Oh, very well," Miss Soames snapped. "Though

I don't see why you bother with her. Title or no, she's not at all fashionable, and as poor as—"

"Good day, Miss Granger, Mr. Davenport," Lady Barclay interrupted, rolling her eyes in a way that almost made Miranda laugh.

"Yes, good day," Miss Soames muttered.

Good heavens, they were leaving her there with Mr. Davenport! Miranda's breath hitched in her chest as the pair of women strode off, the younger one glancing back over her shoulder to where she and Mr. Davenport stood facing one another, entirely silent.

"Mr. Davenport, isn't it?" someone called out.

They both turned in unison toward the voice as a well-dressed gentleman approached. "I'm Howard Tennant." He stretched out one hand, offering a cream-colored card. "I was speaking with Sir Anthony and Lady Bamber-Scott at luncheon today, and . . . well, you must paint my daughter Josephine's portrait. I'll pay you twice what they've offered you."

"I'm sorry, Mr. Tennant, but I'm afraid there's been some sort of misunderstanding. I'm not a portraitist, you see, and—"

"Three times as much. That's my final offer. If you've finished with Miss Soames, we could get started tomorrow."

Mr. Davenport shook his head. "I'm afraid I can't. As I said, I don't normally paint portraits, and—"

"Good God, man. Four times, then."

"If you'll excuse me," Miranda said, seizing the

opportunity to flee while Mr. Davenport was otherwise engaged.

But he looked toward her with pleading eyes, looking slightly panicked. "No, wait. Miss Granger, I—"

"Is your schedule the problem? Next week, then?" the persistent Mr. Tennant pressed as Miranda made her escape toward the hotel's patio. "I realize it's almost Christmastime, but . . ."

She hurried on, their voices fading behind her. Twenty yards, no more, and then she'd be safely inside—away from him, away from temptation. She quickened her pace as much as decorum would allow. Ten more yards. Five.

"Not so fast, Miss Granger," came Mr. Davenport's deep voice behind her, startling her. He fell into step beside her. "I believe you owe me an explanation. About your father."

"You're mistaken, Mr. Davenport," Miranda said sweetly. "I owe you nothing at all. Now, if you'll excuse me, I really must find my sisters."

Chapter 4

Troy sensed Miss Granger's body tense beside him as she attempted to flee. He could not fathom why, but it was almost as if . . . as if she *feared* him. Which was, of course, total nonsense. Yet her sweetly spoken words and her taut, uncomfortable demeanor were at odds with one another. Entirely confounded, he shook his head.

"Oh, Mr. Davenport!" someone called out. Troy and Miss Granger both turned to see a woman waving in his direction, a white calling card clutched in one hand.

"Damn, not another one," he muttered. "What is wrong with these people?"

"Yoo-hoo, Mr. Davenport!" the woman persisted, headed in their direction now.

"I must speak with you, Miss Granger," Troy implored, offering her his arm. "Please. Away from here. Quickly."

She shied away from his arm, shaking her head. "I can't."

"Mr. Davenport?"

He did not have to look back to see that the woman was gaining on them. Instead, he closed his eyes and pinched the bridge of his nose, hoping to dull the ache in his head that was growing in intensity with each passing minute.

"Mr. Davenport? Just a moment of your time," came the plaintive voice from behind.

Troy turned to face Miss Granger and took a deep breath before offering his arm once more. "Please, Miss Granger. You *must* rescue me. Don't make me beg. It isn't a pretty sight, I assure you."

"Oh, very well," she snapped, at last taking his proffered arm.

"Thank you." Relief coursing through him, he nearly dragged her toward the terrace, her feet moving double-time to keep pace.

"Where are you taking me?" she asked breathlessly as they climbed the stone steps leading up.

"I've no idea. Away. Anywhere."

"Well, if you wish to lose her—whoever she is—then I suggest we take the side door and double back outside."

"Excellent plan."

"There's a gazebo hidden away just down that little trail there," Miss Granger continued as they hurried through the side door she'd indicated and stepped back outside. "It's off the main path and usually empty at this hour."

He stole a glance in her direction. "You're quite good at this—evading people, I mean."

"Years of experience," she answered with a

shrug. "You left your easel and paints out on the lawn, by the way."

He waved one hand in dismissal. "I'll go back for it all later."

"I suppose it's safe enough." Several minutes passed in silence before Miss Granger spoke again. "Perhaps now you'll tell me what's going on. Why is everyone suddenly chasing you down?"

Troy couldn't help but smile. "You've noticed?"

"It's hard to miss. I've never seen anything like it. Ladies *and* gentlemen slipping cards into your pockets . . ." She trailed off, shaking her head. "You seem to be quite popular all of a sudden."

"All because I stupidly agreed to paint Miss Soames's portrait. Now everyone wants their darling daughter immortalized on canvas. I'd like to tell the lot of them to go to . . . er, the devil. If you'll pardon me."

Miss Granger hurried her step, pointing just ahead. "There's the gazebo, just beyond that rise."

He glanced up and saw it, just where she'd indicated. Mercifully, it appeared empty. Feeling bold, he reached for her gloved hand and pulled her along.

Miraculously, she allowed the intimacy. "I did not realize you were a portrait artist," she murmured, her hand still clasped in his.

"That's because I'm not," he answered, smiling down at her.

"Then why ever would you agree—never mind." She shook her head. "It's none of my business." Her cheeks turned a delightful shade of pink as he led her up the gazebo's wide, planked stairs.

"Good God, you don't think . . . that I'm . . . with Miss Soames?" he sputtered.

She shrugged. "Truly, it's none of my affair what you do with Miss Soames."

"However true that might be, I hope you give me more credit than that, Miss Granger. Agreeing to paint her was simply a means to an end. Mercenary, I know." He took a seat on the bench and drew her down beside him. "But now that I think about it . . . well, I suppose the result was worth the trouble."

"Dare I ask what you mean by that?"

"Isn't it obvious?" he said, smiling down at her.

Instantly, her eyes darkened. "I should go."

"Please don't."

"You're far too bold, Mr. Davenport. Besides, nothing has changed since our initial conversation."

"Except that I have become acquainted with your father, as you requested. I'm fairly certain I made quite an impression on the man, thanks to your sage advice."

With lashes fluttering, she dropped her gaze to her feet. "Oh, yes. That." At least she had the decency to blush. "Well, you must understand . . . that is . . . you left me no choice. I'm not used to such directness, and—"

"I am sorry for that, Miss Granger. If there had been any other way—"

"I still don't quite understand just what it is you want from me." She looked at him sharply, her deep brown eyes full of mistrust, of skepticism. Troy could only wonder what past hurts had left such an indelible mark on her.

"I told you," he said softly. "I want to paint you."

"Like you're painting Miss Soames?"

He shook his head. "Nothing like that. Not a portrait, not something to hang above a mantel to gather dust. No, a masterpiece, instead. *My* masterpiece."

"But why me?"

"I have no answer for that." He raked one hand through his hair. "Trust me, I've asked myself the same question, time and time again. Why do some people prefer coffee to tea? Game to fowl?"

She simply shrugged.

"They just do," he said forcefully. How could he make her understand? "I crave coffee with my morning eggs and toast; I can't say why, but I must have it. And right now, when I pick up my brush, I must paint you, and only you."

Her lips twitched with a smile. "So you're saying I'm . . . what? Like your choice of morning beverage?"

He couldn't help but laugh. "Precisely, Miss Granger. You are like my morning coffee. What would your father say to that?"

"He would likely offer you some tea."

"After our ill-fated game of hazard, I'm sure you're right. You don't play fair, you know," he chastised.

"You must realize that I have my reasons."

"And I'm certain that they are good ones, Miss Granger. But let me assure you that my intentions are entirely . . . well, professional."

She tilted her head to one side, biting her lower lip as she studied his face for what felt like an eternity but was likely no more than a few seconds. Finally, she nodded to herself. "Still, I doubt my father will be convinced, and without his consent I'm afraid I cannot allow it."

"But if your father *does* allow it? Let's just say, hypothetically. If he did give his permission, then what?"

She rose, clasping her hands in front of her. "Then I suppose I would be pleased to be your subject, Mr. Davenport. Is that the correct term? Subject?"

Relief coursed through him, and all he could do was grin like a schoolboy. "My subject, my model, my muse. Any term will suffice, as long as you allow it."

"How long will you remain here at the hotel?"

"As long as you do," he replied. There was no reason to lie, after all.

A flush stole up her neck, staining her cheeks. "However did you manage it? An invitation to the opening, I mean. I can't help but wonder."

He shrugged, then rose to face her. "I have my connections."

She shook her head. "So very cryptic."

"If you must know, my art dealer has friends who—"

"Never mind," she interrupted. "It doesn't matter. You may keep your secrets."

Oh, if only she knew how deep his secrets ran. Out of necessity, he reminded himself. After all, he would make his way in this world on his talent alone—would make his *own* name, rather than the one he was born with, like a yoke around his neck.

A high-pitched giggle from the path made them both stand to attention.

"Edmund, wait for me!" a girlish voice called out.

"Good heavens, no!" Miss Granger said, then hurried down the gazebo's steps, the color visibly draining from her face.

"What is it?" Troy asked, following a step behind.

"My sister. Silly, stupid girl," she muttered.

Just then, a tall, dark-headed young woman with flushed cheeks appeared in the lane, her hands tucked into a fur muff. Spying Miss Granger there, she stopped short, her smile disappearing at once. "Goodness, Miranda, you scared me half out of my wits! Whatever are you doing here?"

"I could ask the same of you. Where is Grace?"

"Back in our rooms, getting ready for tea. I was

already changed so I thought I'd take a turn—"
Her gaze landed on him, her bright blue eyes
widening with surprise. "I did not realize you had
company," she said sweetly. "You must introduce
me to your companion, Miranda."

Miss Granger ignored the request. "Who is
Edmund, Gertie?"

"Edmund? I have no idea what you mean."
Her expression was all innocence. "I told you, I
was just taking a turn about the grounds, by
myself, and—"

"Oh, Gertie. When will you learn? I suppose
I'll have to tell Father about this. If you'll excuse
me, Mr. Davenport."

"Mr. Davenport?" the girl squealed. "The
artist? Why, everyone's talking about him, saying
what an exceptional talent he is. Even Father
said . . . well, never mind that." She suddenly
looked embarrassed, as if she'd just remembered that he was standing right there, listening to her prattle on about him.

"Your father said what?" Troy prodded, unable
to curb his curiosity.

"Only that he'd read a review of your latest
show in the *Times*. Positively glowing, comparing
your work to some of the most celebrated Post-
Impressionists ever. Father says the reviewer
claimed you'd be famous one day, your name a
household name."

Troy's chest swelled with pride. The show had
been his crowning achievement, perhaps the
happiest moment of his life—even if it had been

in London rather than one of Paris's famed salons. And yet none of his immediate family had been there to witness it, to bask in his success—not even Kate. As far as his family knew, he was still holed up in some shabby garret somewhere, starving for his art in utter obscurity.

Indeed, the mass of his fortune still remained safely in New York, wholly intact except for the lump sum he'd withdrawn when he'd initially set off for France. And despite his threats to cut him off, when his father had realized that there had been no further withdrawals on his son's account at home, he'd opened one abroad in Troy's name, at Lloyd's Bank in London where each month, like clockwork, he deposited a hefty sum—likely a small fortune by now.

Troy had learned of the Lloyd's account through a correspondence from his father's London solicitor, directed to him at Aunt Agnes's home in Wrotham Road. To this date, he hadn't touched the money, preferring to find other ways to make his living between the sale of paintings. He was quite good at carpentry, it turned out. Who would have known?

"Anyway," the girl continued, her color rising, "he said that if you were to paint anyone here at the hotel, it should be Miranda. But Grace and I are far better suited—"

"That's enough, Gertie," Miss Granger interrupted. "Isn't it time for tea?"

"I suppose it is," the girl answered sullenly. "But you can't tell Father—"

"We'll discuss this later. In private," she added pointedly. "If you'll excuse us, Mr. Davenport."

He removed his hat and bowed sharply. "Of course, Miss Granger. Miss . . ." *What was her name?* "Gertrude, is it?"

The girl—not more than sixteen, he guessed—favored him with a dazzling smile. "Indeed, though my friends call me Gertie."

"Gertrude Granger," he pronounced, his brows drawn. "And your sister is Grace Granger?"

"My stepmother was inordinately fond of alliteration," Miss Granger answered wryly.

He laughed, replacing his hat on his head. "It would seem so. Well, I bid you both a good day, then."

With a nod, Miss Granger linked arms with her sister and led her away, back toward the hotel.

Troy stood watching them till they disappeared over the rise. Only then did he let out the breath he hadn't realized he'd been holding. His palms dampened; his heart began to pound in anticipation. He could barely believe his good fortune, but it seemed he would get his way, after all.

Thank God Sir William read the *Times*.

"I don't have to listen to you," Gertie cried, her face a mottled red. "You're not my mother."

Miranda sat on the bed beside her sister with a sigh of frustration. "I'm the closest you've got, and I only want what's best for you, besides."

Gertie reached for a lace handkerchief and

twisted it violently in her lap. "You only want to ruin my life," she wailed, her voice rising shrilly. "That's all you've ever wanted."

"That's not fair," Grace interjected from across the room. "You know Miranda's only trying to help."

Gertie shook her head. "I know nothing of the sort. Why, I think she wants me to be a dried-up old maid, just like her. Sad all the time, and never having any fun. Always threatening to tell Father on me, when—"

"What else can I do?" Miranda interrupted. "You won't listen to me, and poor Bridget can't seem to keep you under control. You seem utterly determined to ruin your reputation, completely disregarding propriety at every turn, and—"

"I wasn't the one hidden away in a gazebo with a man, with no chaperone in sight. Perhaps I should tell Father all about *that*." Gertie folded her arms across her breasts, smiling smugly.

"No!" Grace gasped. "Were you really, Miranda?"

Gertie nodded, thoroughly enjoying her triumph. "It's true—she was. And not even a gentleman, but that painter from New York."

Grace's blue eyes widened. "Mr. Davenport, you mean?"

"Enough of this," Miranda said, striving to keep her voice steady. "Mr. Davenport and I were only conversing. There was nothing improper about it, nothing at all."

"Really, Miranda? Because it seemed quite . . . well, intimate, if you ask me. I'm sure Father—"

"Don't you dare threaten me, Gertrude Granger! I won't have it. It's not the same and you know it. I'm a grown woman, after all, and you're just a child."

"I'm not a child," Gertie whined, sounding exactly like one. "I'm nearly seventeen, and yet you treat me like an infant."

Nearly seventeen? Only two years younger than she was when she and Paul . . . She swallowed hard, refusing to complete the thought. Had she ever been so young, so naïve, as her sister was now? It seemed impossible, a lifetime ago. How could she possibly keep her flighty sister from making the same mistakes she had? From ruining herself, her prospects, her life?

"Don't you see, Miranda? I love him." Gertie reached for her hand and gave it a squeeze, apparently changing tactics. "Edmund, I mean. His father is a baronet, you know. He's charming and rich, and oh, so handsome. I simply *adore* him."

"Don't be ridiculous," Miranda snapped, her patience worn thin. "You only met him the day before yesterday. You barely know him, Gertie."

"You'll never understand. Just because no man's ever loved you, ever wanted you—"

"Gertie!" Grace gasped, goggling now.

Oh, if only they knew. But she could never tell them, not even if she wanted to. Her father wouldn't allow it. Little did he realize that such secrecy put his younger daughters—Gertie, at least—at risk of suffering the same fate as she had endured.

But Sir William Granger had very little interest in his youngest daughters, and even less interaction with them. Gertie and Grace were entirely left to Miranda's care—hers, and a bevy of nursemaids, governesses, tutors, and maids. And though Miranda often threatened to go to their father with their many transgressions, it was mostly an empty threat.

How could she, when any failure on their part was ultimately considered Miranda's failure? After all, she was the one responsible for them.

"Gertie, you must apologize at once to Miranda," Grace ordered.

"I mustn't do anything of the sort. She deserved it."

"Please don't listen to her, Miranda," Grace pleaded, tears gathering in her eyes. "She's just ill-tempered because she saw Edmund taking a stroll with Miss Carruthers at the pier today. Oh, it's true," she added, cutting off Gertie's sputtering protests. "I told you he seemed insincere."

"You're just jealous, Grace."

"Me, jealous?"

"Yes, you. I can't help it that the boys notice me and not you—"

"Simply because I don't go to the lengths you do to get noticed! Why, you'd stroll down the boardwalk in your knickers and vest if you thought someone might—"

"Enough!" Good heavens, what was she going to

do with the two of them? "I won't listen to another word of this. We're to attend a musicale tonight, and I expect you to be on your very best behavior. Especially you, Gertie."

Gertie actually stuck out her tongue at her, the beast.

Wearily, Miranda rose and headed toward the door. "You've less than an hour to get changed. We'll continue this conversation later," she said, one hand on the doorknob. With a heavy sigh, she paused. "If you truly care so much for this boy—this Edmund—then I'm perfectly willing to allow you to keep his company. You must do it properly, that's all, and within the bounds of propriety." She looked over her shoulder to where Gertie sat, and saw her nod.

"I *am* sorry, Miranda," Gertie said, her voice small and contrite. "I . . . I didn't mean what I said before."

"I know you didn't." She never did. It was just the Granger temperament—an ungoverned passion coupled with a quick temper—rearing its ugly head. It would seem that Gertie had gotten the worst of it.

All she could do was hope that her sisters managed to survive it to womanhood unscathed, something she had not managed to accomplish herself.

"I'll send Bridget right in," Miranda said, then hurried off to her own room to change.

Chapter 5

Almost ten years earlier . . .
Weckham, Surrey

Miranda lay back against Paul's shoulder, entirely sated, so happy her heart was near to bursting with it. "I should go," she murmured, shivering as her lover's lips found her ear. "My father will be home within the hour."

"Beautiful Miranda," Paul cooed, his fingertips stroking her side, drawing gooseflesh on her skin. "Don't go."

"I haven't a choice." She sighed, disentangling her limbs from his and reaching for her chemise. "Truly, we should not have done this, not today."

His smile was brilliant. "Don't fret, love. Today's as good as any. I'm going to ask for your hand tonight, remember? Count this as an advance celebration."

She gazed down at his handsome face, wanting to burn the memory of this moment into her brain forever. "I can barely believe it," she said, shaking her head. "These past two months have been like a dream, a wonderful dream."

"Believe it," he said, propping up on one elbow, watching her as she pulled the chemise over her head. "It's fate. I told you I would marry you, my beautiful, passionate Miranda," he added, his fingers skimming up her thigh beneath the thin cotton.

"Stop," she chastised, pushing away his hand with a smile. "I really must go. This is . . . dangerous. We cannot risk discovery, not now."

"Why ever not? Discovery would only hurry the nuptials. Hmmm, now that I think about it . . ." He smiled wickedly, reaching for her hand and drawing her back down beside him. "I don't think I can wait much longer to make you my wife."

His lips found hers—teasing, tormenting. Miranda opened her mouth against his, deepening the kiss. She couldn't help herself; her protests were useless where Paul was concerned. He had her chemise pushed halfway up her stomach when they heard the coach turn off the main road and into the lane.

"He's early," Miranda cried, scrambling to her feet as she attempted to tug down her underclothes. "Oh, dear God, my hair!" Pins were scattered about the cottage's floor beside the narrow iron bed. "My blouse, quickly!"

Rogue that he was, Paul simply leered at her, entirely bare but for the sheet draped across his middle. Miranda tried her best not to stare, not to marvel at the contours of his chest, at the flat planes of his stomach bisected by a line of soft, dark hair that disappeared, tantalizingly, beneath the bedsheet. "Let him catch us," he said with an easy laugh, entirely unruffled by his nakedness, by her father's early arrival. "He'll force us to wed straightaway if he does. And what a beautiful bride you'll be."

"You'll be the death of me yet!" Miranda said with a sigh, forcing her gaze away from the source of temptation. Plucking her waist off the chair beside the bed, she slipped her arms in and began working the buttons up the front, her fingers flying over them. Seconds later she'd stepped into her skirt and located her belt, fastening it around her middle with trembling hands. There was no help for her hair. She'd simply have to dash inside like this and hope no one noticed, especially Grace and Gertie. Lord knows the pair of them couldn't keep their mouths shut, even if they didn't understand what they were saying.

Sullivan would be able to quickly re-dress her hair before her father requested an audience with her. He'd no doubt spend a half hour, at least, with his land steward first. As long as he didn't notice Paul's horse tied in the woods . . .

"Go!" she prodded, tossing his coat to the bed. "And come back after tea, no earlier. You can speak to my father then."

"You're beautiful when you're all ruffled like this, you know," he said, and Miranda couldn't help but laugh at his boyish grin, his golden hair tumbling across his forehead in careless waves. "My lovely bride-to-be."

His bride, her heart hummed. She was going to be his bride! It was almost too good to be true—and yet it *was* true. All her girlish dreams, her fantasies of a handsome, adoring husband. Her father would have no reason to deny his request. Paul Sutcliffe was every inch the gentleman, a baronet's son, an heir to vast holdings in Shropshire—beautiful land, according to Paul, who spoke reverently of his home there.

No, if she hadn't been so certain of her own heart, so certain of Paul's affection, so certain of her father's approval, she never would have given up her virtue before she'd had his ring on her finger. But Paul . . . well, she could not deny him, not when he promised her everything and the moon, the stars, the heavens. Her desire—*their* desire—had been unmistakable, too strong to deny.

And why should they deny it? They were in love—desperately, wondrously in love—and they were going to marry. In her heart they were already joined, their fates forever entwined. They would right the wrong, and soon. An autumn wedding. Sooner, if circumstances demanded it. After all, they had taken no precautions. Why would they, when they were so sure of their future? There was nothing she wanted more than Paul's child—a son, perhaps, as handsome as his father.

"Go, then, if you must," Paul called out, watching

her as she slipped into her kidskin boots and fastened the buttons. "I'll keep the taste of you here, on my lips, and my affections here"—he tapped his chest with one fist—"in my heart."

She hurried back to his side, bending to kiss him one last time before she dashed out the door.

"I love you, darling," he called out just as the door swung shut behind her.

"I know," Miranda murmured to herself, a smile dancing upon her lips. After all, there was nothing in her life of which she was more certain. Paul loved her, and nothing else mattered. She was his, and he was hers.

Forever.

Miranda blinked in confusion, sure she'd misunderstood her father's words. "What do you mean, he's gone? I . . . I don't understand." She shook her head, trying to clear it, to steady her voice, to stop her legs from trembling beneath her. "Surely you did not refuse him."

Her father poured a measure of liquor into a tumbler and downed it in one stiff jerk of his wrist before speaking. "Not so much refused him as offered him an alternative."

She could barely make her mouth form the words. "A . . . an alternative?" she stuttered. "I . . . I don't know what you mean."

Her father's steady gaze met hers. "I gave him a choice. You, or ten thousand pounds. He chose the latter."

Miranda raised a hand to cover her mouth, fearing she might get sick, right there on the Persian rug.

Her father just stared at her, blinking in disbelief. "I never took you for a damned fool, Miranda. How could you allow yourself to be taken in like this?"

Miranda could not speak. Even taking a ragged breath was an effort. Her windpipe tightened, her lungs burning as she willed herself not to faint.

"Not a farthing to his name," he said, pounding on his desk for emphasis. "It would seem that everything he told you was a lie—every last word of it. You think I'd let him sniff around your skirts without thoroughly checking out his story? Took my man long enough to get the details, but get them he did. Entirely done up, he said. A fortune hunter. You, my dear, were his latest prey."

"No," she breathed. It wasn't true. It couldn't be true.

"Yes," her father countered coldly. "Oh, I told your Mr. Sutcliffe he could have you, all right, if he wanted you that badly. Without your dowry, of course. That, or ten thousand pounds to leave the district at once."

"He couldn't," Miranda cried. "He wouldn't. He . . . he loves me."

"It pains me to tell you this, daughter, but he barely blinked before accepting my deal. Though I'm not terribly surprised, as I heard he owes a small fortune to several unsavory characters in

London. I suppose the ten thousand pounds will tide him over until he finds another unsuspecting heiress to toy with." He shook his head, a look of disgust on his face. "I would have gone higher, too, but the fool took my first offer."

Ten thousand pounds? That was all she was worth, no more?

"But I loved him," she choked out. "I love him," she corrected, a fire burning in her breast. "And you . . . what did you do? You ran him off!"

"You would have him, knowing he lied to you?" He began to pace, back and forth before the hearth. Miranda got dizzy, watching him, and had to squeeze her eyes shut. Still, she could not block out his words. "A vast estate in Shropshire, a man of leisure. It was nothing but lies, I tell you. All lies!"

Miranda shook her head, her mind a muddled mess. It didn't make sense; none of it made any sense. "I would have married him, rich or poor," she said, her voice a mere whisper now.

"And that's the difference between you and him—he would not have *you*, poor. When I told him he wouldn't get a farthing if he married you, he turned tail and ran. After he pocketed my cheque, of course."

"No," was all she could say. "No." It wasn't true; it couldn't be true. Paul loved her. He would have told her father to go to the devil; he would have had her without a ha'penny to her name. He would fight for her.

And yet he was doing none of these things. He

was gone. She'd heard the pounding of hooves as he'd ridden down the drive, not a word of good-bye. No explanation, no justification. He was just . . . gone.

He's coming back later, she told herself. Of course. After her father was abed, he'd come for her. They would elope. She was over the age of consent, after all.

Her father poured himself another measure of liquor. "You look pale. Perhaps you should go lie down."

"Yes, of course," she murmured, and yet she couldn't make her feet move, couldn't make them obey her command.

"Truly, he's not worth it," her father added, awkwardly patting her on the arm. "Thank the devil we found out now, before you'd gone and married him. It's a good thing you're a virtuous girl, one with moral fiber. Otherwise, well . . ." He trailed off, waving one hand in dismissal. "At least it wasn't too late."

Too late. The words reverberated in her brain, slowly taking root, planting doubt. Why hadn't Paul told him that it *was* too late? If he had, perhaps her father would have reconsidered. What if he wasn't coming back for her? What if— She shook her head, refusing to allow herself to even think it.

Instead, she began to make her way toward the stairs, barely able to remain upright as her whole world crumbled beneath her. Her thighs ached, chafed, the very core of her tender from where her body had joined Paul's mere hours ago, and not for the first time. Before, she'd thought the pain an exquisite reminder of their coupling, a lingering remnant of the pleasure they'd shared.

Now, however, the ache she'd once cherished was nothing but a painful reminder that perhaps it was already too late, after all.

And if it were, well . . . she was entirely, indisputably, irrevocably *ruined*.

Chapter 6

Miranda paced nervously. The message she'd received from Mr. Davenport said for her to meet him at half past nine, and it was a quarter to ten with no sign of him. Sullivan lounged uneasily on the bench, checking her watch every few minutes or so.

"It's far too chilly to leave you sitting out here waiting," Sullivan grumbled. "Even with your muffler, I'm afraid you'll take a chill."

"I'm fine," Miranda said, pulling her coat more tightly about herself. "Truly, it's unseasonably warm for December, isn't it? If not for the hotel's décor, one would barely know it was Christmastime."

Indeed, it seemed that every possible surface was adorned with boughs of holly and fir. Even the gazebo was draped with silver garlands, enormous red bows placed at pleasing intervals. Yet the air was almost balmy, only the faintest chill to remind one of the season.

"I can't imagine what's keeping him," Miranda murmured. "Are you certain Father got the time correct?"

"Indeed, miss. I saw the note myself. Half past nine, at the gazebo. Do you suppose there's another gazebo somewhere on the property?"

Miranda shook her head. "Perhaps, but I'm certain he meant this one. We'll give him another few minutes, and then—"

She broke off, staring at the lane. There he was, the morning sun glinting off his bronze hair as he headed their way, his pace brisk and purposeful.

At the sight of him, butterflies began to flutter in her stomach. What if she wasn't a good subject? After all, there was nothing special about her, and besides, she knew nothing of being an artist's model. After all the trouble he'd gone to, what if she disappointed him? What if she failed to live up to his expectations? What if—

"Miss Granger, please forgive me," he called out, interrupting her sudden panic. "I've been out for hours, searching for the perfect spot, the perfect background, and I'm afraid I lost track of the time. I did not mean to leave you waiting."

"But I thought you were . . . that we were . . . here," she stuttered, entirely discomposed. "At the gazebo."

"No, this was just a convenient place to meet. If you'll just follow me. It's a bit of a walk, I'm afraid . . . oh, good day," he said as Sullivan rose and joined them.

Miranda ignored his look of surprise. "Sullivan is acting as my chaperone today."

"Chaperone?" His brow furrowed in confusion. "I'm not taking you to tea. Besides, she might find it a bit uncomfortable—"

"I'm sure Sullivan will be fine," Miranda interrupted. "Shall we go?"

He shrugged. "Of course. As I was saying, it *is* a bit of a walk. I apologize for that, but I think when you see the spot, well . . . If we hurry, we can get the best morning light."

He paused, his eyes skimming from the top of her head down to her toes, as if he'd only just noticed her appearance. "I'm glad you wore lavender. It suits you."

Miranda glanced down appreciatively at her ensemble, one of her favorites—a pale lavender serge gown with a matching worsted wool coat. It was warm, yet smart. "Well, you said to dress as if I were going on a picnic." She reached up to finger the brim of her wide straw boater.

"Come, you'll see why." He offered his arm, and Miranda took it, eager to get on with it. Perhaps once they'd begun, her nerves would settle. It was only the fear of the unknown, making her feel so queer.

Setting off at last, they walked in silence, their pace brisk, Sullivan following a few paces behind. As the looming hulk of the hotel grew smaller and smaller behind them, the lane narrowed to a sandy path which then narrowed further as they entered a small wood. Brown, brittle fronds of fern bent toward the path, brushing against Miranda's ankles as she followed Mr. Davenport deeper into the gloom.

Miranda's resolve began to waver, her implicit trust in the man lessening a measure, but then the gloom began to lift, and the forest became lighter and brighter, the footpath more distinct. Dust motes floated in the wide beams of light, looking like small insects. She almost swore she could feel them brushing against her skin, velvety and cool.

"There it is, just ahead." Mr. Davenport released her arm and strode off.

Miranda followed suit, quickening her pace as she chased the bright light penetrating the dense bare branches above. Not ten paces ahead, she burst forth into a small clearing and sucked in her breath.

Magical. That was the best word she could summon to describe the place. It felt almost otherwordly, as if they'd trespassed into a realm of fairies and other mythical beings. A diagonal beam of bright sunlight illuminated the silvery clearing as terns and other seabirds flitted about, diving down toward an ivory blanket spread on the ground. A wicker picnic hamper sat on the blanket, a pair of wineglasses beside it.

Mr. Davenport's easel was there, several paces behind the blanket, a rectangular canvas already propped upon it.

"Perfect," he murmured. "All that's missing is you."

Miranda's hands began to tremble. "What . . . what shall I do?"

He was at her side in an instant. "Just sit, here, facing this direction. Yes, that's good," he said as she sat on the blanket's soft folds, her legs angled to her left. Only an inch or so of her thick, woolen stockings showed above her ankles, but she tugged at her skirt's hem till only her black kidskin shoes were exposed.

"Now," he continued, "either rest your hand on the blanket here, or you can leave them in your lap, whichever is more comfortable. Feel free to leave on your gloves. Good, that's excellent. Now, turn your head to the right, as if you're looking over your shoulder. I'd like to see your profile."

"Like this?" Miranda asked, her voice small. She felt foolish. Sullivan, sitting awkwardly on a mackintosh square at the edge of the clearing with a blanket tucked about herself, watched her curiously, her lips pursed in obvious disapproval.

"Precisely. Now, as to your expression, well, let's pretend that you're dining alfresco with your lover."

Sullivan's *harrumph* of disapproval was surely meant to be heard by all.

"Your lover has moved from the blanket," Mr. Davenport continued, ignoring her. "He's standing over here"—he pointed to the ground at his feet—"and you're gazing at him, perhaps inviting him back to your side."

Miranda nodded, assuming the pose he'd described as best she could.

"Perfect," he said, nodding approvingly. "Relax for now as I get my palette set up. Oh, and there's some cheese and fruit in the basket, along with a thermos of coffee. I can't have you perishing of hunger or thirst while you sit."

Miranda laughed uneasily as she removed the cloth from the top of the basket lid to check its contents. Indeed, it was piled high with fruit—apples and pears and grapes—and several wedges of hard cheese. "How very thoughtful. Really, you needn't have gone to such trouble."

"If you need to take a break, to eat or to . . . er, for any reason at all, just let me know." A flush stole up his neck, and Miranda forced herself to drop her gaze lest he see her smile.

As Mr. Davenport readied his paints, Miranda plucked several grapes from the basket and ate them, one at a time. They were tart on her tongue, but not unpleasant. When she glanced back over her shoulder at him, she was surprised to see that he had shed his overcoat. As if that weren't enough, he had unbuttoned the top buttons of his linen shirt, revealing several inches of sun-bronzed skin beneath his throat. His hair was mussed now, too, as if he'd repeatedly raked his hands through it. He appeared far too casual now. Far too attractive, if truth be told.

Her pulse quickened, her palms growing damp inside her gloves. Guiltily, she glanced over at Sullivan, prepared to face her disapproval, but was pleased to find her maid occupied with the leather-bound book she held in her lap, instead. *Thank goodness*. This was uncomfortable and unnatural enough without having to suffer through Sullivan's disapproving stare the entire time. Perhaps now that Mr. Davenport had taken his seat on the low, spindly stool before the easel, a palette balanced on his knees, Sullivan had decided that he was harmless enough.

"I'm ready now," he called out. "If you could sit as I showed you. Yes, that's it."

And so Miranda sat, entirely silent for what felt like an hour. During that time, nothing broke the silence but the sound of Sullivan turning pages, of the paintbrush stroking the canvas, of seabirds calling overheard as they dipped into the trees, rustling the branches above.

Finally, Mr. Davenport spoke. "You're doing a fine job, Miss Granger. If you feel at all uncomfortable, don't hesitate to stretch or what have you. I don't expect you to turn into marble there."

"I wasn't sure—"

"I do apologize. I was so caught up in my work, I did not realize so much time had passed. Do you need a break?"

"No, not at all." She turned her head from side to side, easing the stiffness in her neck, then resumed her pose. "It's just . . . well, quite boring, isn't it? For the subject, I mean."

"I am sorry for that," he said, now a disembodied voice behind her as she stared at the empty spot

he'd indicated before. *Her phantom lover.* It took
every ounce of her concentration not to picture
Paul standing there, his blond hair turned gold
by the sun.

"There's no helping it, really," Mr. Davenport
continued, oblivious to her inner struggle. "We
can carry on a conversation while I work, if that
will help."

"You're able to focus while conversing?" she
asked, surprised. For some reason, she'd assumed that an artist would require full concentration, that discourse would be distracting.

"Actually, I find it helpful at times. Frees my
mind, so to speak. Allows me to paint what I see
rather than what I think I see, if that makes any
sense."

She resisted the urge to shake her head. "I'm
afraid it doesn't, not really."

"Think of it this way—I want to paint exactly
what I see. Light, depth, color, dimension. I'd
like the image I see to go straight to my paintbrush, to let my paintbrush interpret the image.
If I take the time to think about what I'm doing,
to think about what I'm seeing, to analyze it, then
I've put a filter on the image."

"That makes perfect sense, explained that way.
I only wish my own art tutors had said it so well.
Perhaps I would have been a more apt pupil."

"You paint, then?" he asked, his voice laced
with surprise.

"Not very well. Still, any woman who hopes to
be accomplished must learn the basics."

"Is being accomplished so very important to a woman?"

"Of course," she replied. "To a woman of good breeding, that is. What else have we, but our accomplishments?"

"Your own mind, for one." A trace of disgust had crept into his voice. "If only women of good breeding were allowed to use it."

She said nothing, growing increasingly uncomfortable with the direction their conversation had taken. A few moments passed in silence as Miranda searched her mind for a more suitable topic.

"What of your passions, Miss Granger? Surely you have something that you enjoy above all else. One of your accomplishments, perhaps?"

Why did he make the word *accomplishments* sound so ugly?

"No?" he prodded when she did not answer immediately. "Nothing?"

"I like music, Mr. Davenport. Very much," she added, feeling slightly churlish. He clearly had little respect for ladies of leisure.

"To listen to, or to play?" he pressed.

"Both. I play well enough, I suppose."

"Do you have a favorite composer?"

"Debussy," she said. "I think *Clair de lune* the most beautiful piece of music I've ever heard."

"We have that much in common, then, Miss Granger, as I'm inclined to agree. I've had the pleasure of hearing Mr. Debussy perform the entire *Suite Bergamasque* in Paris." For several minutes he said nothing, yet the silence wasn't the slightest bit uncomfortable now.

On the other side of the clearing, Sullivan was snoring softly. Miranda allowed her mind to drift aimlessly for several minutes while the sun caressed her skin. It seemed almost impossible to believe that, in a matter of weeks, the new year would arrive. Another year, gone.

"What of Ravel?" Mr. Davenport asked, startling her. "Do you find his music pleasing, or vulgar?"

It took her a moment to find her voice. "Very pleasing," she said at last. "He's quite innovative, I think. A fascinating man."

"He is, indeed. Can you tip your chin up, just a bit?"

She raised her chin a fraction of an inch. "Like this?"

"There, that's it."

Miranda plucked a spindly twig from the ground beside her and began to twirl it between her fingers. "Were you in France long?" she asked, unable to staunch her curiosity.

"A little over three years," came his reply.

"And now you make your home in London?"

"For the most part."

"But your family is in New York?"

"They are," was all he said.

Sullivan snuffled noisily, then resumed her rhythmic snoring.

"I suppose we've bored her senseless, poor

woman," Mr. Davenport quipped, then fell silent once more.

Perhaps a quarter hour later, she heard him mutter a curse. "I suppose that's it for today. The blasted light keeps changing. Are you hungry?"

"Famished," she answered, stretching her hands toward the sky. Heavens, but she'd grown stiff.

"Then I'm glad I packed the hamper. Give me a moment to put these things away, and I'll join you. Unless you're too cold?"

"No, I'm perfectly comfortable."

"Very good. We'll picnic, then. Do you suppose we should wake her?" he asked, tipping his head toward Sullivan who still dozed peacefully against the trunk of a tree.

"Not yet," Miranda said, though she could not fathom why. She rose, brushing her hands across her skirts. "Might I see . . . that is, would you mind if I take a look?"

He took a step away from the easel. "I don't mind, though I've still much to do before it's finished."

With a nod, Miranda moved closer, holding her breath in anticipation. As she swept her gaze across the canvas, her eyes filled with tears.

It was her, immortalized there on canvas, and yet it *wasn't* her. The brush strokes were soft and sensual, featherlight and lush. Even with the soft focus, the likeness was somehow revealing. "But . . . but you've made me look beautiful," she stammered, her voice suddenly thick.

He shrugged, his arms folded across his chest. "I only paint what I see, Miss Granger. You *are* beautiful," he said softly. "Only, so very sad."

Her gaze snapped up to meet his. "I'm sure I don't know what you mean," she said crisply, her palms suddenly damp again, her heart beating wildly.

"Even when you smile, I sense it. Sadness, sorrow." He reached for her hand, but she snatched it from his grasp.

"Don't presume to know me, Mr. Davenport."

He raked a hand through his hair. "I want to know you; I can't quite explain it."

Miranda shook her head. "Please, you mustn't. It's impossible—"

"I've thought of nothing else since our meeting on the deck of the *Mauretania*," he interrupted. "I convinced myself that I only wanted to paint you, nothing more, but it was a lie, a damnable lie."

Miranda could only gape, so stunned was she by his outburst. His brilliant green gaze held her, dared her to look away.

Somehow, she did. "If you'll excuse me, Mr. Davenport. Sullivan," she cried out, telling herself that she desperately wanted to get away from this man—and knowing full well that that, too, was a damnable lie.

Chapter 7

Nine years earlier . . .
Lucerne, Switzerland

Miranda glanced down at the clipping she held in her hand, the words blurring as tears filled her eyes. She swallowed hard, trying to tamp down the queasiness that made her stomach roil uncomfortably.

Her father had sent the newspaper clipping, folded inside a page of his personal stationery. "I thought you should know," was scrawled in his familiar hand in the center of the page.

Lord and Lady Dudley of Kent announce the marriage of their daughter, Miss Harriet Birch, to the Honorable Paul Sutcliffe of Hertfordshire. The couple wed quietly, with no attendants. The bride, well-known for her personal charm and beautiful singing voice, wore an ivory gown of silk voile decorated with seed pearls, a pale blue sash tied about her waist. The couple enjoyed a brief wedding trip to Bath, and are now visiting relatives in . . .

Miranda could read no further. She'd studied the same lines, over and over again, but the message remained the same. There was no reason to read on, to further twist the knife that was buried in her heart.

Paul was married. To Harriet Birch, a harebrained heiress from Kent with nothing to recommend her besides her fortune. His betrayal was now complete.

She could no longer entertain the hope that Paul would miraculously appear there in Switzerland to rescue her from her plight, claiming it had all been a big mistake, that he loved her, that he would marry her.

Paul now belonged to someone else. It was over. Done. She had to accept it now, to find a way to move on. But how could she possibly do that when—

"There you are," her cousin Helen called out, her arms filled with brightly colored parcels.

As Helen hurried her way, juggling the parcels, Miranda shoved the clipping back into her bag and wiped the tears from her eyes with one corner of her cloak.

"Can you take these to the carriage?" Helen asked in flawless German, turning toward the servant who had accompanied them into the picturesque, medieval town. While Helen had shopped for Christmas gifts, he had kept watch over Miranda, keeping a discreet distance behind her at all times. For what purpose, Miranda was not entirely sure.

Helen sat on the bench beside Miranda and took her gloved hand in her own. "I should have known I'd find you here," she said, glancing up at the carving opposite them, across the tranquil pond. "It's such a melancholy place. Have you been crying?"

"Just a bit," Miranda said, glad she could blame the carving—a memorial, of sorts—for her current emotional state. "It's . . . quite moving, isn't it?"

Miranda studied it more closely, the giant dying lion carved into the sandstone rock above the pond. His head was bowed, a giant, broken spear protruding from one shoulder, one paw hanging listlessly toward the water. The expression on the lion's face was heartrendingly tragic.

She'd been told that the carving was allegorical, that it represented the defeat of the Swiss Guard during the storming of the Tuileries in 1792. But to Miranda, it seemed to represent the same sorrow, the same hopelessness she felt in her own heart.

"I thought you meant to stroll around the glacier garden," Helen said, drawing her from her thoughts.

Miranda nodded. "I did, but I grew weary. This seemed a peaceful spot to sit."

Helen's brow knitted with concern. "You do

look pale. Are you unwell? Should I get Heinrich to help you back to the carriage?"

Miranda squeezed her cousin's hand, hoping to reassure her. "I'm perfectly well, Helen. Please don't fret over me."

"I just wish there was something I could do to make this situation more bearable for you, Miranda. Truly, I do."

"You're doing enough for me as it is." She swallowed hard, barely able to continue. "You and Johan have been so very kind, so patient." Tears filled her eyes again as she laid one hand on her swollen belly, hidden beneath the folds of her heavy woolen cloak.

"You don't have to do this, Miranda. As much as I want it . . ." Helen trailed off, shaking her head. "I can't force you," she said resolutely. "I won't. It isn't right."

A bubble of hysteria rose in Miranda's breast, but she forced it down. She took several deep, calming breaths. The last thing she needed was to entirely lose her wits, right there in town for everyone to see. She had to rein in her overwrought emotions, to suppress the panic that made her heart beat wildly and her breath come far too fast.

Could she do this? Could she give up the child she carried—her child, and Paul's? She'd asked herself the same question, over and over again. *I have to.* That was the only answer, as far as she could tell. No matter how hard she tried, she couldn't see a way around it.

"I haven't a choice, Helen," she said at last, her tongue feeling strangely thick in her mouth. "My father . . . he won't . . . there are no other options," she stuttered.

She was an unmarried woman of good breeding. She had no useful skills, no education to speak of—no means of making her own way in the world, of supporting herself and a child.

Her father had told her, in no uncertain terms, that she could not keep the child. Her pregnancy had to be concealed, even from the servants. No one could know, or it would mean certain ruin for them all. "Think of your late mother's reputation," he had told her harshly. "Think of Gertrude and Grace. You will ruin their prospects along with our family's name. You will take us all down with you. Can't you understand that?" he had asked, and that had been the end of the discussion. For how could she argue with that? She knew it was true—all of it.

Her father had made the arrangements. Helen was a third cousin on Miranda's mother's side. She had gone to finishing school in Zurich and somehow managed to fall in love with a boy from Lucerne, marrying him less than a year after leaving England. After more than a decade of marriage, Helen and Johan had no children. Helen was barren, it was said. She'd suffered a string of miscarriages before giving up entirely on having a child of her own.

It was the perfect situation, her father had insisted. Miranda would travel immediately to

Switzerland before her condition was detected, under the guise of attending finishing school.

It was a common enough arrangement; no one would even bat an eye over her sudden departure. She would stay with Helen and Johan in Lucerne until the baby's birth, and then return to England and carry on with her life as if this had never happened.

Helen and Johan would have the child they always wanted, and Miranda would not be exposed as the whoring, immoral child her father now believed her to be. He hadn't asked her opinion on the proposed arrangements. It didn't matter what Miranda wanted—she only had to right the wrong, to untangle the mess she'd created.

She had no choice but to accede to her father's wishes. He would put her out, otherwise. Disown her. Strike her name from the family Bible, as if she'd never existed.

And what would she do then? Where would she go? How would she obtain gainful employment? The only situation she was remotely suited to was that of governess, and who would hire a governess who was with child? Who had borne a child out of wedlock?

The answer was simple: no one would.

No, there was no other way. She glanced up at Helen, and attempted a false smile. Helen was one of the kindest people she'd ever known, nurturing and sweet-tempered. Johan was equally kind—a gentle, loving man. They would make good parents, far better than she. They would give the child a loving, stable home. A fine education. A good, happy life. If Miranda hadn't been so certain of it, she might very well have gone mad.

"What about the baby's father?" Helen asked. "Is there no way, no possibility of—"

"None." Miranda squeezed her eyes shut, remembering the clipping in her bag. "There is no way. He's . . . he's married someone else."

She felt Helen lean closer, stroking her hair like a mother might do to a child. "I'm so sorry, Miranda. So very, very sorry. Does he . . . does he know?"

Opening her eyes, Miranda nodded. "I wrote to him. Directed it to his family's home in Hertfordshire. I have no idea if he received it. Anyway, it doesn't matter—not now."

"You *will* move on from this, Miranda," Helen said forcefully. "You will fall in love again, and start a family when the time is right. I do believe that. All things happen for a reason."

Miranda could only nod, though she knew it was a lie. A platitude, spoken to make her feel better.

"Would it make it easier if I promised to write you every year on the child's birthday? An update of sorts? I know Sir William said we shouldn't keep in touch . . . afterward . . . but I'm not certain I can abide by that, not if my silence will pain you."

Miranda shook her head, knowing full well that her father would never agree. "My father won't allow it. He'll make certain I don't receive any correspondence from you or Johan after I return home."

"Is there not somewhere I can write you where Sir William won't know? A friend, perhaps? Someone you can trust enough to receive the letters, and see that you get them?"

She had never considered it before now, never thought about attempting to deceive her father. But perhaps it would give her some comfort, some peace. She deserved that, at least. Caro, perhaps?

"My dear friend and neighbor, Caroline Denby. I trust her entirely." Caro could easily pass on Helen's correspondences to her, though what she would tell her in explanation, she could not imagine. Certainly not the truth.

Helen nodded approvingly. "Very good, then. Before you leave, you must give me Miss Denby's direction."

The blasted tears welled in her eyes once more, blurring her vision. "Thank you, Helen. For everything."

"Don't be silly, Miranda, darling. Thank *you.* You're giving me the best Christmas gift possible, the one thing I want more than anything in this world."

Again, Miranda dropped one hand to her belly. As if on cue, the babe kicked her, hard enough to make her breath catch.

Helen's blue eyes widened. "Is it . . . did you feel him move? May I?"

"Of course," Miranda whispered, taking her cousin's slender hand and placing it on her belly. A moment later, the babe kicked again.

Helen's expression was pure, rapturous joy. "Oh, how wonderful!" she breathed, her entire face lit with a smile. "I meant what I said, Miranda. You *will* fall in love again, with a man who deserves you. Who deserves this," she added, glancing down at her own hand, still on Miranda's swollen belly. "And when you do, the old hurts will begin to heal."

Miranda only hoped she was right. For how could she bear it otherwise?

Chapter 8

Wearing the exact same lavender ensemble and straw boater as the day before, Miranda sat on the ivory blanket spread on the ground in the magical clearing, and took up her pose.

Mr. Davenport had been mostly silent since her arrival at the gazebo, saying very little as they made their way through the bare trees, toward the clearing.

Miranda was glad for the quiet. Yesterday's session had ended badly, and she did not wish to speak of it. He had written her a formal note of apology, and she had quickly responded, affirming that she would uphold their agreement and meet him the following day, as planned.

As it happened, Bridget had taken ill after breakfast, presenting Sullivan with the difficult choice of leaving either Miranda or Gertie and Grace without a chaperone for the day's activities. Deciding that Gertie and Grace were far more of a danger left to their own devices, she had sent Miranda off on her own, imploring her to remember herself.

As if Miranda needed any reminding. She wasn't about to be taken in by a fortune hunter—not this time, no matter how handsome he might be.

Behind her, she could hear his brush stroking against the canvas, almost rhythmical. More than once, she almost dozed off. If not for the chattering gulls, calling to one another as they dipped into the clearing before disappearing back into the trees, she might very well have done so.

Every so often, the sound of the brush would quiet, and Miranda would feel the weight of his gaze on her. Her skin would prickle with awareness, and the moment would stretch on until Miranda thought she could no longer stand it. And then, just as she'd gather her courage to turn toward him, the gentle stroking of his brush would resume once more.

How long have I been sitting here? she wondered idly, noticing that sun's rays seemed brighter, stronger now. It must be nearing noon. Miranda wondered if the post had arrived, and whether it would bring a reply from Caro. She'd written her friend last week, giving her the hotel's direction in case a letter came from Helen in need of forwarding.

Kurt would be nine now. His birthday had come and gone, on the same day as her arrival there at the Grandview. With a heavy sigh, Miranda reined in her thoughts, refusing to allow them to wander that route. She couldn't, not now. Not till she was alone, till she had her cousin's letter in her hand and could savor each and every word in private.

Instead, she breathed in crisp air and exhaled slowly, waiting for Mr. Davenport to say something—anything.

"It's lovely today, isn't it?" she asked, suddenly uncomfortable with the silence.

"It is," Mr. Davenport answered. A rustle of cloth behind Miranda suggested that he was doffing his coat. "Only a winter's day can produce a sky as blue as this one."

Miranda kept her gaze trained on the same spot on the ground, resisting the urge to turn and glance back at him.

"You can relax a bit, if you'd like. I'm mainly working on the landscape now."

Miranda exhaled, inordinately pleased to have the focus shifted away from herself. "You work quickly," she said, readjusting her gloves.

"You're an easy subject. Besides, I've carried your image in my mind for so long now—" He broke off abruptly, clearing his throat. "Anyway, I can finish this canvas back in my studio."

"In France?"

"No, in London. My aunt allows me to stay with her in Town, and I've got a small studio there. Just an attic room, actually, but it serves its purpose. Excellent light."

Miranda could not staunch her curiosity. "Your aunt . . . is she someone with whom I am acquainted?"

He laughed at that. "No, definitely not. Mrs. Agnes Davenport of Wrotham Road. Her late husband was a vicar out in Hertfordshire, but he passed away many years ago."

Miranda nodded, trying to make sense of the relation. "So you're related by marriage, then? Through her late husband's side?"

"No, Aunt Agnes is my mother's eldest sister."

"But you have the same surname. If she's your mother's sister, and she was married to a Davenport—"

"It's complicated," he interrupted tersely. "Where is your keeper today? I assumed that she would eventually turn up."

Miranda turned to face him, her brows drawn. How odd that he wouldn't answer her question; it had been simple enough. Instead, he'd hurriedly changed the subject, as if . . . as if he had something to hide. "My keeper?" she asked, confused.

He didn't even glance her way. "Yes," he said, dipping his brush in the spot of gray on the palette. "Your minder. Your chaperone."

"My chaperone is otherwise engaged today, Mr. Davenport. Minding my younger sisters, who are far more in need of a 'keeper,' as you put it, than I am."

He shrugged, his gaze still trained on the canvas before him. "I should hope so."

"Whatever do you mean by that?"

"Only that you seem perfectly capable of conducting yourself on your own, that's all. I did not mean it as an insult. Just that you're a grown woman—"

"An unmarried woman," she corrected. Rising to her feet, she brushed off her skirts and attempted to straighten her clothing. "Have you any idea how irregular this is? Us, out here all alone like this? And you half . . . half undressed at that," she sputtered. Despite the chill in the air, his coat lay on the grass beside the stool, and he sat there in nothing save his shirtsleeves, rolled to the elbows.

"I see nothing irregular about it," he said with a maddening shrug. "I'm an artist, and you are my model. This is generally how it's done."

"Perhaps in *your* world, Mr. Davenport. I came here alone today against my better judgment, and—"

"Why did you come, then? If you're so very afraid of being alone in my company?" He set his palette down on the ground, laying his brush against it.

"I'm not afraid of you," she said, shaking her head. Her heart fluttered in her breast, her palms suddenly damp. God, but he was beautiful. Far too much so.

He stood, taking two steps toward her. "I think you are afraid, Miss Granger. You're trembling," he said, reaching for her hand. "Do I really frighten you so?"

She swallowed hard, trying to tear her gaze from his. However could she explain it? That she was afraid of her own reactions, her own feelings?

That whenever he stood too close, her heart began to race? That desire coursed through her, nearly stealing away her breath?

She'd denied this part of herself for so very long now—the part of her that craved a man's touch. She'd buried it deep inside, allowing it to wilt away. At least, she'd thought it had.

Why did this particular man have to awaken those long-forgotten feelings? Why an artist—a poor one, if his slightly shabby, somewhat unfashionable clothing was any indication—and an American, at that?

She barely knew him; she could not even claim a longstanding affection that had blossomed into an attraction. He was a stranger to her. And yet . . . and yet she somehow felt as if she knew him. As if he might somehow drag her out from under the veil of darkness she'd been hiding under all these years.

"Miranda?" he asked, so close now that she could feel his heat warming her skin.

"I frighten myself, Mr. Davenport," she whispered, her mouth suddenly dry.

"Troy," he corrected, one arm reaching around her waist, drawing her closer.

Miranda shook her head, but she did not draw away. "I shouldn't feel this way. I can't."

"Why?" A shock of hair fell across his forehead, and Miranda resisted the urge to reach up and brush it back, to tangle her fingers in his hair and draw his mouth toward hers.

She inhaled sharply, dropping her gaze. "What do you want from me? When I asked you this same question before, you said only to paint me. I've allowed that, and now . . . now what?"

"I don't know," he said, shaking his head. "I only know that I want to erase the pain in your eyes. To make you smile. To hear you laugh. Is that really so wrong?"

If only it were as easy as that. "I'm afraid I'm not the best judge of right from wrong. I think perhaps you should release me." His nearness was affecting her ability to think clearly.

"Only if you'll continue to sit for me. Tomorrow, indoors this time, and without your chaperone. I'll set up my room as a studio."

Miranda shook her head, about to refuse, when he quickly pressed on.

"It's one of the less expensive rooms, off the beaten path and without any view to speak of. No one will see you coming or going, I vow. You mustn't say no, Miranda." He squeezed her hand, his gaze imploring. "Just look," he said, drawing her gaze toward the canvas behind them. "This is the single most inspired painting I've done in ages. You cannot abandon me now."

Miranda took a step toward the easel, shaking her head in amazement. He wasn't exaggerating— even unfinished, the painting was exquisite. There was no denying his talent, nor was there any point in denying that she wanted him to paint her, wanted to spend more time in his company.

"Very well," she murmured. "At the very least, I'll try."

She only hoped she wouldn't come to regret it.

"Look, there's Edmund," Gertie said, her cheeks flushing a deep rose. "I must go speak to him."

"Sit!" Miranda ordered, reaching for her sister's hand and pulling her back into her seat. "Good God, Gertie. You can't just waltz over to his table and begin conversing with him."

Gertie fixed her with a glare. "I don't see why not. It's not as if we're going to do anything improper, right here in the dining room."

"Because it's far too forward, that's why. If a gentleman wishes to speak with you, he can approach you, not the other way around. Haven't you any sense of propriety at all?"

"Apparently not," Gertie answered sourly.

With a shake of her head, Miranda released her sister's hand. "Father should be joining us any minute now. Can you at least attempt to behave yourselves in his presence?"

"What did *I* do?" Grace whined, folding her arms across her breasts. "I'm not the one making a fool out of myself over someone who's barely glanced—"

"Be quiet, Grace!" Gertie practically yelled, her flush deepening to crimson.

"Why should I? After the way—"

"Enough!" Miranda hissed. "Please. Can't we get through one meal without the two of you squabbling like children? I told Father we should have left the pair of you at home."

Gertie pouted like an infant. "You'd like that, wouldn't you? Leaving us to rot at home, while you get to have all the fun."

Miranda nearly laughed aloud at that. "Fun? When have I ever had fun with the two of you about, plaguing me all the time? Now shush, here comes our waiter."

"Miss Granger?" the man said, bending over her and holding out a folded slip of paper. "Sir William asked that you get this message."

"Thank you," Miranda said, taking it and unfolding it, her eyes quickly scanning the page. "I'm afraid Father won't be joining us tonight, after all. His meeting ran late, he says. Well, I suppose we should go ahead and order, then."

Once they had made their selections and sent the waiter on his way, Miranda returned her attention to her sisters. However were they going to make it through the meal without Father to distract them? "Why don't the two of you tell me how you spent your day," she said, glancing encouragingly from one to the other. "If you can do it without having a row, that is."

"We played charades this morning," Grace offered. "And then Sullivan made us go cycling after lunch with the Fairfax girls."

Gertie rolled her eyes. "She refused to let us go down to the pier. Said our skin was getting brown, which is ridiculous, of course. It's December!"

"Yes, look at my face." Grace leaned across the table toward Miranda. "Not a single freckle. Won't you have a talk with her? Bridget's still feeling ill, and I just know we'll be stuck with Sullivan again tomorrow. I can't bear spending another day with the Fairfax girls."

Miranda nodded, remembering the promise she'd made to Mr. Davenport. She needed Sullivan out of her hair, and far enough away so that she wouldn't be able to check on her whereabouts. "I suppose I can," she murmured. "I'll tell her to take you down to the pier tomorrow, but only if you both promise me you'll behave. Have I your word?"

"Why don't you come with us, Miranda?" Grace offered. "You haven't even been to the pier yet, and it's quite lovely."

"I already have plans, I'm afraid. But perhaps the day after—"

"What sort of plans?" Gertie asked, wrinkling her nose. "Is that American painter still working on your portrait?"

"His name is Mr. Davenport," Grace said far too loudly, causing the diners at the next table to turn and look in their direction. "The Fairfax girls were talking about him just today. They say he's exceptionally handsome and exciting, even if he is a bit shabby."

"Shhh," Miranda said, glancing about guiltily. "Would you please lower your voice?"

"I'm sorry," Grace whispered. "Anyway, they

were green with envy when I told them he was painting your portrait."

"You shouldn't gossip about him; it isn't lady-like. Anyway, it's not a portrait, not really. Just a . . . a painting, I suppose. But I did say I'd sit for him again tomorrow, so if you girls would like to go to the pier, I'll tell Sullivan to take you."

"Thank you, Miranda," Gertie said, her good humor entirely restored now that she was getting her way—about this, at least. "And speaking of Mr. Davenport, isn't that him dancing with Miss Soames?"

"I'm sure I don't know," Miranda said with a shrug. It wasn't any of her business who he danced with, she told herself rather unconvincingly. It took all the restraint she could muster to continue facing forward, toward her sisters, rather than turning in her chair and craning her neck to search him out amongst the dancers.

But Gertie wouldn't let it drop. "Well, turn around and look. Go on. There, on the far end of the dance floor. Wait, the song has ended. His partner was definitely Miss Soames; I can see her face now. But look, he's headed in our direction."

Grace twisted in her chair, looking over one shoulder. "Do you think he's coming to ask Miranda to dance?"

"I suppose so, as he's coming right toward our table," Gertie squealed. "You must say yes, Miranda!"

"Your sister is right," came the now-familiar

masculine voice, just behind her chair. "You must say yes."

"And what, exactly, am I agreeing to, Mr. Davenport?" she asked, turning toward him with a forced smile.

His own smile was dazzling. "One dance. With each of the lovely Granger women, of course. Starting with Miss Gertrude, if you'll allow it."

"Of course," Miranda repeated, watching in stunned silence as he offered a hand to Gertie and led her out to the dance floor, Grace gaping after them.

"That was rather unexpected," Grace said, finding her voice at last.

"Indeed," was all Miranda could manage.

Chapter 9

Troy glanced down at his dance partner as he twirled her around the ballroom, wishing he were anywhere else but there. The girl he held in his arms was lovely; there was no denying that fact. Diana Livingston looked like a china doll, with wide blue eyes and hair the color of toffee, her mouth a perfect bow, her skin as pale and perfect as the finest porcelain.

Indeed, Diana was exactly the type of girl his parents hoped he would court and eventually marry. She was First Four Hundred, and that was all that mattered to his socially ambitious mother. His father didn't care about a girl's pedigree, only that her family had money. Old money, new money—it didn't really matter to him, one way or the other.

"You seem rather distracted tonight, Mr. DeWitt," the girl murmured. "I do hope I'm not boring you."

"Of course not," Troy answered, attempting to smile. Truth was, he *was* distracted. He was expected to return to Harvard in a fortnight, which meant he was running out of time to speak to his father about his plans.

"Then perhaps you could wipe that scowl from your face. Goodness, Kate said you were in a bit of temper tonight. I should have heeded her warning." Diana tossed her head, a smile tipping the corners of her pretty mouth.

"And miss out on a turn about the dance floor with your favorite partner, Miss Livingston?" he teased. "Surely not."

"You'll ruin my reputation as the most agreeable girl in New York with that frown of yours. Come, let's quit this waltz and get some refreshments, instead."

Diana stepped out of his hold and led him through the crowd toward the refreshment room. "Mmm, champagne punch," she murmured, and Troy took a glass from the serving maid and handed it to her.

"Your mother certainly knows how to throw a ball, doesn't she?" Diana asked, taking the proffered champagne glass and sipping daintily. "Everything is absolutely perfect tonight."

"My mother is nothing if not thorough." She had spent weeks going over every little detail of tonight's festivities—the ball where Troy's sister Kate's engagement would be publicly announced.

Everything, from each flower arrangement to the orchestra's playlist, was agonized over, and nothing more so than the guest list. As always, his mother had made certain that only the cream of New York society graced her ballroom. The irony being, of course, that she herself came from modest means. One could barely believe it, watching her now.

Perhaps she overcompensated, he rationalized. Perhaps her hauteur hid a deep-seated insecurity, a sense of being "different" from her peers. She was English by birth, and he'd seen the little cottage in Hertfordshire where she'd grown up. The entire abode would easily fit inside their ballroom there at DeWitt House.

It would seem that, for all intents and purposes, Lillian's life had only begun the moment she married Cornelius DeWitt and took her place in New York society. Any talk of her life prior to that event was not to be countenanced, not even amongst family. Not once had she invited her sister—her only living relative—to visit. Instead, they traveled to London every few years to visit Troy's aunt Agnes, never staying at her modest flat in Wrotham Road, but taking up residence at Claridge's, instead. As if they were far too fine for Aunt Agnes's hospitality. This, more than anything, filled Troy with shame.

"Shall we take a turn out on the terrace?" Diana asked, setting down her glass on a passing servant's tray. "I've got good news to share—I'm nearly bursting with it."

"Indeed, let's get some air." Eager for the diversion, he offered his arm and led her through the French doors to the stone terrace that over-looked his mother's fragrant rose garden. "Very well, out with it," he said once they'd stepped out into the warm, balmy night.

She glanced up at him, triumphant gleam in her eyes. "I've agreed to marry Francis Vanden-berg."

"That's it?" Troy couldn't help but roll his eyes. "You're getting married? Well, I guess it's to be expected. First Kate, now you."

"Come now, Troy. You could at least pretend to be brokenhearted," Diana said with a practiced pout.

"Oh, I could. But you'd know I was lying." He leaned against the stone railing and sighed loudly. "Though now that I think about it, I *am* broken-hearted that you would promise yourself to such a starchy chap as that. You can't possibly fancy yourself in love with him. No more than Kate fan-cies herself in love with Theodore Baldwin."

Diana shrugged. "Of course not. Don't be ridiculous. Still, we've made excellent matches, your sister and I. You should be pleased for us both."

For a moment, Troy simply stared down at her, the light of the moon reflected in her eyes. Fran-cis Vandenberg was as rich as Croesus, his family descended from New York's original Dutch set-tlers. He was also slightly paunchy, entirely devoid of a sense of humor, and a good ten years older than Diana.

"Does your own happiness mean so little to you?" he asked at last.

Diana tapped Troy on the wrist with her fan. "You see, that's where you're mistaken. We'll both be quite happy, your sister and I. Our lives will go on much the same as before, won't they?"

Troy felt a sharp pain in his gut. "We're different, then. I cannot wait to escape this life."

"You would give this up so readily?" Diana gestured toward the glittering gilt and marble archway beyond the French doors that led toward the vast, chandelier-lit ballroom of his parents' home, DeWitt House—one of the largest and most ostentatious of the new breed of palazzo-style Fifth Avenue mansions.

When Troy didn't immediately answer, Diana nodded thoughtfully. "You're still young, that's all. Wait till you finish at Harvard and go to work with your father—"

"I'm not going back to Harvard," he interrupted with a shake of his head. God, it felt so good to say it aloud!

His companion's cornflower-blue eyes narrowed a fraction. "Whatever do you mean? Of course you are. You've only a year left, and then—"

"I'm going to France. To Paris. In a fortnight."

"But you've only just returned from the Continent," Diana protested.

"Yes, where I met other artists like myself,

young men wishing to study under the masters, willing to apprentice themselves—"

"Have you entirely lost your mind, Troy De-Witt?" Diana's eyes were wide with unconcealed shock. "You can't just drop out of Harvard and abandon your family, not with Kate's wedding coming up, and now mine, too. Besides, you know your father won't have it."

Just imagining his father's reaction made Troy's blood run cold. "This isn't up to my father. It's my own decision, and my family will have to accept it."

"Accept it?" A glint of amusement shone in Diana's eyes. "Surely you know they won't. Besides, what will you do? Go live amongst a set of starving artists, you in your finery with your gold watch and diamond tie pins?" she asked with a delicate snort of laughter.

Troy shook his head. "Of course not. I can't let any of them think I'm some dilettante, whiling away my days on my father's coin while I dabble in art. No, instead I'll take my mother's maiden name, style myself as Troy Davenport, middling-class bloke from New York. I'll find success on my own merit, or not at all. I won't use the DeWitt name or fortune."

"It's a good thing, because your father is likely to disown you. You know he's counting on you to join Gabe at the bank next year."

Troy's jaw tightened uncomfortably. "Gabe doesn't need me. He'll do a fine job carrying on the family business without me."

Diana shook her head. "Gabe is sweet, but not half as smart or competent as you are. You know your father is counting on you—"

"I can't do it." Troy's fist came down hard on the stone railing. Damn it, he hated the way his voice cracked, hated the despair that flooded through his veins at the thought of spending the rest of his life sitting behind a desk at the bank his grandfather—made wealthy by the railroads—had founded. His throat tight, he lowered his voice to a hoarse whisper. "I *won't* do it, Diana. It would kill me to do so. Surely you must understand that."

Diana chewed on her lower lip, then nodded. "When will you tell him?"

"Tomorrow. We're having dinner at the club. I'll tell him and Gabe together."

"Smart." Diana nodded her approval. "He won't be able to murder you in public."

"Precisely. It doesn't matter, though. I'm going, with or without his approval."

She exhaled slowly, her brows drawn. "But how will you support yourself if he cuts you off? Even starving artists must have something to live on."

"I'm of age, and I've got access to my own funds now. I can live off what I've got for a very long time, if I live frugally."

Diana shuddered. "Frugally? You? You mean to say you would actually choose to live like . . . like a common person?"

"Unlike you—and my sister, too, it would seem—I put my own happiness far above my personal comfort. I can easily live without all this." He spread his arms wide, nearly knocking into a servant bearing a tray of canapés in the process.

She shook her head. "I just don't understand you, Troy. I never did. You were always so different from the other boys."

"And yet you adore me anyway," he quipped, raising one brow.

"Of course I do. It won't be nearly as fun here without you. You'll come back next summer for the season in Newport, won't you?"

"For a visit, perhaps, if my family will have me. But nothing more permanent than that."

"Well, isn't that lovely," she said sourly. Tears had gathered on her lashes. "So you're telling me good-bye, then? Just like that?"

Troy just shrugged. "Unless you want to forget about Francis Vandenberg, and come with me to Paris."

"And live in some dusty little rat hole?" Her lower lip curled in disgust. "Good God, no."

"I figured as much," he said, forcing a smile. He was fond of Diana, and yet he'd never understand her. No more than he could understand Kate, or any of the women in his social circle.

Diana had always been such fun, his favorite of his sister's friends. She'd been a free-spirited girl, always up for mischief—right up until her formal debut into society. And then, right before his eyes, she'd morphed into the same creature as all the other girls—girls who assessed a man by the size of his fortune, the promise of his future, the square footage of his mansion. Ever since then, she'd acted her role to perfection—the role to which she was born. *Decoration. Ornament. Accompaniment.*

Now and then, somewhere behind her placid expression and coy smile, he'd detect a hint of the old Diana, the girl whose fingers were always stained from ink, who quoted romantic poets, and allowed a stolen kiss or two in the cloakroom. But then, just as quickly, the spark would fade and he'd stare wistfully at the girl who was now a stranger.

The old Diana would never consider marrying someone as boring and stiff as Francis Vandenberg, yet this Diana viewed such a match as a happy triumph. He could not credit it, could not understand how someone's essence could change so drastically. And yet he'd seen it happen, time and time again. Even his own sister had become a stranger.

He had to leave, had to get away from New York and society's trappings, or he feared his own essence, too, might slip away. He might very well turn into his father, or into his brother, Gabe. Not that he was criticizing either one; it was just that their lives weren't what Troy longed for.

No. He was going to Paris. He would learn from the masters. He would become his own man, damn it.

Chapter 10

"So, Mr. Davenport," Miss Gertrude murmured, "my sister says you are still painting her portrait out-of-doors."

Troy decided not to contradict her. "Your sister is an excellent subject. It's unpleasant at best, sitting for hours on end with no entertainment whatsoever. She bears it with good grace." He cleared his throat and paused a beat before continuing. "Your family's estate is in Surrey, I'm told?"

"Yes, Holly's Close, near Weckham. Dreadfully dull, but Father prefers to rusticate."

"I'm quite fond of the countryside myself."

The girl raised one dark brow. "Aren't you from New York?"

"I am. Perhaps that's why I'm drawn to England's quiet villages. An escape, one might say, from the city's bustle and noise." He could see Miss Granger watching them, her eyes following every twirl, every dip. He could physically feel it—her gaze, making his skin warm as awareness skittered across it.

"And how are you enjoying your stay here at the Grandview?" he asked, dragging his attention back to his dance partner.

"Very much. In fact, I wish we could stay on a bit longer. My father says perhaps we'll come back in the summertime so that we can go sea bathing. Though I'm sure if Miranda has her way, we'll end up stuck at home. She hates to travel, though I've no idea why."

"I'm sure she has her reasons," he murmured, wishing the song would end, allowing him to escort the girl back to the table and claim the youngest Miss Granger. The sooner she had her turn about the dance floor, the sooner he could claim the one woman in the room he truly wished to hold in his arms.

"I love New York," the girl said. "It's so very exciting, perhaps even more so than London. Father took us this autumn—he went on business, of course, though he and Miranda attended a ball at Albany House. He said that Grace and I were too young to accompany them, though I can't see why there should be an age requirement for having fun. Instead we were stuck at the hotel with Sullivan breathing down our necks."

Troy just grunted noncommittally. "So what do you do back in Weckham?" he asked, grasping for a suitable topic of conversation. "Are you in school?"

"My sister and I take lessons with a governess,

hateful creature, though I'm hoping Father will send me to finishing school next year. Miranda was sent to Switzerland, so it's only fair that Grace and I go, too."

At last she quieted, looking past his shoulder toward a table of diners near the orchestra. Moments passed in blessed silence, her attention mercifully diverted by whatever was going on at that particular table.

"Perhaps you'll come to Weckham one day, Mr. Davenport," she said at last, smiling up at him prettily. "There's an old abbey there," she added, and Troy realized she was actually batting her lashes at him. "Weckham Abbey. That's where the village got its name. Some say it's lovely, though it just looks like a pile of stones to me. Perhaps you could paint it."

"And what other diversions might I find in Weckham?" he asked with a laugh.

"Just the usual things. A pub, some shops. Crooked streets and crumbling old houses. I'd be happy to show you around," she added.

Perhaps it was time to take her back to her seat. "I suppose you're missing your first course. I should return you to your sisters."

"If you must," she muttered.

Troy felt a tap on his shoulder, and turned to find a red-faced lad standing there. The boy swallowed hard, his prominent Adam's apple bobbing up and down. "Might I cut in?" he asked.

"Edmund!" Miss Gertrude breathed. "It's so

good of you to rescue me, since Mr. Davenport here was just about to abandon me."

"Then may I?" The boy held out one hand.

"Of course," Troy said with a shrug, glancing over to see Miss Granger watching them with drawn brows. *Damn.* He glanced back at the boy, who looked rather harmless.

He handed over his partner and straightened his coat before returning to the Grangers' table. "I didn't have the heart to refuse him," he said with a wince, waiting for Miss Granger's scolding.

Instead, she smiled a tight smile. "I told her that he could pay his respects, as long as it's done properly. I suppose there's no harm in it." She craned her neck, searching for her sister through the crowd of twirling dancers.

"Oh, go on," the youngest Granger said, shaking her head. "I'll claim my dance with Mr. Davenport another night. Go, where you can keep an eye on her. Lord knows she requires it."

Troy held out his hand to Miss Granger, awaiting her reply.

Her eyes met his, and then she nodded. "If you don't mind, Mr. Davenport?"

"Not in the least," he answered, trying to suppress a grin.

Mere seconds later, he placed one hand on the small of Miss Granger's back. In his other hand, he clasped her gloved one, noting the way it trembled slightly, as if she feared his touch, his nearness. Begrudgingly, he took a step back, putting more distance between their bodies.

As he began to turn her about the floor, he was suddenly reminded of the last time he'd danced like this, five years ago—at his mother's ball, just before he'd left Harvard and upended his life. He'd felt so stifled then, so desperate to rid himself of the confines of New York society, of women who viewed relationships as nothing but a means to an end. And yet here he was, holding a woman who wasn't very different from the girl he'd held then—only, Miss Granger was good *ton* rather than First Four Hundred. Only geography differentiated the two, as far as he was concerned.

What was he thinking, considering making her more than his subject, more than his muse? No doubt he was thinking with his cock, always a dangerous thing. And yet he wanted her, as if she were some French whore for the taking rather than a gently bred woman of means. And yet she was no different from Diana Livingston and her kind, bound to society's rules and dictates, judging a man's worth in pound notes. A trembling virgin, even.

He'd eschewed all that, hadn't he? He'd left it all behind when he'd taken off for the Continent, when he'd abandoned the DeWitt name and entitlements.

Then why couldn't he get the sweet-smelling, sad-faced Miss Granger out of his thoughts? Why did he spend every spare moment mentally undressing her, imagining the curve of her breast, the slope of her belly, the dark curls between her legs that he desperately wanted to bury his face in, to explore with his mouth?

Bloody hell, just last night he'd set his as-yet-unfinished painting of her on the easel and stared at it while he'd grabbed his cock and stroked himself till he came with such urgency that he'd had to clench his teeth to keep from crying out.

It made no sense, and yet it made perfect sense as he held her in his arms, twirling her about the dance floor.

"You dance well," Miss Granger said, a note of suspicion in her voice.

"Yes, well, we're not entirely uncivilized in New York."

"Of course, but I thought—" She broke off abruptly, biting her lower lip.

That he was uncultured. He'd never said he was; he only let her make her own assumptions. Not that he could fault her conclusion—she'd first met him on the second-class deck of the *Mauretania,* after all, and the Davenports were not people of means or connections.

He was suddenly struck with a twinge of regret for misleading her. Still, his desire to tell her the truth battled with another, more powerful one—a desire to be wanted for himself.

Troy DeWitt had been wanted for his name, his place in society, his deep pockets. Women had wanted Troy Davenport, too—women who sought the attentions of artists, who hoped to be made famous by his brush. But to be wanted for

no other reason than his own personal worth—
indeed, to be wanted despite what Miss Granger
would see as his unsuitability . . . yes, *that* was
what he truly craved.

After all, he *was* Troy Davenport now. He was
an artist, a man with no permanent home, no ties
to society. To claim his DeWitt heritage in hopes
of securing a woman's affections seemed wrong,
somehow misleading.

He was never going back to that life, to the glittering Fifth Avenue mansions and affected manners, to the familial obligations that came with
being Cornelius DeWitt's son.

"She seems to be behaving herself well enough,"
Miss Granger murmured.

Troy shook his head, momentarily confused.
"Who is?"

"My sister. Gertie."

Troy nodded. "Of course. Lovely girl," he said,
just to be polite. "She reminds me a bit of my
sister, Kate." In looks, anyway. Certainly not in
temperament, at least from what he could dis-
cern from the short time spent in her company.

"Heaven help your mother, then," she said,
glancing up with a bemused expression on her
lovely face. Their eyes met and held, her smile
slowly fading as seconds passed. Troy could have
sworn he saw a flicker of desire, of longing, as if
he'd caught her off guard. And then, just like
that, the moment passed. She dropped her gaze,
her lashes fluttering as she glanced down at
her slippers.

Troy cleared his throat, wishing desperately he could somehow get that moment back. Better yet, that he could capture it on canvas. "Your sister tells me that your family's estate is near Weckham. I've always wanted to visit that part of Surrey."

She glanced back up at him again, a faint smile tipping the corners of her mouth. "Why on earth would you want to do that? There's nothing particularly special about Weckham. Lord knows my sisters find the village boring enough. I never hear the end of their complaints."

"Isn't there an old abbey there?" Thank God for young Miss Gertrude's chatty nature. "Or the ruins of one, at least? It's quite picturesque, I'm told."

Miss Granger shrugged. "I suppose it is."

"So," he pressed, "if I were to visit Weckham, is there an inn of some sort nearby that you'd recommend?"

"You're not serious?" she asked, her brows drawn over suspicious eyes.

He nodded, hating the way she seemed to shrink away from him now, as if he'd gone too far. Still, he could not help himself. After all, he had no intention of quitting her company anytime soon, and if that meant traveling to Surrey, then so be it.

She let out a sigh. "Don't you have any obligations whatsoever? Or do you simply travel about like a vagabond to wherever you please?"

"That's precisely what I do." He shrugged, glancing down at her with an uneasy smile. Disappointment shot through him. Why had he allowed himself to hope that she was different from the rest, that she could set aside her expectations where he was concerned? "I travel wherever my muse leads me," he said, affecting an air of nonchalance. "Occasionally I'll take a commission or two, if the mood strikes me. I'm not quite certain why that should offend you."

"It doesn't," she answered absently, glancing past his shoulder. "I do wish she'd stay where I could see her."

"Your sister and her young suitor?"

Miss Granger visibly flinched. "Suitor? I hope not. She's far too young for that."

"You're very protective of your sisters, aren't you?"

She shook her head. "No more than any other elder sister would be. Besides, they haven't a mother, so they're my responsibility. I only want what's best for them."

"And what about what's best for you? Who sees to *your* happiness?"

She smiled then, a taut, uncomfortable smile. "In case you did not notice, Mr. Davenport, I am what's affectionately called an 'old maid.' It's *their* time now, and my job is to see them both happily settled."

"Surely you can't mean that. You're far too young to set aside your own life—your own hopes and dreams—for theirs."

"What do you know of my dreams?" she snapped. "My hopes? You presume to know me—"

"I *want* to know you," he corrected.

She let out her breath in a rush, her cheeks flushed a deep rosy pink. "Why, Mr. Davenport? Why must you know me?"

Frustration ripped through him. He drew her closer, her breasts nearly pressed against his coat. "Don't pretend you don't feel it, Miss Granger," he whispered, dipping his head toward her ear. "This . . . this electrical current between us. You feel it, too—I'd stake my life on it." He'd seen it there, in her eyes, before she drew that maddening curtain across them.

"You're holding me much too closely," she said, her voice a hoarse whisper. "And the song has ended, besides."

"Has it? I didn't notice." He took a deep breath, his eyes scouring her face, looking for some sort of encouragement. He got none. "To-morrow, then, Miss Granger. At ten A.M."

She said nothing, only nodded, her lower lip caught between her teeth.

"Room 214," he murmured, then released her.

"Good night, Mr. Davenport," she said, her voice as calm, as serene as ever.

She walked away without a backward glance, damn it.

Dawn would not come fast enough. Troy lay on his back, his arms folded behind his head and the bedclothes tucked about his waist, as he waited for the sun to pierce the darkness. Bit by bit, the deep, impenetrable black turned to violet, then lavender, then silver before the sun's pale yellow rays began to warm Troy's skin. Anticipation coiled in the pit of his stomach—an artist's curiosity mixed with a sexual hunger that he hadn't felt in ages. Hell, maybe *ever.*

What would the day bring? He couldn't wait to find out. There was such an air of mystery about Miss Granger—*Miranda,* he corrected, saying her name aloud, letting the syllables roll off his tongue. There was a certain lyrical quality to the name. It suited her somehow.

Sitting up, he reached for his pocket watch and checked the time. Still far too early for breakfast. Ten A.M. seemed eons away, and he was restless. He considered taking an early-morning walk down to the boardwalk, but feared he might encounter other guests doing the same, and he did not feel up to making idle chitchat. Or, even worse, deflecting the requests of those still eager for him to paint their loved ones, as he'd done for Lady Barclay.

Even now, total strangers waved him over, requesting a word, shoving their cards into his reluctant hand. He'd refused each and every request since painting Miss Soames. Word had gotten out that he was now painting Miss Granger—no doubt aided by her sisters' gossip—and now everyone was vying to be his next subject.

Indeed, when he'd retired to his room after quitting the dining room last night, he'd pulled no less than a half-dozen cards from his waistcoat pocket. He'd tossed them into the rubbish bin, along with three he'd received earlier in the day.

François would no doubt chastise him if he knew. A lucrative commission could come from any of them, his always-wise art dealer would likely say. No reason to burn bridges. But right now he had a good feeling about the work he was currently producing. He'd organize a show—in the autumn, perhaps. By then he hoped to have several paintings of Miranda.

Perhaps he'd even invite Kate and her husband, Theodore. Gabe and his wife, too. Not his parents—surely not. They still refused to receive him, after all. But Kate . . . he might very well be able to convince her to come. After all, she'd defied their parents' wishes when he was last in New York and come to see him at his hotel.

Throwing off the bedclothes, Troy stood and stretched, then reached for his trousers. He might as well do something constructive to pass the time, he decided, as he pulled up the trousers and fastened them. Striding over to the desk in the room's corner, he took out a piece of stationery embossed with the hotel's name and rummaged for a pen. He'd write a letter to François, tell him his ideas for an autumn show.

François could start working on the details now. Troy was certain that he'd have enough new paintings to warrant it. Not necessarily by the time he left the Grandview, but certainly after a few months in Surrey.

After all, there was no doubt in his mind that that's where he was going next. The village of Weckham. In fact, perhaps François could start looking for a place there for Troy to let for a few months—something modest, inexpensive. His only requirement was that it was nearby Sir William's estate—Holly's Close, according to Miss Gertrude.

With a newfound sense of anticipation, Troy picked up the fountain pen and began to write.

Chapter 11

Miranda glanced at her reflection one last time, swallowing hard as she repositioned a hairpin that had slipped. It was nearly ten A.M. Bridget was still ill, leaving Gertie and Grace in Sullivan's care, which meant that Sullivan was fully occupied for the day. Her father was busy with his own affairs, and wasn't likely to appear before dinnertime. Indeed, no one was the slightest bit concerned with how Miranda might spend her day.

Leaving her free to do as she wished. And the truth was, she wished to go to Mr. Davenport's room, to let him paint her in whatever intimate setting he proposed.

There, I've admitted it. Somehow doing so gave Miranda a great sense of relief. After all, she was no longer a naïve girl of nineteen, easy prey for a fortune hunter. She wasn't quite certain what Mr. Davenport's intentions were, but she could no longer deny her own needs, her own desires.

She desired Mr. Davenport. And why not? He

was young and handsome, charming and virile. He certainly acted as if he desired *her*. If that proved to be the case, then she would be using *him,* not the other way around. She was older, wiser than she was last time, when Paul had stolen her heart, her pride. And if Mr. Davenport only wanted to paint her . . . well, then, she would be his muse.

Something he'd said last night had stuck with her, keeping her up long into the night. "Who sees to *your* happiness?" he'd asked, and the simple answer was "no one." No one cared that Miranda was a woman with feelings, with dreams and desires. Her father considered her ruined, soiled goods to eventually pawn off on one of his associates, if he so deemed it fit. He would consider it a favor to one of his cronies. A widower, perhaps with grown children of his own, who hoped for a young, pretty wife—one with a fat dowry, no doubt—to see him through his twilight years.

But first her father expected her to see that both Grace and Gertie made advantageous matches and were happily settled. Which meant several more lonely years until she could look forward to her own bleak future—becoming a middle-aged bride, likely to a man nearly twice her age. She'd be nothing more than a pet, a mere possession.

As far as her father was concerned, that was all she was worth. Less, really. How many years would he punish her for her mistakes? As if her painful memories weren't punishment enough, suffered in silence. Even Caroline, her dearest friend in all the world, had no idea about the depth of her sorrows.

No one cared about her happiness—that was the simple truth. And now a handsome young man was pursuing her, awakening feelings long forgotten, desires long abandoned. Was it so wrong to give in to them, just once in all these years? To allow a measure—however brief—of pleasure to creep into her desolate, dreary existence?

Still staring into the looking glass, she took a deep breath, amazed at the thinness of her cheeks, the hollowness in her eyes. Her loneliness was leaching away what girlish bloom was left in her countenance. She no longer recognized the woman who stared back at her—this thin, delicate, fragile woman with haunted eyes.

She did not want to be that woman, not anymore. She wanted to live again. To bloom again. And what better man than Troy Davenport to bring her back to life? He was a man of no commitments, no home, no responsibilities. He would expect nothing from her, and he would make her no promises. They were from two different worlds, after all. Different spheres. Their lives had only briefly intersected, and would just as quickly move on, each on their own path, with no regrets and no recriminations.

At least she hoped that was the case. If, indeed, her instincts were wrong and he *was* a fortune hunter, well . . . he would soon learn that she wasn't so easily manipulated, not this time. Besides, she would never be as careless as before. She wouldn't dare risk such heartache, such heart-wrenching sorrow again. If nothing else, she'd learned her lesson, and learned it well.

She would conduct an affair like a modern woman would—a woman of the world, a woman who placed value on her *own* happiness. She certainly would not be the first of her class to do so. No one looked askance at a widow who took lovers—indeed, some women were nearly famous for just that. And though she wasn't a widow, she often felt like one. Like Caro.

She nodded, as if giving herself permission. She met her own gaze in the glass, saw the determination there in her eyes. She would do this now, before she lost her courage.

With one more deep, calming breath, she straightened her shoulders and strode briskly toward the door, letting herself out and locking the door. Her legs wobbled slightly as she maneuvered the hotel's long corridors, passing briefly through the lobby where an enormous fir tree reached the ceiling, twinkling with hundreds of tiny electric lights and decorated with red velvet bows and colorful ornaments made from blown glass.

Continuing past the tree, she made her way toward the near-deserted corridor where Mr. Davenport's room was located. He'd told the truth—the few people she did pass coming and going on this particular wing were not of her acquaintance. Their dress was simpler, not shabby, but not the height of fashion, either. Who were these people? she wondered. What brought them to the hotel's opening?

She didn't have long to puzzle over it, as she soon enough found herself standing before a black-lacquered door at the far end of the corridor, the number 214 engraved on a brass plaque beside it.

She did not risk glancing about, but instead rapped sharply and quickly, holding her breath as she awaited a reply. When the door opened, Miranda wordlessly slipped inside. Unlike her own room, this one had no antechamber, and she found herself standing directly inside Mr. Davenport's bedchamber.

"You've come," he said, standing so close that she could feel his heat, smell his scent—an odd mix of tobacco, perhaps, and turpentine.

For a moment, Miranda simply stood there trembling, her heart beating like a rabbit's. She glanced around the room, which he'd clearly prepared for her sitting. He'd closed the drapes and lit an electric lamp in the room's far corner where he'd dragged a deep blue velvet chaise and draped it with a throw a shade lighter. Directly across from the chaise, his easel was already set up, a blank canvas on its stand, a palette and brush lying on the low stool before it.

He was behind her now, his broad chest pressed against her back, one hand resting on her shoulder.

She found herself unable to speak, unable to do anything but stand there, her chest rising and falling with rapid breaths.

"Come," he said softly, turning her so that she stood facing him, only inches separating them. He reached for her hand and placed her palm against his heart, laying his own hand on top of hers.

She could feel his heartbeat, as rapid as hers, thumping insistently against her palm.

He tipped his chin down, his gaze seeking hers. "This is what happens to my heart the moment I lay eyes on you. Why do you suppose that is?"

"I . . . I cannot say," she stuttered.

A shock of bronze hair had fallen across his forehead, over one eye. That sight alone made her pulse leap. The simple fact that she was alone with a man in a room—a room with a bed, so utterly and completely taboo—excited her and terrified her, all at once.

"But I suppose mine does the same," she ventured, her voice nearly a whisper. "The moment I lay eyes on *you*, that is."

His gaze shot up to meet hers, his eyes wide with surprise, as if he hadn't expected a response like that. A shiver worked its way down her spine, and she realized she was glad—oh, so glad—to have startled him so. That meant he had been unsure of her reaction, perhaps as insecure as she was.

Nothing like Paul, who would have only quirked

a brow and smiled a cocky smile, entirely sure of his effect on her.

Her hand still pressed to his heart, he drew her closer still, his head dipping down toward her neck. She tipped her head to one side in invitation, shuddering when his lips touched her skin, his breath warm and moist through the lace of her collar.

"Dear God, Miranda, have you any idea how long I've wanted . . . how I've dreamed of this?" came his muffled voice, a hoarse, ragged whisper. "Since that night on the *Mauretania,* I've thought of nothing else. You've near enough driven me mad with wanting."

Miranda swallowed hard, terrified to say the things she felt inside, to describe the physical need she'd experienced since that very same night. The fact that he'd called her by her given name did not escape her notice. How she longed to say his name, to hear it roll off her tongue. If only she weren't so terrified, so afraid to give in to her feelings, afraid to go down the path that had led to her ruin in the past.

His mouth moved higher, shoving aside the top of her collar, his lips insistent beneath her ear where her pulse leapt wildly. "I want to touch you," he murmured. "I want to feel your skin against my fingertips. I want to trace every inch of your body, to memorize it. Like a painting."

His words pushed her over the edge, and his name slipped out on a moan. "Troy . . . please."

She hadn't any idea what she was begging for, not the slightest notion of what she wanted.

"Please, what?" he asked, his lips still moving against her throat, over her jawbone, toward her mouth. "You must be more specific."

At last he took a step away from her, his mouth retreating, leaving her breathless, wanting more. Grasping her chin, he tipped her gaze up to meet his. "You must tell me, Miranda. Say something," he begged. The unconcealed desire there in his eyes made her tremble, made her thighs dampen as she grew slick with wanting.

Heaven help her, but he looked so young, so eager. So entirely perfect that he took her breath away. Steeling every ounce of courage she possessed, she found her voice at last. "Undress me," she answered, her voice steady and sure.

She half expected him to rip her clothes off with clumsy fingers, before she could change her mind. Instead, he reached for the square buckle of her kidskin belt, his movements slow and unhurried. Once the belt was discarded, he grasped her shoulders and turned her, his fingers moving to the row of pearl buttons at her back.

She shivered when his fingers made contact with the skin at the nape of her neck, raising gooseflesh across her skin. He undid each button maddeningly slowly, one by one, as if he had all the time in the world. Gently, he slipped the delicate garment down, the lacy material sliding sensuously across her skin till it fell to the carpet at their feet.

Miranda stood as still as a statue as he moved to her skirt, pushing it down past her hips, her silk waist-petticoat following in its wake. Her camisole came next, unbuttoned down the front, exposing her pink boned corset. As soon as the camisole slipped to the floor, Troy paused and took a deep breath, his eyes heavy-lidded and glazed with desire.

Standing there in nothing but her corset, knickers, stockings, and slippers, Miranda shivered despite the room's warmth. Almost instinctually, she wrapped her arms around herself.

"Are you cold?" he asked, his eyes flickering back to life.

Miranda shook her head. "Not at all." Indeed, she felt flushed all over.

He nodded, taking a step toward her. But instead of continuing to undress her, he reached up and removed a pin from her simple hair arrangement. Inhaling sharply, she closed her eyes. One lock fell across her shoulder, then another, tickling her skin. Soon enough, only the two carved ivory combs remained in her hair, holding the sides off her face.

"You are the most incredibly beautiful woman I've ever seen," he said, his voice thick. "So very delicate. I don't want to hurt you."

Miranda swallowed hard, thinking of how she'd been hurt in the past. "Just be . . . gentle."

"Of course I will. Dear God, I'm almost afraid . . ." He trailed off, shaking his head.

He thinks I'm a virgin, she realized with a start.

Of course he would. And however could she possibly explain that she wasn't? That she'd meant for him to be gentle with her heart, not with her body?

He said no more; instead, he dropped to his knees, reaching up to unfasten her garters. His fingers moved more quickly now, more impatiently, pushing down the fragile silk and slipping off her dainty shoe before sliding the stocking off and tossing it aside. Soon both legs were entirely bare.

He rose, sliding a hand sensuously up one leg, across her hip as he did so. And then he took a step away from her, his gaze sliding from the top of her head down to her toes, and back up again. He began to unbutton his waistcoat; only then did she notice that he wasn't even wearing a coat. In seconds, the waistcoat slipped to the floor and his fingers began to undo the buttons on his crisp linen shirt.

Miranda held her breath as the fabric parted, revealing a broad, muscled chest with only the faintest dusting of deep bronze hair. His skin was tanned, taut over hard planes and defined muscles. He looked more like a man who made his living with his hands than one who did so with a paintbrush.

The shirt slipped off his shoulders, revealing arms as muscled as his chest. Dear Lord, what did he do with those arms? In seconds they were around her, reaching for her corset's lacings. Miranda stood stock-still as he began to unlace her.

He paused as soon as the top loosened and parted, freeing her breasts from their tight constraint.

She gasped as his hand reached inside the front of her corset, cupping one breast as he pushed aside the stiff fabric and captured one erect nipple in his mouth. Without thinking, she fisted her hand in his hair, arching her back as he began to stroke the sensitive peak with his tongue, circling the areole before suckling her.

Her womb clenched in response, her sex growing wetter and slicker as she clasped his head to her breast, biting her lower lip to keep from crying out. Finally, she could take no more. Her fingers still tangled in his hair, she drew away, tugging his face up to her mouth, her lips searching for his.

"Kiss me," she murmured.

He wasted no time, his lips crushing hers. She heard him groan, her name a muffled cry as he opened his mouth against hers. His tongue skated along her lower lip, dancing across her teeth before retreating. It seemed as if his hands were everywhere at once—her breasts, her hips, then reaching between her legs, his fingers pressing against her delicate, convent-made knickers.

As soon as his fingers found her entrance, her legs grew weak, trembling as he began to stroke her. As if sensing her melting against his hand, he stumbled back toward the chaise, dragging her with him, his lips never once leaving hers.

And then she felt herself being lifted, set gently against the chaise's cushions. He braced himself above her, his body held rigid as his mouth moved from her lips to her throat.

"Mmm," he murmured. "So lovely. Perhaps I should hold you hostage here, make you my concubine."

"You'd grow bored of me soon enough," she teased, feeling strangely lighthearted.

He shook his head, his mouth moving lower, trailing kisses across her collarbone. "I assure you, I wouldn't," came his muffled reply.

Miranda felt herself arch off the chaise as his mouth continued its downward trail to her belly, and then farther on toward the juncture of her thighs. His mouth pressed hotly against her knickers, making them damp, his tongue drawing lazy circles around the center of her sex till she thought she might go mad.

Once, twice, his tongue flicked across her bud, the wet fabric abrading her tender flesh. Faster, harder, his mouth moved against her, till her hips began to buck and all rational thought flew from her mind. Her breath came faster, her fingers clutching at the sides of the chaise, her hips rising from the velvet cushions in a frantic rhythm as she desperately sought her release.

"Go on," he urged, his voice rough. "Come for me, Miranda."

She hovered there on the precipice for only a moment before plunging into sweet oblivion, crying out as wave after wave of pleasure crashed over her.

As she caught her breath, Troy gathered her in his arms, cradling her against his chest. His erection pressed against her bottom, reminding her that he had not found his own pleasure yet, that he had only sought to please *her*.

Somehow it didn't quite seem fair. And yet he seemed satisfied enough as he held her in his arms, his heart beating frenetically against her ear. The silence stretched on for what felt like several minutes, and then he released her, setting her gently back on the velvet cushions.

"I must paint you right now," he said. "Just like this, your skin still flushed, your hair falling across your shoulders."

Miranda nodded. "How shall I pose?"

"Just like you are now, but turn your head away from the window," he instructed. "Yes, like that, so I can see your profile. Perfect."

Out of the corner of her eye, she saw him nod, then hurry to his stool. A feeling of vague unease skittered across her consciousness as she considered the notion that perhaps *this* was how he found his pleasure, instead. Perhaps he lived like a monk, giving himself fully to his art.

Or perhaps he feels he must protect my virginity. If that were the case, then he was more a gentleman than she supposed him to be. Why did that surprise her so?

Behind her, she heard his brush begin to move

against the canvas. "Are you comfortable?" he asked.

"Perfectly so," she answered, surprised to realize that she meant it. Despite the intimate nature of what they'd just shared, despite the fact that she now lay in nothing but her knickers and her partially unlaced corset, she felt warm and languorous, entirely feminine, and wholly comfortable in his presence.

He made her feel beautiful, desirable—things she never again expected to feel. Whatever his motives were, his true desires, they were immaterial, really. All that mattered was that she had this interlude, this time to feel like a woman again, before she returned to Surrey and her responsibilities there.

At least now she knew there was some part of her—some small, insignificant part of her—that still lived and breathed.

That meant there was a measure of hope for her. She would cling to it, that glimmer of hope, for the rest of her days.

It would have to be enough, for it was all she had left to see her through.

Chapter 12

"Gertie, stop fidgeting," Miranda said, tapping her sister lightly on the wrist. "Why do you keep twisting in your seat like that?"

"What?" Gertie answered distractedly, peering over her left shoulder.

"She's looking for Edmund," Grace offered.

Miranda shook her head in frustration. "Must you use his given name? It's far too intimate for someone you barely know. The boy *must* have a surname."

"Stratmore," Gertie replied dreamily. "Edmund Thomas Stratmore, of Kent."

"Well, you don't need to be craning your neck this way and that, looking for Mr. Stratmore, that much is certain. Anyway, the show's about to begin."

Gertie screwed her face into a frown. "I hate the theater. Why must we sit through this tonight? I'd rather be dancing. Where's Father, anyway?"

"Playing cards, as usual," Miranda answered.

"Or dice, perhaps. I forget. Anyway, you know he doesn't enjoy the theater any more than you do."

"Well, I love the theater," Grace chirped, smoothing down the folds of her pale blue skirts. "I've heard Simone DuBois is lovely. Ethereal, someone called her, though I've no idea what that means, exactly. But everyone is so excited about her performance. What are we seeing tonight, anyway?"

Miranda handed her a folded playbill. "Excerpts from *A Midsummer Night's Dream,* it appears. Mrs. DuBois as Titania."

"I *do* hope they're brief excerpts," Gertie said, casting one last glance over her shoulder. "I despise Shakespeare."

Miranda felt the hairs rise on the back of her neck as an odd feeling of awareness shot through her. "Why didn't you stay back with Sullivan, then?" she snapped, forcing herself to look straight ahead at the curtained stage. "No one made you come tonight."

Somehow she knew Troy was nearby; she could feel the weight of his gaze. He was there, somewhere. Watching her. But unlike her sister, she would not turn and search for him amongst her fellow theatergoers. She would not seek him out. Still, she couldn't help the warmth that flooded her cheeks at the memory of the morning's events. If she closed her eyes, she could still imagine the sensation of his hands on her body, the scent of him there beside her. It almost seemed like a dream, a wonderful dream.

Yet it had been real. He had undressed her. He had touched her intimately, till she cried out in pleasure. And afterward, he had painted her as she lay sated on the velvet chaise. Hours had passed in what seemed like mere minutes, till eventually the peaceful sound of his brush stroking the canvas had ceased.

"That's all for now," he had said, setting down his brush and palette and coming to stand beside her, one hand resting on her shoulder.

There had been very little awkwardness between them as he'd helped her dress and then sat silently watching her as she'd attempted to restore her hair to its usual orderly fashion.

She'd left his room minutes later with genuine reluctance, wishing she had the courage to stay longer, to allow more than his touch, his kiss. And now here she sat, her skin still slightly flushed and her body still humming as she contemplated their next meeting.

"You're sitting on my dress," Gertie whined, tugging at her skirts while she glared at Grace.

"I am not," Grace shot back.

"Please," Miranda pleaded, ill-tempered at being whisked back from her memories, back to her unpleasant reality, instead.

Mercifully, the house lights dimmed then, the scarlet-colored velvet curtain parting to reveal the chestnut-haired Simone DuBois standing on the stage, looking ethereal indeed as she held her pose.

Beside her, Gertie giggled.

"Shh," Miranda whispered one last time, casting Gertie a quick glare before focusing her full attention on the stage.

Two and a quarter hours later, Miranda rose stiffly, applauding enthusiastically as the troupe took their bows. Heavens, but she was glad it was over.

Oh, the production had been diverting enough, certainly well acted and interestingly staged. Gertie had managed to limit her bored sighs to exactly three, far less than Miranda had anticipated.

But Miranda had been distracted the entire time, unable to focus. Mere minutes into the performance, she'd leaned forward in her seat, her gaze inexplicably drawn to her left.

And there he was, near the end of her row, where it curved sharply to the left. He had turned toward her in the same instant, and their gazes had collided with an intensity that had nearly knocked the wind from her lungs. Flustered, she'd quickly averted her eyes back toward the stage, but from then on, she couldn't concentrate on the drama, couldn't focus on the performers. Instead, she repeatedly fought the urge to watch him, to see if he were watching her.

By intermission, she'd lost count of how many times she'd done just that, briefly meeting his gaze before flicking hers back to the stage. Despite her sisters' protests, they'd remained in their seats throughout the brief intermission.

She wasn't quite ready for him to approach her, not yet.

And so the next interminable act had passed much as the first—Miranda's skin flushed, prickling with awareness, her concentration entirely dashed. Now, as the actors took their final bows, she let out her breath in a rush, hoping that Gertie and Grace hadn't noticed her discomfiture.

"There're the Fairfax girls," Grace said as soon as the applause quieted. "Look, over there, with Edm—I mean, with Mr. Stratmore."

"Where?" Gertie asked, nearly shoving Miranda out of the way. "Miranda, you must let us join them for a few minutes. Mrs. Fairfax is there, too, so you cannot say it's inappropriate. Please say yes!"

"Yes, go on," Miranda conceded with a sigh, following the girls out into the crowded aisle, watching as Troy made his way toward the same spot. Without a word, he slipped into the aisle behind her, perfectly timed.

Finally they made their way into the crowded, chandelier-lighted lobby, where Grace and Gertie went off to join their friends. Troy continued through the crowd, with Miranda leading, till they reached a pair of double doors that led back into the emptying theater.

Only then did he speak to her. "Did you enjoy the show?"

Miranda nodded. "Well enough. I was . . . a bit distracted, however."

"As was I." He took a deep breath, his eyes never leaving her face. "You look lovely tonight."

She swallowed hard, inexplicably shy now. "Thank you," she murmured. She smoothed her hands down her gown, a dusty mauve evening dress trimmed in creamy Belgian lace.

"Troy Davenport? Ees zat really you?" a feminine voice called out, startling them both.

Both Miranda and Troy turned toward a tall, willowy woman headed their way, a feathered dressing gown wrapped around her narrow frame. Troy's eyes widened, a smile spreading across his boyish face.

"Chantal?" he called out, his voice laced with surprise. "Miss Rousseau," he corrected, but Miranda did not miss the casual use of the woman's given name. Wasn't she just lecturing Gertie on the same thing? "I can barely believe it!"

Waving gaily, the woman hurried over. She was beautiful, of course. Her hair was an unnatural shade of red, obviously aided with the help of dye, but the curls that fell across her shoulders seemed natural enough. Her china-blue eyes were wide and thickly lashed, her cheeks and lips stained a deep rose as she hastened to Troy's side and offered her hand.

Troy took it and bent to press a kiss to her knuckles while Miranda looked on curiously.

"I thought you looked terribly familiar up there," Troy said, "but the wig confused me, I confess. What a pleasant surprise!"

She threw her head back and laughed. "I almost

forgot my lines, watching you in zee audience, trying to decide if eet was indeed you sitting there, or if my eyes were playing cruel tricks on me, eenstead."

"So you've left the Moulin Rouge, I take it?" Troy asked.

"Oui, months ago. I'm touring now with Madame DuBois's company. You've left Paris?"

"Yes, long ago. I'm making my home in London these days, with my aunt. My art dealer, François Joyant, is there, as well."

"And what of dear Marcus and Sébastien? Are they in London now, too?"

"Sébastien is, yes. Last I heard from Marcus, he was enjoying the delights of Düsseldorf." At last he seemed to remember Miranda's presence there beside him. "You must forgive me, Miss Granger. Allow me to introduce you to an old friend of mine from Paris, Chantal Rousseau. Miss Rousseau, I present Miss Miranda Granger of Surrey."

"Charmed, Mademoiselle Granger," Miss Rousseau said with an affected curtsey.

"Likewise, Miss Rousseau," replied Miranda. "The performance tonight was lovely. I quite enjoyed it."

"Madame DuBois ees an amazing talent, ees she not?"

"Indeed. I very much hope to see her perform again soon. Has your troupe any plans to come to London's West End?"

"Oui, next spring. Perhaps Monsieur Davenport will escort you?"

Miranda felt her cheeks warm. "I . . . we're not . . . that is to say, I've only just made Mr. Davenport's acquaintance. Here at the hotel."

"Ah, I see." She raised one brow. "But he ees painting you, non?"

Troy nodded. "I am. She's a lovely subject and I'm afraid I could not resist."

"Of course you could not." She patted his sleeve in a familiar fashion. "Monsieur Davenport has painted me, as well," she said, her voice filled with pride.

Troy cleared his throat uncomfortably. "And did I tell you that the painting sold to a private collector? It now hangs in a château in the Loire Valley, along with several others from my Moulin Rouge series."

Miss Rousseau clapped her hands together in delight. "How very exciting that ees! I'd love to sit again. Perhaps when I'm in London with Madame DuBois?"

"Perhaps," Troy said noncommittally, shifting his feet uncomfortably.

"Well, I must go and clean zee paint from my face," she said, peering up at Troy with a coy smile. "The troupe ees here only one more night—perhaps we can talk later, catch up, as they say, oui? Eet has been way too long."

"Of course," he answered, his cheeks coloring slightly.

"It was lovely to meet you, Miss Rousseau," Miranda offered, refusing to seem discomfited by their obvious familiarity. She was willing to bet that he had done far more than just paint her.

"You, too, Mademoiselle Granger." Her eyes were suddenly cold as she stared down at her, a false smile pasted on her painted lips before she turned her attention back to Troy. "Au revoir, Troy, *mon ami*."

They both turned to watch her retreat, her hips sashaying from side to side in an alluring manner that Miranda could never accomplish, even if she tried. The woman simply reeked of sexual appeal—there was no way that Miranda could compete with someone like her, she realized. To even entertain the notion that Troy would want her when such an alternative presented itself made her feel foolish; ridiculous, even, despite what had happened earlier that day in his room.

"Will you meet me later?" Troy asked, his voice low. "At the glasshouse, perhaps? It will be empty at that hour."

She nodded, taken by surprise by his request. Did that mean he was choosing her company over Miss Rousseau's? "It will have to be after my sisters have retired. They're usually abed by ten."

"Half past ten, then?" he pressed, reaching for her hand.

Miranda could only nod mutely.

"I'll be counting down the minutes till we meet again."

"I'm sure Miss Rousseau would be delighted to

help you pass the time," Miranda said, hating the pang of jealousy that prompted it.

He ignored her jibe. "I'll work on my latest painting until then. If I cannot have you by my side, then your image will have to keep me company, instead."

She fought to keep her voice steady. "You speak like a romantic, Mr. Davenport. I suppose it's the artist's sensibility in you."

"Or perhaps you've simply enchanted me," he answered with a shrug.

Oh, if only it were so.

"Au revoir," he said meaningfully, releasing her hand. *Till we meet again.*

Without another word, they parted, a triumphant smile spreading across Miranda's face as she headed back to the theater's lobby to retrieve her sisters.

Chapter 13

Miranda paused at the bottom of the grand staircase, surprised to find the hotel's glass-domed lobby so crowded, despite the late hour. Christmas was two days away, and carolers stood 'round the ornamented tree, singing one of her favorite hymns in loud, clear voices.

> *"It came upon the midnight clear*
> *That glorious song of old*
> *From angels bending near the earth*
> *To touch their harps of gold . . ."*

A roaring fire crackled in the hearth behind them, the smell of roasting chestnuts—strong and heady—wafting through the air. Around the carolers, hotel guests sat enjoying glasses of hot mulled cider or rum toddies, joining in with boisterous voices:

> *"Peace on the Earth, goodwill to men*
> *From heaven's all-gracious King*
> *The world in solemn stillness lay*
> *To hear the angels sing."*

There was a feeling of merriment, of excitement, in the air. For the first time in nearly a decade, Miranda allowed a bit of that merriment—however small—to creep into her heart. She was glad they had come to the Grandview for the holidays, after all.

"Dear me, Miss Granger," a voice said, startling her. She turned to find Lady Barclay there, frowning at her. "Whatever are you doing about at this hour?"

"It's barely ten, Lady Barclay," she answered with a smile, her entire body tensing with the fear of discovery. She would play her sympathy card. "Now that my sisters are abed and my day's responsibilities complete, I thought I might take some air. You know, enjoy the peace and quiet."

Lady Barclay's face softened at once. "Of course you should, poor girl." She leaned closer and whispered to her, almost conspiratorially, "They're quite a trial, those two, aren't they?"

"They *are* a handful, I admit. But I find a walk about the grounds in the cool, clean air a comfort after a long day. I'm sure you understand."

"Of course I do, dear. Would you like me to accompany you?" Lady Barclay offered.

Miranda shook her head. "That's so very

kind of you, but I fear I'm not good company at present. However, it's nothing that a bit of brisk exercise won't cure."

"I entirely understand." Lady Barclay waved her cane in the air. "I'm afraid I'm not quite up to brisk exercise, myself. Dratted rheumatism."

"Won't you give my regards to Miss Soames?" Miranda offered in parting.

"Indeed." The woman nodded. "And you tell your father that I won't continue to take 'no' for an answer. He simply must dine with us before the week is out."

"I'll do that. Well, good night, then."

"Good night, Miss Granger. Enjoy your exercise."

Miranda let out a sigh of relief as Lady Barclay left her and continued on her way. She glanced down at the watch she wore around her neck— she had a quarter hour to get to the glasshouse. She hadn't any idea what to expect there, but it didn't matter, not really. She just wanted to see Troy again. *Had* to, though she couldn't say why.

It occurred to her that she had felt much the same about Paul, inexplicably drawn to him, craving him and his company with a sheer recklessness that defied sensibility. Yet this was different . . . wasn't it? It had to be; there was no way to countenance it, otherwise.

I'm not that same girl, she reminded herself. *I won't let it happen again.*

Quickly, she made her way outside, down the lighted path toward the glasshouse, her heart beating wildly in anticipation. The temperature had dropped considerably, and few guests braved the grounds. Why would they, when they could be inside the lobby before a roaring fire, a warm drink clutched in one hand as they joined in the seasonal festivities?

Still, she kept her head ducked, her gaze lowered to the path that led to her destination. As she came around a sharp bend, it appeared, the full moon reflecting off the roof's curved glass panes. All was quiet; there was no sign of activity, yet she knew he'd be there, waiting.

And he was. As soon as she rounded the bend, he appeared there in the lane, the moonlight glinting off his hair, the lapels of his coat raised against the cold. "Come," he said, holding one hand out to her. "It's warm inside."

Without a word, she allowed him to take her hand and lead her in.

"So, you managed to escape," he said, releasing her and closing the door behind them.

Miranda took a deep breath, inhaling the warm air redolent with the scent of hothouse flowers. "They think I'm out for a late-night stroll. Lady Barclay, at least. I ran into her in the lobby." She glanced around, taking in her surroundings that were fully illuminated by the light of the moon. It was lush and verdant despite the season, with paving stones wending around manicured beds of blooms. In the glasshouse's center, a gurgling fountain led to a small, man-made stream that meandered throughout the structure.

"It's beautiful here," she murmured. "How did you know it would be open at this hour?"

He shrugged. "I've come here several nights during my stay to pass the time. Alone," he added with a smile. "The groundskeepers don't lock up till midnight."

"We haven't much time, then."

"Time enough," he said, favoring her with a heated gaze that made her blood sing. "Come, would you like to sit? There are benches beside the fountain. Don't worry, the greenery will shield us from passersby. No one will see us sitting there."

Yet anyone could walk in, she realized.

"If someone comes in, we'll hear them," he said, as if he were reading her thoughts. "Plenty of time for me to hide. Or hide you." He reached for her hand once more.

"Very well, then. I'd like to sit, and take off my coat. It's so very warm in here."

"Here, give me your coat," he said, helping her slip it off her shoulders. Once she'd shrugged out of it, he folded it over his arm. "There, is that better? Now come, let's sit."

She followed him down the path, her heels tapping sharply against the stones, keeping rhythm with her heart. Once they reached the fountain—a stone quatrefoil with a cherub statue in its center—they found a bench tucked beneath a leafy palm, and sat.

Water gurgled from a stone fish carried by the cherub—a peaceful sound, soothing Miranda's jangled nerves as she stared at the enormous green lily pads covering the surface of the water and waited for Troy to speak.

"You'll have to excuse me if I have paint on me," he said at last, doffing his own coat and laying it across the bench's back with hers. "I was working on my latest canvas, right up until it was time to meet you here. My aunt often claims I have paint in my whiskers." He reached up to rub his jaw with the palm of his hand, drawing Miranda's gaze away from the fountain and to his face, instead.

Again, she was struck by his youth, so evident now. How had she missed it that night on the *Mauretania*'s deck? *Because it hadn't really mattered then.* He'd been nothing to her then. And now? *He was just a diversion,* her mind insisted. An interlude, soon to be forgotten.

Though she would not let herself forget the feelings he'd awakened in her. How well she remembered those words that Helen had spoken that day in Lucerne, sitting before the statue of the dying lion—one day the hurt would fade, and she would love again.

And perhaps she would. But not this man, this penniless young painter who stirred her blood into reckless passion. No, no matter how badly she wanted him. But someone . . . someone her father would approve of, someone who would want her for herself, not for her fortune. There was no other way to protect herself from heartbreak.

She glanced over at him, sitting silently beside

her, so close that his shoulder brushed intoxicatingly against hers. His clothing was simple, a working-man's attire, and well-worn at that. She was struck with the uncomfortable thought that perhaps her evening's ensemble—the silk evening gown from one of London's finest modistes, paired with multiple strands of pearls worn around her neck and matching pearl drops at her ears—was likely more costly than his year's earnings.

She sighed heavily, wishing that it didn't matter.

Almost abruptly, he turned toward her, one hand moving to her face, cupping her cheek. "Sometimes I feel as if you must be a vision, a mirage. After all those months thinking of you, dreaming of you . . ." He trailed off, shaking his head. "You can't possibly be real, sitting beside me in flesh and blood."

"I never imagined we'd cross paths once more."

"We might not have if I hadn't seen your photograph that day in the *Mirror*. It was pure dumb luck—I never read the society page. Perhaps it's fate."

She recoiled at his use of that word. *Fate* was a word Paul had liked to throw about—fate had brought him to Weckham, had brought them together, had justified their lovemaking, making it right.

She had believed it, then.

After all, fate had been far more palatable an excuse than greed, or lust. Her blind belief in fate had protected her pride, her ego. And in the end, it had ruined her.

His head dipped toward hers—slowly, achingly slow. It was time enough for Miranda to draw away, had she wanted to. He moved closer still, till their lips were inches apart, their breath mingling. He paused, as if awaiting her permission, or perhaps he was only trying to drive her mad.

Gripping the bench's wooden slats with both hands, Miranda leaned forward, her lips searching for his. At last they met, tentative at first, as gentle as a whisper. Releasing her grip on the bench, Miranda rose up, her hands cradling his face now as she returned the kiss, hungry for more.

She heard him groan—a low, deep sound—as she pressed against him, urgent now. In response, he suckled her lower lip, taking it inside his mouth, his hands fisted into her skirts, clutching her to him.

Miranda's pulse leapt, her thoughts a jumbled mess now as his mouth retreated and then reclaimed hers, over and over again, growing more insistent as the seconds passed.

Nearly in his lap now, Miranda dragged her mouth from his, pausing to catch her breath. Only a moment passed before he took her mouth once more, his body straining against hers now. His hands encircled her waist, then slid up, across her ribs, till they cupped her breasts. His thumbs brushed sensuously across her nipples, tightening them beneath the fabric of her gown. Beneath her, his erection pressed against her bottom, making her squirm against it.

The friction caused the familiar pleasurable sensation to well inside her, making her breath come faster. How her body ached for his! How she longed to feel him inside her, moving against her.

But she couldn't take that risk—it was far too dangerous, even if he supplied protection, which she assumed he would. But that didn't mean she couldn't give him pleasure, couldn't help him find his own release. It was only fair, after the pleasure he'd given her there on the chaise in his room.

Dragging her mouth away from his, she wrenched out of his grasp, lowering herself to the ground at his feet, reaching for his trousers' fastenings before he had a chance to react. Shock registered on his face as she completed her task with shaking hands, knowing what she was about to do was unspeakably wicked, entirely wanton. Certainly no woman of good breeding did such a thing, and yet heaven help her, how she wanted to!

"Miranda," he pleaded, his voice a low growl. She had no idea if his plea was a warning or an invitation. Without waiting to find out, she slipped her hand inside his trousers and freed his erection, clasping it in her hand, running her fingers along its velvety length. And then, rising on her knees, she took him into her mouth.

She heard his gasp, felt his entire body tense as

her tongue stroked the length of him, circling
the tip before taking him fully inside her mouth
once more. His eyes became unfocused, almost
glazed as she continued to pleasure him.

"Good God, Miranda," he ground out, reaching a hand around to clasp the back of her neck,
guiding her, setting a rhythm. Seconds passed,
and then she felt him stiffen. With a low groan,
he abruptly pushed her away. The force of his release was etched into his face, his eyes heavy-
lidded, his jaw clenched.

"Good God," he repeated, sounding slightly
dazed. "How did you even know . . . where did
you learn . . ." His voice trailed off, and only then
did Miranda realize her error.

How would a virgin know of such acts, much
less be willing to perform them? She'd been so
caught up in the moment that she hadn't even
thought . . . hadn't realized the implications of
what she was doing. Not that she'd claimed to be
a virgin; still, it was clear that he assumed as much.

What does it matter what he thinks? Her own
worth was not decided by his opinion of her, after
all. Besides, if nothing else, Troy didn't strike her
as a man who would judge her in that sense, who
would expect a woman to come to him a virgin.
Why would he? He wasn't bound to society's
dictates. And the women with whom he likely
associated—women like Miss Rousseau—weren't
either. They could do whatever they pleased.

And so could she.

Her fears slightly eased, she rose, returning to her

seat there on the bench beside him. He reached for her hands, clutching them both in his as he leaned toward her, resting his forehead against hers as he caught his breath.

"You're a puzzle waiting to be solved," he said at last. "So full of contradictions. I've never met anyone like you."

She leaned away from him, a faint smile tugging at her lips. "Perhaps that's why you're drawn to me, then. I'm a challenge. A sport to you."

"You're so much more than that," he said, his gaze direct and unflinching. "Still, I cannot figure you out."

"Good," she murmured. "I'd like to remain a mystery."

Still clasping her hands in his, he massaged her palms with his thumbs. "Soon enough I'll unlock your secrets, Miranda. I can be quite tenacious when I want to be. Just give me time."

She knew she couldn't allow that. "Troy, I—" She paused, hearing the unmistakable sound of voices just outside, growing louder.

Troy stood and helped her to her feet beside him. "Shhh," he whispered close to her ear. "I think they're just passing by. Don't move, not yet."

Her eyes wide with fear, she stood stock-still, listening in horror as the voices grew louder still, drunkenly slurring the words to some unrecognizable Christmas carol. The door rattled, and Troy pulled her backward, behind the palm.

"What's in here?" a male voice boomed, though the door remained shut.

"It's just a greenhouse, 'arry. C'mon, let's go down to the Pier and have another pint, eh?"

Miranda held her breath, mentally willing the man to listen to his friend. *Please, please go!* Her legs began to tremble, her knees nearly knocking together in fright. She clutched at Troy's sleeve for support, her palms damp and slippery.

"Now that's an idea!" came the first voice, and then launched merrily into the carol's second verse as they moved on.

Miranda let out her breath in a rush. Whatever had she been thinking, taking such risks? It was that damn Granger recklessness, leading her astray once more.

"They're gone," Troy said, leading her back toward the bench where their coats still lay. "See?"

The drunken voices had entirely faded away. All that greeted them now was the gurgling of the fountain.

She closed her eyes, inhaling sharply as fear raced through her veins. "I can't believe how close that was, how close we came to discovery. How can you be so calm? Have you any idea what my father would do, were he to find us alone like this? Or worse, hear about it from someone else?"

"I've the general idea of it." He sounded almost amused, she realized. As if it were all a joke to him.

"No, I'm not sure that you do," she snapped, drawing away from him. "It's taken me years to gain back his trust, years till he could meet my eyes without flinching with disgust. And to risk it all again, and in such a fashion as this . . ." She trailed off miserably, shocked at her own outburst.

Dear God, I've said too much.

His brow knitted over curious eyes. "Earn back his trust for what, Miranda? Whatever are you talking about?"

"Nothing," she lied.

"You won't tell me? Even after what we've shared, after—"

"No. Never." She shook her head so vehemently that a pin clattered to the ground beneath her.

"Will you tell me what I can do to help you, then?" he pressed. "To ease whatever pain is eating you up inside? Because it is, isn't it? It's eating you alive. I'll do anything . . . just name it."

She took a deep, steadying breath, hating what she had to say. "I'm afraid the only answer to that is to leave me be. Forget me, forget what's happened here."

"I can't do that, Miranda. I won't." He reached for her hand, but she tugged it from his grasp, feeling like a horrible, cruel woman even as she did so. How she hated herself, hated her fears.

"You haven't a choice. What's happened here"—she swallowed hard—"what's happened between us has been . . . lovely. Like something from a dream. But we'll leave the Grandview soon enough, and then we must put this all behind us. There's no other way."

He shook his head. "This isn't over, Miranda.

It's only just begun, and I won't give you up so easily."

"Don't you see?" she cried in frustration. "You haven't a choice in the matter. It can't continue, not once we leave here. Under any circumstances," she added.

"That's it, then?" he asked, his eyes suddenly blazing. "And what was this, then—this intimate act you just performed on me? A parting gift of some sort? A consolation prize?"

His anger took her by surprise. "I don't know what you want from me," she said, her voice barely above a whisper. "I can't give you any more than what I've already given—perhaps far too freely."

"You wanted to be my whore, then, and nothing more? Is that what you're saying, Miranda?" His voice was cold, clipped. He sounded haughty, almost aristocratic, she realized.

Tears sprang to her eyes, blurring her vision as she reached for her coat. "I must go."

"Of course," he said. "And you can take comfort in the knowledge that, technically speaking, you did not give up your virtue to me. You can give it to someone far more deserving, instead, can't you?"

A single tear spilled over her lashes and traced a scalding path down her cheek. "Good-bye, Troy," she said, then turned and fled without a backward glance.

* * *

Troy clenched his hands into fists by his sides as he watched Miranda go. He wanted to break something, to smash something into a million little bits. Damn her! And damn his masculine pride, too.

And yet—he took a deep, calming breath— what *had* he expected from her? Had he truly expected her to engage in a lengthy affair with him, to declare her everlasting love and hang about waiting as he chased his muse? As Chantal had done, until she'd grown bored with him—as other women had done both before and after her? Miranda was a baron's daughter, for fuck's sake, not some dance hall girl. She did not live in his world. There was no way she could play the role he wished her to play, whatever that was.

He reached for his coat, hurrying out into the cold, clear night. The door to the glasshouse slammed shut behind him with a bang. He hadn't any idea where he was going, but he had to get away, had to forget the sight of Miranda on her knees before him, pleasuring him with that beautiful mouth of hers. Damn it to hell, but he could barely believe what had just happened— undeniably any man's fantasy. How he wished he could get his hands on those drunk bastards who had intruded on them, and wring their necks! If not for them . . .

Pausing, he shoved his arms into his coat, buttoning it up to his chin before continuing on his way, back toward the looming hotel. If not for them, what? Things might have ended just as badly, what with him foolishly pressing her for more than she was willing to give. Perhaps he would go find Chantal, after all, he decided, though to what purpose, he could not say. To soothe his pricked male ego?

No, it would never do. Another woman would never do. And he hadn't any idea what he was going to do about it. He wasn't done painting her; he'd barely even begun. But it was more than that, damn it, and there was no denying it.

Yet she was clearly done with *him*. And why? As best he could tell, because he was Troy Davenport, and not Troy DeWitt. He knew her kind, after all; had grown up among them. Still, he would not confess the truth to her. He couldn't. He'd worked too hard, come too far to give up the ruse now. He was only just beginning to make a name for himself in the art world, only beginning to garner respect.

No, he wouldn't reveal himself, not now. Not even for Miranda. Still, he was not finished painting her. He would not—could not—abandon his muse. Not now, not with the brilliant work he was producing, work that was sure to gain him entry into some of Paris's finest salons. And if that made him a selfish bastard, then so be it. After all, Miranda had clearly used him for her own purposes, whatever the hell they might be.

Not that he was complaining, mind you, but he could not possibly fathom why an unmarried woman of good breeding would allow the liberties she'd allowed him that day—and not just allowed, but eagerly participated in—and then cast him aside just as quickly. A young widow wishing to make conquests might do so, yes. Or a married woman wishing to make a wandering husband jealous. But a woman like Miranda Granger?

A sudden thought pierced his consciousness— perhaps she was more sexually experienced than he believed her to be. It made sense, after all, considering the act she'd just performed on him. He would not hold it against her if she was— surely she would know that.

He rounded the path that led toward the theater and paused, thinking perhaps he would pay a call on Chantal, after all. Just to catch up, nothing more—he would make that clear from the outset. The actors' guest quarters were connected to the theater, purportedly for their convenience, but he knew better than that. It was to keep the performers separate from their so-called "betters," of course. To make sure they knew their place. He bristled at the thought, feeling more kinship with their kind than the fancy ladies and gentlemen who currently filled the hotel, preparing to pass the holiday in opulent elegance, waited on hand and foot, as was their custom.

His mind made up, he continued on, though he had no idea how he would know which room was Chantal's. His heels clicked against the paving stones as he hurried his step, thinking he'd have to find someone in the theater to ask.

There must be someone about, someone who would know—

"Troy, darling!" a voice called out, and he turned to find Chantal herself behind him. "There you are. I was so worried," she said with a pout.

"Worried?" he asked, confused.

"Oui, after zee commotion, I thought for sure it must have been you, you and your Mademoiselle Granger. Zat ees the name I heard, I'm certain."

Troy shook his head, his heart accelerating alarmingly. "I have no idea what you're talking about. What commotion? What does this have to do with Miss Granger?"

"Oh, everyone ees talking! The girl was nowhere to be found, they say. Her father went searching, and found her, oui. In flagrante delicto." Her brows raised suggestively, Chantal paused for dramatic effect before continuing on. "In an amorous embrace with a gentleman. Can you blame me for thinking eet was you?"

Dumbfounded, Troy just shook his head.

"Anyway, whoever he ees, they say they were kissing most passionately, his hands on her breasts, though I cannot fully comprehend zee outrage. She's old enough for such things, your Miss Granger, oui?"

"I don't understand," was all Troy could muster. It made no sense, no sense at all. Miranda had been with him, right up until she'd left him there at the glasshouse. There hadn't been time enough—*wait*. He let out a sigh of relief as realization dawned on him at last. *Of course.*

"Whomever you had the story from, are you sure they said Miss *Miranda* Granger? Not Miss Gertrude or Grace?"

"Gertrude!" Chantal exclaimed, looking very pleased with herself. "Oui, zat's the name. Ah, but your Mademoiselle Granger is Miranda, non?"

"She's not *my* Miss Granger, but yes. And Gertrude is Miranda's sister. Her very *young* sister."

Chantal shook her head. "Now I understand zee outrage, then. Well, there was quite zee scene, they say. I wouldn't be at all surprised if they were packing their bags right now, zee whole family. Everyone says eet's a terrible scandal."

Of course it was. Troy reached a hand up to his temple, wondering what the hell he was going to do if they were, indeed, packing to leave at that very moment. He couldn't let her go, just like that, without another word. Without apologizing for his harsh words, damn it.

He'd all but called her a whore.

It suddenly felt as if all the blood had left his head in a rush, leaving him strangely lightheaded. "If you'll excuse me," he choked out, brushing past a gaping Chantal as he hurried toward the hotel.

It couldn't end like this. It wouldn't.

Chapter 14

Miranda lobbed the ball over the net, wincing when it made contact with Caro's shoulder and bounced off into the grass behind her.

"Good God, Miranda," Caro cried out. "Are you trying to maim me?"

"I'm sorry," she said, dropping her racquet and sinking to the springy lawn beside it. "Let's quit. I'm hopeless, after all."

"I wouldn't say you're hopeless. Just not quite suited to the game, that's all. Perhaps you should try golf instead." Caro swiped the back of one hand across her forehead as she came around the net and joined Miranda there on the grass. "It's warm today, isn't it?"

"Terribly so." Miranda readjusted the skirt of her tennis costume, and then lay back on the lawn, staring up at the cloudless sky. A butterfly fluttered past; a bee buzzed in the hedgerow beside them. It was a beautiful summer's day, despite the heat. "Have you had a letter from Jamie lately?" she asked, turning her head toward her friend. "Or has he entirely forgotten us here in Weckham by now?"

"I had a letter from him last week. He said very little, though. I wonder if perhaps he's gone and fallen in love. It's long overdue, I suppose."

Miranda just laughed. "Can you imagine a woman putting up with Jamie and his bluster? Permanently?" James Garland was nothing if not pugnacious. It was part of his charm, really.

"Well, he *is* nearing thirty. At some point he must settle down. Though I suppose it's more acceptable for a man to be unwed at thirty than it is for a woman."

"I suppose you're right," Miranda said with a sigh.

Caro suddenly reached for her hand. "Oh, Miranda . . . I didn't mean . . . that is, it's different with you. You've got Gertie and Grace, and a household to manage already."

She and Jamie were the same age, after all. Nearly twenty-nine, as was Caro. They'd all grown up together, there in Weckham. Playmates, confidantes.

Yet, of the three of them, only Caro had married and settled down. Robert Cressfield, a dashing junior naval officer, had swept her entirely off her feet, and she'd married him within a year's time and set up housekeeping in Liverpool, where he was stationed. They'd been wed less than three years when Robert had died of influenza while at sea. Following his funeral, Caro had packed up her belongings in Liverpool and returned to her parents' house in Weckham—to the same room she'd grown up in, as if her marriage had never taken place at all.

It was all horribly tragic. Still, Caro could comfort herself with the knowledge that she had been wanted. She had loved and been loved in return, however briefly.

"Do forgive me, Miranda," Caro said miserably. "I didn't mean to be insensitive."

Miranda sat up with a sigh, giving her friend's hand a reassuring squeeze. "You weren't insensitive at all. Truly, I knew exactly what you meant, and I couldn't agree more."

Caro eyed her suspiciously. "I hope you aren't just trying to placate me. Feel free to clobber me with a tennis ball again, if you'd like. Truly, I deserve it."

Miranda laughed, rolling her eyes heavenward. "Oh, shush. Just let me enjoy the peace and quiet, won't you? I haven't long till Gertie and Grace finish with their lessons for the day. They'll both be plaguing me soon enough."

There was nothing Miranda treasured more than the hours Grace and Gertie spent with their tutors, doing lessons. Their last governess had quit just after the New Year—the two went through governesses at an alarming rate—but that still left them with several tutors each day. French,

German, music, dancing. Even without a governess, lessons took up a good portion of their day, and during that time, Miranda was free to do as she pleased.

"Is Sir William still angry with Gertie?" Caro asked, plucking a blade of grass and twisting it between her fingers.

"Deservedly so. I don't know what she was thinking. But then, I never do." The silly girl had tried to sneak a letter to Edmund Stratmore into the post. Miranda had intercepted it, and hadn't a choice but to tell their father.

Miranda had felt like the worst sort of hypocrite, tattling on her sister when she'd done far worse things in her own youth. But if their father had somehow found out—and worse, that Miranda had known and not told him—she would have been held responsible. It was a risk she wasn't prepared to take at present. As it was, he still blamed her for the horrible scene back at the Grandview just days before Christmas.

The night in question had been dreadful. Soon after retiring, Grace had awakened and found Gertie's bed empty. Alarmed, she sent Bridget for Miranda, but Miranda had been nowhere to be found. She'd been with Troy, of course, out in the glasshouse, doing things far worse, far more scandalous than what Gertie had been caught doing.

So Bridget had been forced to summon Sir William, instead. He'd searched the grounds for Gertie, and found her just as Lady Bamber-

Scott—a notorious gossip—had. In Edmund's arms, one of his hands on her breast, the other up her skirt. Or so the story went.

When Miranda had arrived back at her room, Sullivan had been waiting for her, and from the look on her maid's face, Miranda knew that something horrible had happened. Her father wanted to see her right away, Sullivan had told her, filling her in on the evening's events. Father had been furious, so much so that Miranda feared he might have an apoplexy right then and there—and it would have been entirely *her* fault, for abandoning her duty to her sister in favor of her own amorous pursuits.

But Sir William hadn't collapsed. Instead, he'd ordered them to pack their bags at once. They'd left at dawn, Gertie sobbing the whole way, insisting over the roar of the motorcar's engine that she loved Edmund, that she was going to marry him once she came of age. Her histrionics had grown so unbearable that Father had threatened to put her out on the road.

Miranda had known exactly what her father was thinking throughout that interminable drive home—that it was her and Paul, all over again. But it wasn't—Gertie and Edmund's indiscretion had gone no further than a few stolen kisses and some forbidden touches. Though Gertie's disgrace had been embarrassingly public, at least her virtue had remained safe.

And so they'd returned to Holly's Close where they spent a quiet, joyless Christmas, tiptoeing around one another for fear of further outbursts. For a short while, Gertie had seemed truly repentant, as if she finally understood the gravity of what she'd done.

But now it would seem she was back to her old tricks, plotting and planning ways to contact the boy. Worse, Miranda felt sure it was only a matter of time before Gertie succeeded, despite their father's strict order against it. She could not remain vigilant every waking moment, after all. She was tired of hovering over the girl, watching her like a hawk.

"Oh, I've some news from the village," Caro said, drawing Miranda from her thoughts. "Did you hear that someone's let the Rawlings' cottage?"

Miranda shook her head. "No, I didn't even know they were planning to let it. Are the Rawlings staying in Bath as long as that?"

"Yes, through the end of the year, I'm told. Anyway, a man's taken it, though he's not yet arrived. A painter, from New York. A Mr. Troy Davenport. Isn't that the man you met at the Grandview over Christmas? The one who painted your portrait?"

All the air left Miranda's lungs in a whoosh. *Good God, no.* It couldn't be. It wasn't possible. Why would he come to Weckham now, after all these months? She'd almost allowed herself to forget him, to forget the feelings he'd stirred in her.

She'd asked him to leave her be. Other than the portrait—the painting of her sitting on the ivory blanket—that had arrived at Holly's Close wrapped in brown paper with a note addressed to Sir William, there had been no communication whatsoever from him. She'd taken that as a sign that he was accepting her wishes. She'd been grateful yet disappointed, all at once.

But with time, the disappointment had slowly faded away, till eventually she'd been able to look back at those days at the Grandview with fondness. It was a closed chapter in her life now, as far as she was concerned. And now, just like that, he was going to open it up again? *Why?*

She glanced over at Caro, realizing she was still speaking to her. "Whatever is the matter?" she was saying, her blond brows knitted with concern. "You look positively ill, as if you're going to faint."

"It's . . . it's just the heat, is all," she stammered. "I suppose it's getting to me more than I realized."

Caro didn't look convinced. "Are you certain that's all? I vow, as soon as I mentioned Mr. Davenport's name, it was if the blood drained from your face. Is there something about him you're not telling me? I thought he only painted your portrait, nothing more. Did he . . . that is to say, is there any reason that you fear his presence here?"

Good God, was Caro suggesting that the man had assaulted her? She had to put that fear to rest, and right away. "No, of course not." She reached over to pat Caro's hand reassuringly.

"I'm surprised by the news, that's all. He did suggest an interest in visiting Weckham, to paint the abbey, but I never truly believed . . ." She shook her head, searching for the right words. "I suppose it's just that I never expected to see him again."

Caro was far too perceptive by half, Miranda realized. There was no point in pretending herself entirely unaffected by the news. That didn't mean she would tell her everything—goodness, no. But still, she could not entirely lie to such a dear friend, one who only had her best interest at heart. It just wasn't fair.

She swallowed hard before continuing. "If I tell you something, something . . . personal, do you promise not to tell a soul?"

Caro looked wounded. "Goodness, Miranda, need you even ask? We've been friends all our lives, shared so many secrets throughout the years. Have I ever given you any reason to doubt my discretion?"

"Of course not." Only, Caro had no idea how deep Miranda's secrets ran, how many she kept locked away in her heart. A feeling of shame washed over her. "You must forgive me. But the truth is, I met Mr. Davenport before my family traveled to the Grandview. Months before. Onboard the *Mauretania*."

Caro's gray-blue eyes widened with surprise. "Really? You never mentioned him before you left for Eastbourne."

Miranda shook her head. "I never thought I'd

see him again. I hadn't even given him my name, you see. But he claims to have come to the Grandview specifically to find me."

"But however did he know—"

"The society page, of all places," Miranda supplied. "There was a picture, an article mentioning that I was planning to attend the hotel's opening."

"But . . . but why? Why did he want to find you, I mean?"

"He said he wanted to paint me." Miranda shrugged. Reaching for her racquet, she ran her fingers over the smooth wooden handle. "As ridiculous as that sounds, he insisted it was the truth."

"And so he painted you. It's lovely, you know. Truly inspired. But . . . then what? Did anything come to pass between the pair of you that would bring him here to Weckham?"

Miranda dropped her head into her hands. "It's far too embarrassing to admit."

Caro reached for her hands, pulling them away from her face. "Come now, Miranda. Don't be ridiculous. I was a married woman, remember? I won't be so easily scandalized."

Gathering her courage, Miranda took a deep breath. "Let me put it this way—while Gertie was off with her gentleman, I was with Troy Davenport. Doing much the same as she was." It was close enough to the truth. Heaven knows she'd never admit the full extent of it, not to anyone. "The only difference was that I didn't get caught."

Caro shook her head. "It's not the same, Miranda. You're a grown woman, after all, and Gertie is just a child. She's not old enough to use good judgment, to know her limits, to make up her mind on matters such as that. But you . . ." Caro's eyes gleamed with mischief. "Why, I say it's high time you let yourself have a bit of fun."

Miranda just goggled at her friend. "Good God, Caro. That's positively outrageous!"

"So you must tell me," Caro continued on, ignoring her protest, "is he terribly handsome? I assume he must be. I've never before seen anyone catch your eye well enough for you to actually *act* on it. Well, not since Paul Sutcliffe, all those years ago."

Oh, she didn't know the half of it. "I suppose you can decide for yourself, if he's truly coming to Weckham. Anyway, it doesn't matter. Nothing can come from it. It was just an . . . an ill-considered indiscretion. Nothing more than that."

Caro's face widened into a grin. "It does sound terribly romantic, though. An artist, sweeping you off your feet. He's penniless, I suppose?"

"By all appearances. No connections whatsoever. He has an aunt in London, in Wrotham Road." It was a respectable address, though slightly shabby and entirely unfashionable. "She was married to a vicar, he says. I know nothing of his family in New York, but I don't recall meeting any Davenports there. It's not a name I'm familiar with." And she'd met all of New York's high society during her last trip there: Vanderbilt, Astor, Vandenberg, Livingston, Cooper-Hewitt, DeWitt. The list went on and on, without a single Davenport gracing it.

"Nor I," Caro agreed. "Though I'm slightly out of touch, having spent those years in Liverpool."

"You weren't even gone three years," Miranda reminded her, then wished she could take back the careless words. Those years were all Caro had had with Robert, though he had been at sea more often than not.

"Don't look like that," Caro said with a smile, obviously sensing her distress. "Honestly. It's been, what? Four years now? I'm not as fragile as that."

Miranda let out a sigh of relief. "Of course you're not. Still, it was my turn to be insensitive."

"Then it's my turn to tell you to shush, isn't it? Anyway, back to the topic at hand. Just because you can't marry this Mr. Davenport doesn't mean you can't enjoy his company. Why not? These are different times, Miranda. Goodness, ladies smoke and curse now, drive motorcars and campaign for the vote. If you want to have an affair, I say you should."

Again, Miranda could only stare at her friend in disbelief. "Do you know what your mother would do were she to hear you say such things? She'd lock you up and throw away the key for certain. Besides, I'd long since forgotten about Mr. Davenport, until you'd brought him up today," she lied. "And I certainly don't intend to carry on some illicit affair with him right under my father's nose."

"Sir William barely notices what you do, Miranda," Caro said with a shrug. "Anyway, he's far more focused on Gertie and her transgressions at present."

That was true, but it didn't change things. Not in the least. "When is he due to arrive?" she asked.

"Next week, I think. You won't have long to make up your mind," Caro warned.

"Make up my mind about what?"

"Why, what you're going to do about him, that's what." Caro rose, brushing grass from her skirts. "Just promise me you won't offer to play tennis with him. I won't have you murdering him, just to get rid of him. At least, not before I've had the chance to meet him."

"Very amusing." Miranda rose to stand beside her.

"Sorry, I couldn't resist. Anyway, have no fear, my lips are sealed." She mimed turning a key by her mouth and tossing it over her shoulder. "I shall be the model of discretion where your Mr. Davenport is concerned. Oh, dear," she added, just as girlish voices sounded from the direction of the house, growing louder by the second. "Here come Gertie and Grace. And with that, I think I'll take my leave."

If only Miranda could do the same.

Chapter 15

Troy couldn't help but grin as he cut the motor-car's engine and removed his driving goggles, staring at the modest little cottage in front of him. It would do nicely. He'd have to send a telegram to François right away and tell him how pleased he was with the accommodations. Of course, he hadn't seen the inside of the place yet, but it didn't matter overmuch.

All that mattered was that Holly's Close was less than a mile away, just down the dusty road from his temporary home. They'd passed it as they'd driven in. It had taken all of Troy's restraint to keep on course rather than turn down the narrow lane that led to the tidy stone manor house that Miranda called home.

"This is it?" Sébastien said beside him, removing his own goggles and tossing them to the black tufted seat beside him. "Well, I suppose it's not that bad, though I can't possibly imagine why you'd want to spend more than a fortnight in this grim little outpost."

"You haven't yet seen the abbey. We'll drive out later, once I get settled. I can't quite explain it, but something has drawn me to it," Troy lied. He'd seen only photographs, never having laid eyes on the place in person. "You know how that goes," he added, hoping to appeal to Sébastien's artist's sensibility.

"I suppose so, but couldn't your aesthetic instincts have drawn you somewhere more lively than this? You could always change your mind and join me in Greece. I'm not sailing for several more weeks, you know."

Troy pulled off his thick, leather driving gloves, shoving them into the little compartment on the dash along with his goggles. "I'm sure you'll have a jolly old time without me. Isn't Marcus planning to meet you there?"

"Indeed, he is. Marcus, at least, understands the attraction of such a place. As opposed to, say, *here.*"

Troy just shrugged. "You must admit there's a certain pastoral charm to Surrey."

Sébastien turned to him with a grin. "Yes, and you must admit there are certain charms to Greece, too. Beautiful, scantily clad charms, I'm told."

"I'm sure you'll sample enough of them for both of us." Troy could barely believe it, but the very idea seemed almost distasteful to him. Before, such a notion would have been incentive enough to set sail immediately. An exotic locale, beautiful women, cheap wine, and easy fucks. Now, he was inordinately satisfied to let Sébastien and Marcus have their adventure—and their women—without him.

"Well, let's get your trunks inside, man," Sébastien said with an exaggerated grimace. "I'm anxious to see this abbey of yours. It's in ruins, you say?"

Troy nodded as he stepped down and hurried to the rear of the motorcar, where his trunks were strapped, Sébastien's smaller traveling case on top. "Extensive ruins, though there are some standing vaulted ceilings and columns in places. Should make an interesting study of light. Here, take your valise."

It took a good ten minutes to drag Troy's trunks up the cottage's uneven steps and deposit them into what must be the front parlor. The walls were painted a pleasing soft green, a nice complement to the foliage just outside the dusty windows curtained in simple white lace. The furniture was simple, yet attractive and well made. Yes, it would do well enough.

He could barely believe how long it had taken him to get there. He'd meant to go as soon as he left the Grandview—on Christmas Day, it turned out. Once Miranda and her family had made their sudden and unexpected departure, there had been no reason for him to remain, so he'd checked out and hastened back to Aunt Agnes's flat in London, anxious to spend the holiday with her before making the necessary arrangements to travel to Surrey.

But when he'd arrived back in Wrotham Road, he'd found his aunt feverish and ill, far worse than she would admit to. He'd summoned a doctor at once, who had diagnosed her with pneumonia. Following a tense few days where a quickly deteriorating Agnes had refused to leave her own bed, Troy finally convinced her that she needed to be in a hospital.

For weeks, her very life had hung in the balance. Finally, she'd begun to improve, only to relapse again weeks later. Back to the hospital she'd gone for another lengthy stay, before returning home once more, weak and frail to the point of being almost unrecognizable.

Troy wanted to move her to a sanitarium—not one that specialized in tuberculosis, but more a private health resort where she could fully regain her strength and vigor in the fresh, clean air of the countryside. The only problem was, such places were costly. He could not afford one, not without dipping into the London account funded by his father.

In the end, he'd swallowed his pride and withdrawn enough funds from his account to pay for his aunt's care. She'd spent two months at a well-regarded sanitarium in Bath, and returned home, at last restored to good health.

Then, despite Aunt Agnes's protests that she didn't need any help, that he'd already done enough as it was, he'd engaged a young woman to serve as both his aunt's nurse and companion. He could not leave Agnes until he was convinced of her comfort and satisfaction with the situation.

At last, his aunt seemed well and happy. Her companion, Miss Hart, was competent and effective, but more importantly, she seemed utterly devoted to her new charge. Indeed, from all appearances, the pair got on famously.

When Troy was finally able to begin making arrangements to travel to Weckham, he'd been shocked to see that nearly six months had passed. Six long months—long enough for Miranda to have forgotten the spark of passion that had ignited between them. *Even if I accomplish nothing more than filling several more canvases with her image, it will be worth it,* he convinced himself.

Just before he left London, he'd dipped into his account once more, taking out just enough to buy an inexpensive motorcar, thinking he'd find it useful in the countryside. After he left Surrey, he could sell it, he reasoned. Turned out he enjoyed the little roadster far more than he'd anticipated. Now, glancing out at it, its shiny brass fittings glinting in the waning afternoon sun, he realized that he would have a difficult time parting with it. Would it be so very bad to allow one luxury, one extravagance into his life?

"Do we need to take these trunks upstairs?" Sébastien asked, startling him. He'd been so lost in thought that he'd almost forgotten his friend's presence there.

Troy glanced with displeasure at the steep,

narrow staircase, and then back at the pile of trunks. Considering his options, he rubbed his chin with the palm of one hand. "Let's just leave them down here for now. I'll sort it all out later."

"Good idea. I'm suddenly quite parched. Do you suppose there's a pub in this godforsaken place where a man can get a pint or two?"

Troy shrugged. "Surely there must be. I'd say a pint or two is well deserved in this instance. My treat, old friend."

"It'd better be, after I allowed you to drag me away from London. For this," he said, spreading his arms wide.

"Oh, go fuck yourself," Troy shot back.

"I'll wait for the Greek goddesses instead," Sébastien retorted with an exaggerated leer. "If you don't mind, that is."

Troy nodded, ready to head out into Weckham and meet his new neighbors. What better place than a pub?

And then tomorrow . . .

He shuddered in anticipation. Tomorrow he'd go to Holly's Close, to Miranda. Under the guise of checking to see that the painting was delivered. At least, that would be his story if Sir William were home to require an explanation.

The very idea that his muse was close by was enough to make his imagination soar, his creativity come alive. If only she would cooperate.

* * *

The curiosity was killing her. Troy was there, in Weckham. He'd taken up residence at the Rawlings' little cottage, a modest house covered in creeper vines there at the bottom of the main road.

He'd actually had the nerve to call at Holly's Close the day before. Luckily, she had gone with the housekeeper to the market in Dorking, so she'd been absent at the time. Grace and Gertie had been home, however, and they were still chattering on about the coincidence, about how exciting it was to have a real artist there in Weckham, immortalizing the village on canvas.

Apparently, he'd had a friend with him, as well. Sébastien something-or-other. Her sisters had been too excited to remember, but he was handsome and charming, they claimed, about to set sail for Greece. They reported that Troy had been pleased to see his painting hanging in the drawing room—a gift, he'd insisted, refusing to take any payment from an insistent Sir William.

She had no idea why he was there—besides his supposed purpose of painting Weckham Abbey—but she intended to find out. *Soon enough.* Today she would simply walk past the cottage with Caro. And if he happened to be about, well . . . if he was, then she would stop and speak with him. The conversation would have to remain vague and impersonal, what with Caro standing there.

She glanced down at the watch worn round her neck, wondering what was keeping Caro. For perhaps the fifth time in so many minutes, she peered around the gate, out into the lane, looking for the familiar figure headed her way.

This time, she was not disappointed. Caro rounded the bend and lifted a hand in greeting, the other shielding her eyes from the bright afternoon sun. *Thank goodness.* Miranda was growing restless waiting, losing her nerve more and more as the minutes ticked by.

"I'm so sorry I'm late," Caro called out, hurrying her step. "The post came and I had a letter. I simply lost track of time!"

Miranda hurried out into the lane to meet her. "Don't fret, you're only a quarter hour late. There's still plenty of time for our errands. I was thinking afterward we could stop at the hotel for tea."

Caro nodded, falling into step beside her. "That sounds lovely. I have to stop by the milliner's, too, if you don't mind. I took a hat in for trimming just last week. It should be ready by now."

"I don't mind at all. I'd like to purchase a boater with a slightly smaller brim, I think."

"You do realize we'll have to pass right by the Rawlings' cottage," Caro said, taking Miranda entirely by surprise.

"I hadn't thought of that," Miranda murmured, unable to meet her friend's questioning gaze.

"Of course you did," Caro said with a laugh. "I can only assume that means you hope to see him.

Lord knows I'm dying to meet the man myself. I heard he was at the pub two nights ago. Closed down the place with some friend of his, another artist, I'm told. You'd think we'd never before had strangers here in Weckham, by the way people are going on about him."

"He came by Holly's Close yesterday, while I was out. Grace and Gertie have not shut up about him since. I had to get up and leave the breakfast table this morning, I was so tired of listening to them prattle on. Besides, I fear they might read something in my expression." Miranda exhaled in a rush. "It's a dreadful situation."

"Oh, it's not so bad as that. Come now. Where's your sense of adventure?"

Miranda had to laugh at that. "Me? Whenever have you known *me* to have a sense of adventure? I've always been the cautious one, remember? The one standing on terra firma while you and Jamie climbed a tree or jumped in the swimming pond with your clothes on. I'm far too prudent for adventure."

"I suppose you're right. Anyway, can't you walk faster?"

Miranda turned toward Caro with a frown. "I vow, this isn't a footrace. We'll get there soon enough. Besides, we might not even see him today. Unless he just happens to be standing outside at the precise moment that we come strolling past. And what are the chances of that happening?"

"You really *do* want to see him, don't you?"

Caro said, her voice full of amazement. "I can hear it in your tone."

Miranda rolled her eyes. "Oh, just be quiet and walk. I can't continue to converse; I'm getting winded."

For several minutes more they continued on in companionable silence. At last they reached the end of the lane, and turned onto the main road leading into Weckham. The Rawlings' cottage came into view, set back only slightly from the road. A shiny red motorcar was parked in front, blocking their view of the front door.

But as they drew closer, a figure near the front stairs became visible. A tall, masculine figure, Miranda realized, with deep bronze hair glinting in the sun. She had to reach for Caro's arm to steady herself as her heart began to race at a dizzying speed, her breath coming faster now— and not because she was winded.

It was him. There was no doubt about it. Any minute now, they'd draw abreast of the cottage, mere yards away from where he stood. If only he were to turn around . . .

Almost as if in slow motion, he did just that. Miranda could feel the weight of his stare, saw the flicker of recognition, of surprise there in his eyes as he wiped his brow with the back of one hand.

He looked almost like a laborer in his brown trousers and white linen shirt, his sleeves rolled to his elbows. In one hand, he held something by a long, wooden handle. A hammer, perhaps? What on earth was he doing?

"Miss Granger?" he called out, squinting against the sun.

"Good day, Mr. Davenport," she called out in reply, endeavoring to make her voice as steady, as cheerful as possible.

He took several steps toward where they stood frozen on the walk. "What a pleasant surprise. I came by Holly's Close yesterday, and was sorry to have missed you. I must say, I did not expect to meet you like this."

"Well, Mr. Davenport, I have no choice but to pass by the Rawlings' cottage on my way into the village. I suppose we'll meet like this frequently enough as long as you remain here."

His gaze swept over her, from the top of her head to the tips of toes, and then back up again. She swallowed hard, forcing her expression to remain neutral, forcing herself to seem entirely unaffected.

"And how long *were* you planning on remaining here?" she asked, unable to staunch her curiosity.

He shrugged. "I've got the cottage till the end of the year. That should be time enough to accomplish what I came here to do."

So he was going to speak in riddles, then.

Beside her, Caro cleared her throat loudly.

"Oh, you must forgive me. Mr. Davenport, this is my dearest friend, Mrs. Caroline Cressfield. Caroline, I present Mr. Troy Davenport. The artist who painted my portrait, the one that hangs in the drawing room," she added unnecessarily. Best to seem as if they hadn't discussed him at all.

"Of course," Caroline said, holding out one hand. "I've heard so much about you."

Miranda shot her a pointed glare, but Caro ignored her.

Troy dropped the hammer and wiped his hand on his trousers before taking Caro's hand. "It's a pleasure, Mrs. Cressfield. You live here in Weckham, as well?"

Caro nodded, smiling broadly. "Indeed. My family's estate neighbors the Grangers'."

"And . . . Mr. Cressfield?" he prodded.

"Passed away unexpectedly several years ago," she supplied.

"My deepest condolences," Troy said softly.

Caro nodded her acknowledgment. "I live with my parents now, Mr. and Mrs. Thomas Denby. Just up the road a piece from Holly's Close, though our house isn't nearly as grand. I'm afraid ours doesn't even have a name," Caro babbled on. Whatever had come over her?

"I'm fairly certain this little cottage doesn't have a name, either." Troy hooked a thumb toward the house behind him. "Besides 'the Rawlings' place.' At least, that's what everyone I've met has called it."

"The Rawlings have lived here as long as I can remember," Caro said with a nod. "Mr. Rawlings is the best farrier for miles about. It's such a shame that he's taken ill. I hope their time in Bath does wonders to restore him."

Troy's gaze trailed back to Miranda, his eyes seeming to search her face. "My aunt has only just returned from Bath, where I sent her to recuperate from pneumonia. She was ill for quite some time—since Christmas, actually—but mercifully she returned from Bath entirely recovered."

"I'm so glad she made a full recovery," Miranda murmured. "You must be terribly relieved."

His gaze was direct and unflinching. "You've no idea. I was forced to set aside my plans far longer than I'd intended."

Miranda swallowed hard. "Whatever were you doing with that hammer?" she asked, deciding it prudent to change the subject.

"Reinforcing the front stairs. One side was beginning to sag. I figured I might as well make myself useful."

"And . . . and that's something you know how to do?" she asked in amazement.

"Quite well, actually. I did a fair amount of carpentry work in France. I'm good with my hands," he added, smiling wickedly.

Which meant it was time continue on their way, Miranda realized, her cheeks suddenly warm.

Oh, I remember just how good you are with your hands. Her knees went weak with the memory.

"Well, I'm afraid we must be off," she said brightly. "We've got business in the village today."

"Perhaps you could stop in for tea on your way home," he offered, and Miranda's heart skipped a beat.

"I don't think—"

"That would be lovely." Both she and Caro had spoken at once, and Miranda looked pleadingly at her friend.

"Miranda's right," Caro amended with a nod. "I'd forgotten that we . . . um, we promised we would, er—"

"That we're expected for tea at the Batemans' this afternoon, remember?" Miranda prodded.

Caro nodded. "Right, of course. The Batemans. But it was a pleasure to make your acquaintance, Mr. Davenport, and welcome to Weckham. I do hope we'll meet again."

"I'm sure we will," he answered with a boyish grin.

Miranda nodded sharply. "Good day, then, Mr. Davenport."

"Good day, Miss Granger, Mrs. Cressfield," he returned, then bent down to retrieve his hammer.

Miranda let out her breath in a rush. That had been worse than she'd anticipated—far worse, if her body's reaction had been any indication.

Maybe it's time to travel abroad, she told herself sourly as they continued on their way toward the village's shops. Antibes was lovely this time of year, or so she'd heard.

She shook her head, hoping to clear it. But it was no use; no matter how hard she tried, she couldn't banish the image of him standing there in his shirtsleeves, his familiar green gaze boring through her.

I'll just have to try harder, that's all.

Chapter 16

"You didn't tell me he was so young," Caro said, reaching for a strawberry tart. "Goodness, just how young do you suppose he is?"

Miranda just shrugged. "I haven't any idea. I didn't ask. Younger than we are, that much is certain."

"Yes, but how much?"

"Does it matter?" Miranda reached for a tart herself. Blueberry, her favorite.

"I suppose it doesn't matter. Still, I hadn't expected him to look so boyish. I had expected handsome, yes. And he is, terribly so. Those eyes of his . . ." She sighed dramatically, looking almost dreamy. "I can certainly understand the attraction. And the way he looks at you . . . I swear, it's as if he wants to eat you up."

"I wouldn't go that far." Miranda bit into the tart, wiping pastry crumbs from her chin as she did so.

"Then you must be blind. The tension between

the two of you—it's almost electric. I could positively feel it, crackling between the pair of you. There's no way you'll be able to hide it from Sir William."

"There won't be anything to hide from him. I'll simply avoid Tr—Mr. Davenport," she corrected. "It isn't as if he can just come calling at Holly's Close whenever he takes a notion to."

"I suppose that would be quite irregular," Caro agreed with a nod. "But can you honestly say you *want* to avoid him?"

Of course not, but she didn't have a choice. "I'm smart enough to realize that what I want and what I must do are not necessarily the same thing."

"Oh, please don't go and get all melancholy on me again. You know I can't bear it when you start talking that way."

Because Caro would never understand. She hadn't any idea what Miranda had gone through all those years ago. Oh, she'd known that Paul had broken her heart; everyone in Weckham knew that. But she'd never quite understood why Miranda had gone off to Switzerland—purportedly to finishing school—and come back an entirely different woman. One who no longer smiled, who no longer laughed or teased like the younger version of herself had done.

Swallowing a painful lump in her throat, Miranda reached for her tea, now lukewarm, and took a sip.

"Miss Granger?" came an all-too-familiar voice

behind her, and Miranda nearly spilled the tea down her lap.

Across from her, Caro's eyes widened with surprise.

Setting down her teacup with unsteady hands, she turned to find Mr. Davenport there, an impossibly tall, dark-haired man beside him. She tried to speak, but found she could not. Just how long had he been standing there?

"I didn't expect to see you here," he said. "I thought you had an engagement for tea. The Batemans, wasn't it?"

He had an excellent memory, it would seem.

"We were mistaken," Caro said, saving her. "We're expected there tomorrow for tea, instead."

Now they would have to make certain that they stopped by the Batemans' house tomorrow—just in time to get asked to stay for tea.

Miranda found her voice at last. "I did not expect to see you here, either."

A smile spread across his face. "Yes, obviously. But my kitchen's not yet stocked, and I could not let my guest go hungry." He gestured toward the man still standing silently beside him. "Sébastien, allow me to introduce what must be the two loveliest ladies in all of Weckham, Miss Miranda Granger, and Mrs. Caroline Cressfield. Ladies, this is Sébastien Dumas, rake and roué extraordinaire. We're old friends, having studied together in France. He was kind enough to accompany me down from London and see me settled in. But don't let his kindness fool you. He's a dangerous man. I wouldn't recommend you get too close."

Mr. Dumas nodded in greeting, his straight, white teeth flashing as he smiled down at them from a considerable height. He was handsome, with tanned skin and eyes so dark they seemed almost black. He looked like Miranda imagined a pirate might look—swarthy and devilishly charming. All that was missing was the eye patch.

"A pleasure," the man said in perfect English with only the slightest hint of a French accent. "But please, don't listen to a word my friend here says. He simply can't stand the idea of competition where beautiful ladies are concerned." His dark gaze traveled from Caro to Miranda and back to Caro again, lingering there. Indeed, it seemed as if the man couldn't take his eyes off her. "What a pity that one of you is already taken," he added. "Not enough of you to go around."

"I'm . . . a . . . a widow," Caro stammered, her cheeks coloring slightly.

And not because the reminder of her loss upset her, Miranda realized, but because she was flustered. In fact, Miranda couldn't remember the last time she'd seen Caro blush like that.

"You must forgive me, Mrs. Cressfield," Mr. Dumas said, his voice soft and respectful. "I spoke hastily and carelessly."

Caro reached out to lay a comforting hand on his wrist. "No, it's quite all right, Mr. Dumas. You did not offend me. After all, I lost my husband many years ago."

Troy cleared his throat uncomfortably. "Anyway, Sébastien here is only staying on a few days. Then he's off to Greece to paint sunsets and ancient ruins."

"I wish I had more time to spend here in your charming little village," Mr. Dumas said, and Troy's questioning gaze snapped immediately to his friend's, his brows drawn in what looked like genuine surprise. "Now I see why Troy was so drawn here," Mr. Dumas added.

For several seconds, no one said a word. Finally, Troy broke the uneasy silence. "I suppose we should leave you two to your tea. We're on our way out to the abbey so that I can do some preliminary sketches."

"You really *are* going to paint the abbey, then?" Miranda asked before she'd thought better of it.

"Of course," Troy answered, his gaze meeting hers. "Why else would I be here in Weckham?"

It was Miranda's turn to blush. "Indeed, why would you?"

Troy smiled, apparently pleased with her discomfiture. "Well, good afternoon, then," he said, gesturing toward his friend. "Shall we?"

"Yes, of course. It was a pleasure to meet you both," Mr. Dumas said, bowing to them, each in turn. "Perhaps the next time I'm in Surrey . . ." He trailed off, staring meaningfully at Caro.

"That would be lovely," Caro answered, her cheeks flushing scarlet now.

They watched in silence as the men took their

leave, weaving their way through the maze of tables.

"Whatever just happened there?" Caro asked as soon as they moved out of earshot.

Miranda's smile was full of mischief. "Why, I'd say you have an admirer, Mrs. Cressfield. *Non?*"

Troy stood, setting aside his palette as he regarded the canvas before him. He nodded, pleased with the day's work. The abbey had turned out to be a far more interesting subject than he'd anticipated. He'd only been there in Weckham a fortnight, and he'd made some interesting studies. He'd chosen one structure in particular to focus on, what used to be the abbey's refectory. It was surprisingly intact, all four walls with classic Cistercian vaulting and columns inside.

He'd set his easel up inside the structure's far corner, looking out toward the archway that was its front door. At different times of day, the light inside changed dramatically, casting the most interesting shadows on the stones that had turned greenish-yellow in places with age. Protected from the elements, he could paint in any weather. He carried tarps in his motorcar, just in case.

It was a peaceful place. Though its proximity was close to the village's main thoroughfare, there were no homes out this way, or at least not in the immediate vicinity. The abbey lay just in the bend of the River Wey, accessed by a picturesque stone medieval bridge. He'd driven out there every day since he'd arrived in Weckham, sometimes staying for hours. Other times, he'd find himself unable to focus, unable to think of anything but Miranda, so close by, and yet so unapproachable.

He could not simply sit at home, staring at the road in front of the cottage all day, waiting for her to walk by. Yet so far he'd found no other way to see her.

And so he could do nothing but wait. Somehow he felt sure she would seek him out eventually. Still, his patience was wearing thin. At least his work was not suffering for it, he decided, pleased with the painting he had been working on.

He would go home for the day, he decided. Have his tea, and watch the road. And then perhaps he'd go to the pub and have a pint.

A flash of color on the bridge caught his eye, and he strode toward the structure's open doorway, raising one hand to shield his eyes from the bright afternoon sun. Something metallic flashed in the sunlight. A bicycle, he realized. A cyclist, headed across the bridge toward the abbey.

He hadn't had many visitors in all the time he'd spent there. A pair of village boys now and then, off to fish in the river. The shopkeeper and his wife, picnicking on a Sunday after church. But most days he saw no one, as if the place held no charm for those who'd lived beside it for years.

He went back to gather his things, carrying his easel under one arm back toward the motorcar when the cyclist came back into view, heading straight toward him now. He blinked hard, sure he must be seeing things. But no, it was Miranda, wearing a wide straw boater on her head, ribbons trailing out behind her as she rode up beside the motorcar and braked.

"Good afternoon," she called out formally, stepping over the bicycle and peeling off her gloves as she strode toward him. She wore odd-looking knickerbockers, gathered between her legs like billowy trousers, along with a fitted jacket. Some sort of cycling ensemble, he decided.

"Whatever are you doing all the way out here?" he asked, putting his easel on the motorcar's seat.

"I needed to speak with you. I hope you don't mind the interruption."

"Not at all," he said with a grin. "In fact, feel free to interrupt me in such a fashion every day, if you'd like."

He saw her take a deep breath, her chest rising and falling before she answered. "Why are you here, Troy? In Weckham, I mean? I must know."

He decided to tell her the truth—at least, partially. "I wasn't through painting you."

Her cheeks, already flushed from her ride over, colored further. "What makes you think I'll sit for you again? My father won't allow it."

"Did your father allow you to ride out here today, knowing I'd be here?"

"No, he's gone to London for the day." She

shook her head. "Anyway, that's beside the point. You had no right to come here, Mr. Davenport."

She'd called him Troy back at the Grandview, allowed him to address her as Miranda. Now it would seem she was back to formality, as if she'd entirely forgotten the intimacy they'd shared. "I have every right to be here. I've paid for the cottage, and as you can see, I'm painting the abbey, just as I said I would. I'd like you to sit for me, of course, but I cannot force you—"

"That's it, then?" she cried, her hands balled into fists by her sides.

He took two steps toward her, then stopped. "What do you want me to say, Miranda?" he pleaded. "I'm trying to give you the answer you want to hear, but I'm not quite certain what that is. You want the truth?" He closed the distance between them, reaching for her hand. "The truth is I'm here because of you. Yes, I want to paint you, but you know it's more than that. It's always been more than that."

"It's been so long," she said. "Since Christmas."

Six very long months. "It was unavoidable. I hoped you would not have forgotten me."

She shook her head. "I haven't. I couldn't. Still, you should not be here." She looked pale, distraught. He hadn't meant to frighten her. But he could feel her hand trembling in his as she stared up at him, wide-eyed.

He was asking too much of her. Women like Miranda Granger did not have affairs of the heart. Women like her were gently courted, and then they married some chap. So why did he continue on, pursuing her, when he knew he couldn't marry her, and knew that having an affair with her would destroy her?

What had he hoped to accomplish? What kind of bastard was he, toying with her like this, simply because he wanted her, liked a spoiled boy wanted a shiny new toy?

She tugged her hand from his grasp. "That night at the glasshouse, I asked you to leave me be, Mr. Davenport. I told you in no uncertain terms that we could not . . . could not continue," she stammered. "It was a mistake, a terrible mistake. And now that you're here, I'm looking over my shoulder constantly—afraid to see you, and yet afraid that I will not. I'm acting strangely, and everyone has noticed. My father, my sisters, even Caroline. Can't you see what you're doing to me?" Tears had gathered in her eyes, threatening to fall.

"I'm sorry," he said, feeling like a selfish bastard. "I know it's not enough, but I am."

"Then you'll leave? You'll leave Weckham, and go back to London? Or France, or wherever else you might go?"

Pain ripped through his gut. "Is that what you want me to do, Miranda? Can you look me in the eye and tell me that you truly want me to go? That you never want to see me again? Because if it is, God help me, I'll go." He would get in the motorcar and ride back to the cottage, pack up his belongings and drive back to London posthaste.

She dropped her head into her hands, standing like that for what felt like an interminable time. At last, she looked up again, her gaze meeting his. "No. Devil take it, no. I can't tell you that. I don't want you to go."

Thank God. "We could start over, then. As friends," he suggested. "You could come out here, with Mrs. Cressfield, perhaps? As a chaperone. You'll be safe enough, I vow."

"Do you . . . come here every day?" she asked tentatively, and his heart soared with victory.

"Yes, it would seem so. Either to paint, or to swim in the river."

She shook her head. "The current is much too strong out here. You shouldn't, not alone. There's a swimming pond, you know, not far from your cottage. There's a path through the woods, just beyond your garden gate. It would eventually lead you straight to Holly's Close, but if you go left at the fork instead of right, you'll find the swimming pond, instead."

He allowed that information to sink in—some sort of path that would lead him to Miranda's home. To the grounds, at least. And a swimming pond, one she might frequent herself.

"Thank you," he said.

She nodded sharply. "I should go. I promised to take Gertie and Grace into town for tea when they finished with their lessons."

"I'll be here tomorrow," he said. "In the late morning. Perhaps I'll bring a picnic lunch."

She took a step away from him, her face entirely unreadable. "Good-bye, Troy" was all she said. At least she was back to using his given name.

"Good-bye, Miranda," he answered, watching her retrieve her bicycle and climb on, pedaling away as fast as she could. He watched until she was nothing but a speck against the green landscape, then disappeared entirely from view.

And then he let out his breath in a rush. *Friends?* How in the hell was he going to manage that?

Chapter 17

"How is it that he speaks such flawless English, then?" Caro reached across the blanket and plucked a fat, ripe strawberry from a fruit-filled straw basket.

"His mother was an Englishwoman," Troy answered, tipping his face upward, toward the sun. "Sébastien spoke English long before he spoke a word of French. Much to his father's displeasure, I'm told."

"Fascinating," Caro said brightly.

Miranda watched her friend in amazement, wondering just what fantasies Caro was entertaining about Troy's darkly handsome friend. It seemed her fascination with the man was unending—they'd been talking about him for the better part of an hour. However, her friend's obvious enjoyment of Troy's company assuaged her guilt, if only a bit. She'd suggested a picnic out at the abbey, never letting on that she'd known for certain that Troy would be there.

And so she'd acted surprised when they'd seen his red motorcar parked on the far side of the bridge. If Caro suspected the truth—that their meeting was not accidental—she did not let on, thank goodness. As it was, Miranda felt like a fool.

What must he think of her? First she demanded that he leave her alone, that he leave Weckham altogether—and then she admitted that she wanted him to stay, after all. As if she couldn't make up her mind where he was concerned. And then she'd foolishly agreed to try and be *friends* with him—a man she couldn't stop thinking about, couldn't stop dreaming about, no matter how hard she tried.

She'd spent the past hour trying to pretend that he was no different from Jamie, she and Caro's usual third. After all, the three of them had enjoyed many a picnic there on the banks of the River Wey throughout the years. And yet there was no escaping the fact that he was nothing like Jamie, that her feelings for him were entirely different from the comfortable camaraderie she always felt in Jamie's presence.

After all, she could watch Jamie eat an apple without her gaze lingering on his lips, without imagining how his mouth would taste were she to lean across the blanket and trace his lips with her tongue. She could sit beside Jamie without her entire body tingling with awareness every time he inadvertently brushed against her, without staring at his calloused hands, remembering how they felt against her flesh.

This was madness, she realized. Pure and utter madness. She shook her head, trying to clear it, trying to concentrate on the conversation that continued on around her. ". . . would love to go there myself one day," Caro was saying. *Greece*, she realized. Of course.

"As would I," Troy answered, and Miranda allowed her gaze to roam over him hungrily. He sat between them in his shirtsleeves, the cuffs rolled up to his elbows, exposing his tanned, muscled forearms. One long leg was stretched out straight, the other bent at the knee, his scuffed oxford resting on the blanket. He wore no hat, and the days spent out-of-doors in the summer sun had streaked his hair with threads a shade lighter than the rest, like burnished gold mixed with bronze.

His hair looked mussed, as always, and she could have sworn there was a spot of paint in his whiskers, another there on his wrist. His fingernails were neat and rounded, yet stained with pigment.

He looked every bit the handsome, romantic, penniless painter, entirely unconcerned with appearances, consumed with his art, with enjoying life to its fullest. Or at least, that's how she imagined him. Yet, in many ways, the reality of Troy Davenport contradicted her imaginings. She'd never really thought about it before, but he spoke like a gentleman—an educated one. His accent was cultured, his manners refined.

"You seem rather distracted today, Miranda," Caro said, startling her from her musings.

"What? Oh, I'm sorry. It's just this business with Gertie," she lied.

"What now?" Caro asked with a sigh. "She isn't still angry with you, is she?"

Miranda sighed. "Gertie is perpetually angry with me, more so since the Grandview."

"You were only following your father's instructions," Caro said with a shrug. "God knows I wouldn't cross Sir William."

"It's just Gertie's nature, I'm afraid. She's overly"— Miranda searched for the right word— "passionate, about everything. There're no shades of gray where she's concerned—everything is black and white, one extreme or the other."

"I suppose you're right," Caro agreed, uncorking the bottle of wine and refilling her glass. "Well, one day some poor man will marry her and take her off your hands. I suppose Sir William already has a list of possible candidates?" She held out the bottle toward Miranda.

"Thank you," she said, raising her glass to be filled. "Nothing less than an heir to a baronetcy will do, according to Father. I think there might even be one of Lord Spencer's grandsons on his list. He has extraordinarily high hopes for Gertie."

"And what if Miss Gertrude were to fall in love with the butcher's son, instead?" Troy put in. "Then what?"

Miranda shook her head. "It would never even occur to Gertie to fall in love with the butcher's son."

"No?" he asked.

"No," Miranda affirmed. She took a sip of wine, hoping it would calm her nerves. "It doesn't work that way, not with, well . . . people like us," she finished lamely.

He turned toward her, his brows drawn. "What doesn't work that way? Love?"

"It's just that she couldn't marry him," Miranda explained in exasperation. "So there's no point in even looking at him in that way. And what would a butcher's son want with her, besides? Except her inheritance."

"So you're saying, what?" Troy pressed. "That one can control with whom they fall in love? That they can reserve their affections for a small pool of acceptable candidates, and simply ignore the rest?"

"One hasn't a choice," Miranda said icily, "when there are fortunes involved. I don't suppose you'd understand."

"I suppose not," he said coldly, rising and stalking away from the blanket.

"Good God, Miranda!" Caro whispered harshly. "What were you thinking? Go, apologize to the man!" She tipped her head toward where he stood, off staring at what looked like the remains of an old, stone tower by the bank of the river.

She took a deep breath, weighing her options. She hated the way he'd made her feel, like some cold, calculating shrew. How dare he suggest that there was something wrong with a woman being careful where her heart was concerned, guarding herself against heartache?

And yet . . . she supposed he saw himself in the same ranks as the butcher's son. She'd hurt him, as if her words were an affront to him personally. She hadn't meant them that way.

Blast it. Caro was right; she owed him an apology. Nodding, she rose, straightening her hat as she slowly made her way down the gentle grassy slope toward him.

Before she even had a chance to consider her words, he turned toward her with a tight smile, one that did not reach his eyes.

"You'll have to excuse my temper," he said, shoving his hands into his pockets. "My apologies." With that, he strode off into the crumbling remains of the tower, leaving her standing there alone.

She sighed, inhaling the warm, heather-scented air. She couldn't leave it at that, couldn't just go back to the blanket without having her say. After all, his unexpected apology had only made her feel worse.

She followed him inside the structure where it was shady and cool. He turned to face her, looking almost surprised to see her there.

"I'm the one who should be apologizing," she said, feeling entirely discomposed. "You must forgive my careless words. I only meant—"

"I know exactly what you meant, Miranda," he interrupted. "I only wish I knew what happened to make you so bitter, to give you so little faith in human emotion."

She couldn't bring herself to look him in the eye. Instead, she studied the shiny, dark river stones beneath her boots. "I have my reasons, Troy. You must know that by now."

For a moment, he said nothing. She felt the weight of his stare, boring through her, daring her to look up.

At last, she did, their gazes colliding with what felt like a physical force. "Or perhaps you're just a terrible snob," he said with a shrug.

His lack of faith made her eyes sting. Did he truly believe that of her? She took a deep breath, gathering the courage to expose herself, to make herself more vulnerable than what was comfortable. He would see her for the silly fool she was, but at least he would understand.

"His name was Paul," she said at last, her voice tremulous. "I loved him, and it turned out he only loved my pocketbook. There, are you satisfied?" she asked, her hands clenched into fists. She turned back toward the structure's opening, toward Caro and the picnic blanket, prepared to flee.

But before she could, he reached for her hand, drawing her back to his side. "Don't go," he said, his voice low.

"I know exactly how much it took to buy him off, too," she continued on, her cheeks burning with mortification now. "Surprisingly little. To say that I was taken by surprise . . . well, I suppose that's quite the understatement."

His hard face softened at once. "How old were you?"

"Old enough to have known better. Now you must understand why I remain so wary where men are concerned. Especially those whose motives seem unclear. Whose"—how to say this delicately?—"whose pocketbook might suggest a motivation besides that of affection."

His eyes narrowed, a muscle in his jaw flexing perceptibly as he stared down at her. "So what are you saying, Miranda? That you suspect I might very well be a fortune hunter, too? Like the bastard who broke your heart?"

"I'm only saying that I need more time, more time to be certain—"

"More certain of what?" he interrupted angrily. "That I'm not going to rob you blind? Do you honestly believe that's why I'm here?"

She shook her head. "No, but I'd have said the same of Paul, had he asked me that question. I'm unquestionably a fool, you see."

He reached a hand up to her cheek. "You're not a fool, Miranda. I'd prove it, if you'd allow me."

"We'd best be getting back," she said, taking a step away from him, no longer able to think clearly, her brain muddled by his soft words, his gentle caress. "Caroline will be wondering what's happened to us."

She had to get away from him at once, before temptation overcame her sensibility.

Because at present, she believed him—believed he wasn't after her fortune, believed he would have pursued her had she been the butcher's daughter, instead.

And that couldn't *possibly* be sensible.

Without looking back, she hurried out into the bright sunlight and up the grassy slope toward Caroline.

"So it does lead here," came a voice behind Miranda, startling her so badly that she dropped the book she was reading and scrambled awkwardly to her feet.

Troy stood there behind her, at the edge of the woods, hidden in the shadows. "You said this path led to Holly's Close," he said, "but I had to see for myself."

"Good God, Troy, you just about frightened me half to death! You shouldn't sneak up on people like that." Her heart was pounding violently against her ribs, her breath coming far too fast.

"I didn't mean to startle you. What were you reading?" He took a step toward her, moving out of the shadows and into the brilliant sunshine.

"A novel," she answered. "You shouldn't be here. If anyone were to see you . . ." She took a deep breath, trying to calm her racing heart.

"What sort of novel?" he asked, ignoring her warning.

"*Anne of Green Gables.* By a Canadian authoress,

L.M. Montgomery. Quite charming, actually. Do you read much?"

He shook his head. "Not at all."

"Hmm, a shame. There's nothing I enjoy more than losing myself in a book."

"I suppose my art affords me the same escape. Do you play tennis?" he asked, tipping his head toward the net behind her.

"Very, very badly," she answered. "Just ask Caroline. Do you play?"

He shook his head, taking another step closer to where she stood. "Not in a very long time."

She turned, glancing back over one shoulder toward the house in the distance. The lawn was empty. Her sisters had music lessons, and her father was locked away in his study with a business associate from London, discussing yet another investment opportunity. Likely another hotel—her father was inordinately fond of hotels, it would seem.

"Are you expected somewhere?" Troy asked. "Or might you consider joining me for walk? To the swimming pond, perhaps?"

She turned back to face him. "I really shouldn't."

"But?" he prodded, the hint of a smile dancing on his lips.

It's only walking, she told herself. The paths through the woods weren't private, and if anyone asked . . . well, she'd simply say that they'd run into each other.

"But I will," she answered, before she had time

to change her mind. "I'd like that. Only, not to the swimming pond, if you don't mind."

"I don't mind at all. Where shall we go, instead?"

"I'll show you," she said, leaving her book there in the grass and hurrying to his side. "There's a place I like to go and sit—very peaceful and quiet. It might appeal to your artist's sensibilities," she offered. "It reminds me a bit of that clearing at the Grandview, the one where you painted me."

"Lead the way, then," he said with the sweep of one arm.

She set off, Troy falling into step beside her. "You're not painting out at the abbey this afternoon?"

He shook his head. "I painted some this morning, at the cottage. I'm working on another series besides the abbey at present," he added cryptically.

"Oh?" Miranda ducked beneath a low branch, keeping her eyes on the path ahead instead of the man beside her.

"Perhaps you can come by the cottage one day and I'll show you."

"Really, Troy, you know I can't do that. Ever," she clarified. "It's simply beyond the rules of propriety."

"Silly rules, if you ask me."

"Even so, I can't even consider it. If we're to meet, it will have to be like this. Outside, in the open. As if by accident. And better yet if Caroline is with us."

"And how is Mrs. Cressfield?" he asked, mercifully changing the subject. "Well, I hope."

She nodded. "Very well. She enjoyed the picnic last week; perhaps we should do it again soon."

He turned toward her, his eyes wide with surprise. "I'd like that. I suppose we can be more, ahem, honest with Mrs. Cressfield from now on? Or must we continue pretending to her that our meetings are purely accidental?"

"We no longer have to pretend with Caroline. Though I'd still appreciate your discretion, if you don't mind. It's one thing for her to think us all friends, but another for her to suspect, well . . ." She trailed off, unsure of what she meant to say. She sighed in exasperation, knowing full well he wasn't going to let that pass unnoticed.

"For her to suspect what, Miranda?" he prodded, just as she'd expected.

"Must I say it aloud?" With a huff of annoyance, she hurried ahead of him. He easily caught up with her, reaching for her elbow.

"Suspect what?" he repeated, as tenacious as ever.

She licked her lips before she spoke, moistening them. "Back at the Grandview. What happened there between us—"

"Is perhaps one of loveliest memories I own, Miranda," he interrupted. "Please don't take it away from me, pretending that it was something less than what it was. Or worse, pretending that it never happened."

Her breath caught in her throat. "What was it, Troy?" She shook her head, unable to staunch her curiosity. "I look back at those weeks and it all seems as if it must have happened to someone else. But then I see the painting, there on the drawing room wall, and I know they must be real, those memories."

He drew her close—so close that her breasts brushed against his coat. Her heart was pounding, and all she could think was that she hoped he kissed her; she *wanted* him to kiss her, so senselessly that nothing else mattered.

Instead, he simply gazed down at her, his own chest rising and falling at an alarming rate. "It's what's called a sexual affair, Miranda. I wanted you then, and I want you now. Nothing's changed on that count. Surely you must know that?"

"And . . . and is that something you engage in often?" she stammered, her cheeks burning now. "Sexual affairs? Conducted in the absence of a committed relationship?"

"Are you asking if I make a habit out of it? Yes," he said, not waiting for her answer. "I suppose I have. I've certainly never had anything that I'd describe as a committed relationship before. Still, I'm not a monk, Miranda."

"I never supposed you were." She swallowed a painful lump in her throat, willing herself to speak the truth. "And you must have noticed that . . . that I was not entirely inexperienced myself."

"The thought did occur to me," he said. "After all, in the glasshouse . . ." He shook his head. "That's not what one might consider a beginner's technique."

She hadn't thought it possible, but her cheeks burned hotter still. Her chin began to tremble, and he grasped it between his forefinger and thumb, refusing to let her look away. "I don't hold your experience against you, Miranda. In fact, I like that we're even on that count."

Tears gathered on her lashes, blurring her vision. "It's not like that. There was only Paul. No one else, and it was so long ago."

"How long?" he asked, his mouth so close to hers now that all she needed to do was rise up on tiptoe, and their lips would touch.

"A decade," she answered, her voice a hoarse whisper. "Ten very long years." Even now, she would not go near the little stone gatekeeper's cottage at the edge of their property, the place where she'd so carelessly given up her virtue.

Troy flinched, dropping his hand from her chin. "Good God, Miranda. Ten years? You've denied yourself that long, ignored your needs? Why didn't you marry in all that time? There must have been ample opportunity, must have been offers."

"Don't you see?" she cried, hating the way her voice broke. "I'm"—she swallowed hard—"I'm soiled goods. Who would have me?"

"Who told you that?" He was angry now, his green eyes flashing. "Damn it, I hate what your kind does to women, hate the double standard. A gentleman is perfectly entitled to his sexual experience—hell, it's expected of him. But a lady must come to the marriage bed entirely pure, without any experience whatsoever. It's entirely unfair, completely unbalanced."

Miranda just stood there, entirely mute, stunned by his outburst. She'd never heard a man say such things, never heard a gentleman speak so frankly.

"You're a passionate woman, Miranda," he continued, his voice softer now. "You've got the same needs as a man, the same desires. Why should you be ashamed of them? This is the twentieth century, after all, not the goddamned Middle Ages."

"That's just . . . just the way it is," she stuttered, though in her heart, she wanted to believe him, wanted to believe he spoke the truth.

"No," he said, raking a hand through his hair. "No, that's *not* the way it is. It's barbaric, is what it is. You, thinking you're some kind of failure, not good enough for men of your breed—'soiled goods,' you call yourself. It will not do, Miranda. I won't have it."

She blinked rapidly, trying to make sense of it all. What was he saying? "So . . . so you're saying that I should marry?"

"No, I'm only saying that you should do whatever you damn well please. That you shouldn't deny a vital part of yourself, the part that craves physical affection, just because of some outdated social mores that only seek to subvert women of your class."

Miranda stared up at him in amazement, still entirely speechless. By the way he talked, it seemed as if he was some sort of champion of women's rights. Either that, or an anarchist, she decided. She wasn't entirely sure which.

He reached for her hand, holding it in his, stroking her palm with his thumb. "Will you at least promise me that you'll think about what I've just said? Consider that there might be an entirely different version of the truth than the one you've been led to believe?"

She nodded her agreement.

"Good," he said, smiling now. "And now you can show me this secret place of yours. The one that the artist in me might appreciate."

"Let's go," she said, finding her voice at last. It seemed as if a weight had been lifted from her heart, inexplicably lightening it. With a sigh of relief, she led him deeper into the woods—and deeper into her heart, no doubt.

Chapter 18

Troy raised his arm, then tossed a stone across the surface of the swimming pond, watching as it skipped over the water in graceful arcs. "So it sounds as if the three of you got into plenty of mischief," he said. "And what does this Jamie do now? Is he in London?"

Caroline laughed. "Yes, believe it or not, he reads law. Ironic, isn't it?"

"Especially considering the number of times he was kicked out of school," Miranda put in. "Though he didn't care a bit. His father beat him with a switch the last time, and after that he was schooled at home with tutors. It's a miracle he's turned out as well as he has."

Troy shook his head in amazement. "And does he ever venture back to these parts? Or is he far too afraid of his father and his switch?"

Caroline looked toward Miranda, sitting on the bank beside her. "How long has it been since Jamie's been back to Weckham? Two years, I'd say," she answered when Miranda just shrugged. "I hoped he'd come home this year for the Founder's Fair, but I suppose he's not, or I would have heard from him by now. The fair's this weekend, after all."

His curiosity was piqued. "The Founder's Fair?"

"The village celebrates its founding each year with a summer fair on the green, followed by a dance in the assembly hall," Miranda supplied. "I'm surprised you haven't heard about it. Everybody's talking about it this time of year."

"Hmm, perhaps that's what they were talking about at the pub last night, then. Someone was going on about dancing, but I couldn't make heads or tails of it."

"You spend an awful lot of time at the pub, don't you?" Caroline asked, her voice laced with amusement.

"Well, it *is* only a half dozen doors down from my cottage. Besides, I'm a bachelor, remember? Where else am I to get a decent meal?"

"I'm sure you could hire a cook," Miranda said with a shrug. "At the very least, you could take your meals at the hotel. It's far more respectable, you know."

He couldn't help but notice the nudge Caroline gave Miranda in the ribs.

"I wasn't thinking," Miranda murmured in response, her cheeks coloring at once. "About a cook, I mean. The expense. But the hotel . . . it would be a better choice. Far better company, at least."

"I like the company at the pub just fine," he said with a shrug. "And I'm not the least bit concerned with respectability."

"Apparently not," Miranda muttered.

Time to change the subject. "Anyway, about this Jamie fellow. Surely he must have been in love with one of you, at least."

Caroline laughed at that. "Jamie? Not in the slightest, I assure you. We were natural playmates, all three of us so close in age, and all of us neighbors. Anyway, he and Miranda were always fighting, always at each other's throats."

"If he'd listened to me, he would have been in far less trouble most of the time," Miranda said, sounding defensive.

"Let me guess," Troy drawled. "You were always trying to make him act more respectably?"

"Something like that," Miranda agreed, rising and checking her watch. "He and Caro were always into some sort of mischief or another."

"Remember the time my brother caught us swimming here in our underclothes? I thought he was going to murder me, right there on the spot."

Miranda nodded, dropping her watch back against her blouse's high lace collar. "You're lucky Jack didn't murder poor Jamie. I told you both it was a bad idea."

"Yes, but that didn't stop you from eventually joining us, anyway. Sir William didn't let Jamie anywhere near Holly's Close for months afterward, if I remember correctly. Poor boy; it had only been innocent fun, but everyone treated him as if he'd . . . well, as if he'd forced us to do something horribly wicked. I don't know why Jack had to go and run his mouth like he did."

Troy couldn't help but laugh at the poor boy's misfortune. Then again, he wondered if the boy's intentions had been less innocent than Caroline and Miranda believed them to be. At thirteen, he certainly would have had wicked thoughts about two girls in their wet underclothes.

Regardless, it was hard to imagine Miranda the carefree youth the pair of them described. If only he could help her recapture that bloom, that joie de vivre. Perhaps he was, to some extent, he realized.

After all, the past few weeks had been nothing short of miraculous. Almost every day she'd cycled out to the abbey where she'd sit patiently for hours on end, watching him while he painted. Some days it was just the two of them; others days, Caroline joined them.

Miranda had seemed to laugh more in recent weeks, particularly when the three of them were together. Perhaps it reminded her of the dynamics they'd had with this Jamie fellow, of the easy camaraderie they'd shared. Whatever the case, she seemed more comfortable in his company now, and he hadn't pushed her, hadn't risked making her uncomfortable by his advances, even when they were alone.

It was killing him, however. His desire simmered just beneath the surface at all times, threatening to spill over with just the slightest inadvertent touch. The brush of her shoulder against his arm or her sleeve against his was all it took to set his blood afire, his attention focused solely on the sensation that skittered across his skin in the wake of her touch.

He couldn't last much longer, not like this. And yet . . . and yet they were friends now. Damn if he wanted to risk that, to risk taking the smile from her lips, the laugh from her throat. For now, this would have to suffice.

"So are you going to the dance?" Caroline asked him, her pale hair reflecting the sunbeam that penetrated the canopy of trees above them. "On Saturday night, I mean?"

"Should I?" he asked, glancing over to where Miranda stood leaning against the trunk of a slender tree. He tried to read her expression, to search her dark eyes for any encouragement whatsoever.

"Of course you should," Miranda answered. "Everyone comes, after all. From Sir William down to the butcher's son."

He wondered where she placed him on that order. Probably best not to ask. "Then I suppose I will go, but only if I'm promised dances from both of you. Or would that be considered inappropriate?" he asked.

Miranda shook her head. "Of course not. Grace and Gertie will undoubtedly want their turn, too."

"I'll be on my best behavior, then. I would not want to give Sir William cause for alarm. But until then, are you certain that neither of you are up for a swim? It's unbearably hot, and the water is growing far too tempting."

Caroline shook her head, rising to join Miranda by the tree. "I believe we learned our lesson all those years ago. But don't let it stop you; go right ahead."

"I think I will," he said, grinning up at the pair of them standing there, no doubt perspiring in their multiple layers of clothing. Indeed, even in the heat, they were modestly covered from neck to wrist to toe.

Both pairs of female eyes widened as he unbuttoned his coat, tossing it to the branches beside them before moving on to his waistcoat. As soon as his fingers began working the buttons on his shirt, they'd taken several steps away, laughing merrily.

"Good-bye, Mr. Davenport," Caroline called out, disappearing over the rise that led back toward the path.

Shrugging out of his shirt, he tossed it aside. Miranda still stood there, as still as a statue, watching him. Slowly, sensuously, even, her gaze slid down to his waist, then back up again. Their eyes met and held for a fraction of a second, long enough for Troy to see unmistakable desire smoldering in her gaze—long enough for his cock to grow immediately hard, damn it.

And then she turned and fled without a backward glance.

With a groan of frustration, he dove into the

water, trousers and all. He only hoped the water was suitably cold enough to douse the fire she'd just stoked.

"Miss Granger," Troy said with a slight bow. "You look lovely tonight."

"Thank you," she answered, inclining her head toward him, trying her best to ignore the way her heart leapt in her breast at the sight of him.

She glanced over her shoulder to where her father stood, deep in conversation with Mr. Denby. Grace and Gertie surrounded him, both of them watching her closely.

"Did you enjoy the fair today, Mr. Davenport?" Caroline said beside her, and Miranda sighed in relief at being rescued. Her mouth was suddenly dry, her palms damp. When she looked at him now, all she could think of was the sight of him just days ago, standing there at the swimming pond in nothing but his trousers, his chest entirely bare.

Oh, she'd seen him shirtless once before, back at the Grandview. But that seemed a lifetime ago, and even then she hadn't taken the time to really look, to appreciate the sight as she had done there by the pond, in broad daylight.

How she'd wanted to hurry back to his side, to press herself against those hard muscles, to feel her bare skin against his. She'd had to force her feet to flee, to hurry and catch up with Caroline before she'd been able to change her mind.

She couldn't risk discovery in such a public place as that. She wouldn't have gotten off as lightly as she had when she'd been thirteen and caught swimming with Jamie in her underthings. Indeed, no. But that didn't mean she hadn't wanted to—desperately, even.

And worse, he knew it. She'd seen it there in his eyes as he watched her watching him. She could see that he was thinking about it now, too, just as she was. Just how long had she thought she could deny it? It seemed almost silly to try, now that she thought about it.

And yet now, in public like this with her father just across the room, they had no choice but to hide it. After all, if her father got a whiff of it, she had no doubt that her freedoms would be restricted. As it was, he mostly let her do whatever she pleased while her sisters were in lessons. He assumed she spent her time with Caro, or off walking in the woods alone as she always did. As far as she could tell, he had no knowledge that she had any contact with Troy whatsoever. Best to keep it that way.

"Will you dance, Mir—Miss Granger," he corrected, and Miranda let out a sigh of relief. It seemed he would remember the rules, all right.

She cleared her throat, finding her voice at last. "I think I shall have a glass of lemonade first. But I'm certain that Mrs. Cressfield will oblige you, instead."

She turned toward Caro with hopeful eyes. Her friend just nodded, understanding the message. He must not seem to single out Miranda, not at first.

"Of course," he said, offering his arm to Caro. "Mrs. Cressfield?"

"Thank you, Mr. Davenport." Caro took his arm and allowed herself to be led out to the dance floor. Both of them acted extraordinarily formal, as if they were but the merest of acquaintances.

Miranda let out a sigh of relief as Troy began to turn Caro gracefully about the dance floor, seemingly oblivious to the pairs of curious eyes trained on them.

"Do you suppose he'll ask us to dance?" Grace asked, sidling up beside her, Gertie at her heels.

"Yes, it does seem odd that he'd ask Caroline first." Gertie stood on her toes, craning her neck to find them in the crowd. "After all, we made his acquaintance first, didn't we?"

"Well, she *is* a widow," Grace reasoned. "Perhaps he feels bad for her."

Gertie nodded. "I suppose you're right. Do you suppose that's his best suit? I vow, he looks a bit like the baker's son, don't you think?"

No, Miranda wanted to say. He looked nothing like the baker's son, nothing at all. The baker's son was tall and gangly, awkward looking and ill at ease in his finest suit of clothes.

And though Troy's suit was similarly simple and plain, he wore it without the slightest bit of awkwardness. He had the regal bearing of a duke, as graceful a dancer as any peer of the realm. In fact, he'd look equally at home in the finest ballroom in Mayfair, she realized with a start.

He was easily the most handsome man in the room, as evidenced by the scores of young ladies following his every move, his every step.

If only he *were* a duke. A viscount, even. Any sort of gentleman, really. If he were, then they wouldn't have to play these foolish games. If he were, her father would be looking on approvingly as he turned her about the polished floor.

Instead, it seemed as if every woman in the room had their turn before her. Grace, Gertie, the butcher's wife, the barmaid from the pub. He was doing it on purpose, she realized with a start, watching as he claimed the shopkeeper's daughter for a second waltz. He was making her suffer, drawing out the anticipation till she was nearly mad with it.

"Don't be angry with him," Caro whispered in her ear, as if she could read her thoughts. "You know exactly why he's doing it."

"I know," she muttered, feeling almost churlish now.

"He's quite the hit, though, isn't he? I do believe he's charmed every woman in the room. Even my mother is saying how delightful he is—can you believe it? He's offered to paint my portrait, you know. That's what we were discussing while we danced. I agreed, but only if you come to keep me company while I sit."

A pang of jealousy shot through her, though she'd never admit to it. "Of course," she agreed.

"I vow, it's dreadfully warm in here. I don't know why our founders couldn't have chosen a cooler month to establish our little village. I think my face browned a shade out at the fair today."

"Should we take some air? I don't see Mr. Davenport, anyway. Perhaps he's in the refreshment room."

"Lemonade?" came a voice behind them, and both women turned to find Troy standing there bearing two glasses.

"Why, thank you," Caro said, taking one of the proffered glasses.

Miranda said nothing.

"Would you care to dance instead, Miss Granger? I don't believe I've yet had the pleasure." He held out one hand to her.

She placed her hand in his, hoping he didn't notice how it trembled. "That would be lovely. Thank you, Mr. Davenport."

Glancing up, she saw her father watching them. His expression was unreadable. He couldn't possibly complain, however. Gertie and Grace had already danced two dances each with him, and he hadn't raised an eyebrow then.

"They're all wondering where you learned to dance so well," she murmured as Troy clasped her hand in his, his other pressing against the small of her back.

"They don't think very highly of Americans, do they? Your father is watching us, by the way."

Miranda swallowed hard, trying to ignore the excitement that coiled in her belly, just from his touch, his nearness. "Just don't hold me too closely," she answered, feeling the weight of her father's stare.

He smiled down at her, a lock of his hair falling across his forehead. "I won't. But just know that I want to," he added, his voice low. "I want to press my body up against yours; it's all I've thought of, all night long."

"Shh," she warned, shocked yet excited by his words, all at once.

His grip around her waist tightened ever so slightly. "No one can hear me over the music. I want to kiss you, Miranda. What do you say to that?"

"I say that you're teasing me. And that you should stop. You're making me blush." She caught sight of Caro out the corner of her eye as they spun past, a blur of pale yellow silk.

"You like it, though, don't you?" he pressed, his smile wicked now.

"Did you talk scandalously to all the ladies as you twirled them about the floor?" she murmured.

He feigned shock. "Of course not. It's you I want, and no one else. You've ruined me for anyone else. Surely you know that by now."

"Please stop." She didn't want him to, not really.

"Very well, but only if I extract a promise from you first."

Miranda was growing slightly dizzy. "What sort of promise?"

"I'll quit, and I'll take you back to Caro and your sisters as soon as this waltz ends, but only if you'll promise me a waltz in the moonlight later."

She rolled her eyes. "And how do you suppose I manage that?"

"Easy. Once you get back to Holly's Close, you excuse yourself and pretend to go to bed. And then you sneak out and meet me by the edge of woods. One dance, that's all, and then I'll let you go back to bed."

Miranda shook her head, thinking he'd lost his mind. "Don't be ridiculous. You know I can't do that."

His gaze was heated now, warming her skin. "You can do it, if you want to. And I'll be there waiting, just in case. I'll wait all night, if I have to."

"I'm afraid you're going to be disappointed, then. I can't possibly do what you're asking."

He shrugged. "Just today you and Caro told me about sneaking out into the woods with Jamie when you were thirteen. How is this any different?"

"Because I'm not thirteen anymore, that's how," she snapped. "I'm not a girl. And you're not Jamie, besides." It would be far too dangerous, too tempting.

"The song is ending," he said, his voice urgent now as the last strains of the waltz faded away. "Say yes, Miranda. Say you'll try."

"Thank you, Mr. Davenport." She stepped away from him, refusing to meet his eyes, fearing she wouldn't be able to refuse him if she did.

"I'll wait all night," he said in reply, his voice so low that she wasn't sure she'd heard him right.

Her father was watching her still; she could feel his gaze following her as she made her way back to where Caro stood watching, an expectant look on her face.

"Well?" Caro whispered once she reached her side.

"Goodness, Caro," she said, endeavoring to keep her tone light and playful. "Don't be so dramatic. It was just a dance, after all."

But of course it was so much more than that—anything with Troy was more than it was meant to be, filled with promise and expectation.

Would tonight be any different?

Chapter 19

Troy glanced up at the full moon, then back down at his pocket watch. It was just after midnight. Would she come? She'd said she wouldn't, of course, but he'd convinced himself that she wanted to, that she'd somehow find a way. Wishful thinking, perhaps. But damn, he would give anything to hold her in his arms beneath the light of the moon.

The one dance they'd shared tonight wasn't enough, would never be enough. He wanted more, needed more. He began to pace a circuit at the edge of the woods, his gaze trained on the silvery house in the distance, entirely dark now. He willed her to come, as if wishing alone could bring her there.

Surely she could feel his presence out there, waiting. Hoping. A quarter hour later, he paused his pacing and checked his pocket watch again. *Damn.* He'd been so sure she'd come, despite her

protests. He'd said he'd wait all night, however, and
he would. He would stand there till the sun rose.

The breeze stirred, carrying with it the scent of
grass, of earth. It felt cool against his skin, bring-
ing with it a hint of autumn. Soon enough the
season would change. The leaves would fall from
the trees and it would grow colder. He only had
the Rawlings cottage till the end of the year, and
then what?

He didn't want to think about it now, didn't
want to consider his options. But the truth was,
they could not go on like this forever. He knew it
was so, and yet he was unsure of what he could
possibly hope for where Miranda was concerned.

Why did it have to be so complicated?

And then he heard a noise—faint yet distinct.
A rustling. Just the wind in the leaves, perhaps?
He looked toward the house, squinting his eyes,
scanning the shadows for movement.

And then, like a mirage in the desert, a vision
shimmered and took shape. Miranda, moving
toward him stealthily and silently. She looked
almost like a specter, wearing what seemed to be
a pale-colored dressing gown, her dark hair loose
about her shoulders.

"Miranda?" he called out, his voice a hoarse
whisper.

"Shhh," she replied, though she kept moving
toward him, her feet seeming to float just above
the ground.

For the briefest of moments, he wondered if
he was dreaming, if he'd somehow fallen asleep

there at the edge of the woods and was now enjoying a lovely dream where Miranda heeded his call and came to him.

Only, it wasn't a dream—she was really there, in flesh and blood. He could feel her warmth as she drew closer, her dark eyes reflecting the moon as she gazed up at him expectantly.

"One dance," she said. "Just like you said. And then I must hurry back to bed."

Reeling with surprise, he opened his arms, gathering her in his embrace. Her skin felt flushed, hot to the touch as he wrapped his arms around her waist, drawing her closer.

She reached up to wrap her arms about his neck, laying her cheek against his shoulder. For several minutes, they stood just like that, not moving a muscle. And then he couldn't stand it any longer—he had to feel his fingers in her hair. He combed it back from her face, marveling at the texture, at the heady scent of lavender that wafted up from the deep chestnut strands that slipped through his fingers like silk.

The breeze stirred, ruffling the hem of her dressing gown, exposing one pale ankle for the briefest of seconds. She was barefoot, he realized with a start.

"You look like some sort of goddess," he murmured. "I'll never get this image out of my head. I'll have to paint it, as soon as I return to the cottage."

His fingers skimmed over her sides, up to her shoulders, and he felt her shudder in response. "What about that dance you promised?" she asked, reaching for his hand, placing the other at her back.

His eyes never leaving her face, he nodded, burning the beautiful image into his brain. He'd never seen her more beautiful, never wanted to forget the way she looked at that very moment. And then he started to hum, low and quiet beside her ear. *Clair de lune,* the piece they'd agreed was the most beautiful one ever written. Slowly, he began to move—a leisurely waltz, turning her beneath the stars, the moon, the heavens. His heart kept time, thumping against his ribs as he gazed down at her in wonder, wanting this moment to last forever.

Miranda gazed up at her partner, wondering just what she'd done to deserve this—this perfect moment in time. No dance would ever compare, no matter how fine the ballroom, how excellent the orchestra, how exquisite the gown she wore. This was the perfect waltz, and nothing would ever surpass it. She was sure of it, as sure as she'd ever been about anything in all her years.

For a good five minutes, he continued to hum her favorite piece of music, gazing down at her as if she were the most beautiful woman in the world. The heat in his gaze was unmistakable, yet his touch was gentle, exquisitely so. At last, his movements slowed, his voice quieted as he hummed the movement's final bars. He pulled her close, up against his chest. Her breasts flattened against his coat, her nipples rubbing deliciously against the fabric between them. Her thighs were damp with need, her sex swollen and sensitive.

That was all it took—a dance beneath the stars, with only the moon as their witness—to make her ready for him. And yet she knew that she couldn't have him, couldn't allow him to take her. Because if she did, it would be akin to opening Pandora's box. Once she had him, she'd never be able to give him up, and then where would that leave her?

His mistress? Someone like that Rousseau woman, to warm his bed as long as it was convenient for them both? No, that would never do. But what else could she possibly hope for, where he was concerned? She certainly could not risk finding herself in the same situation as she had a decade ago. The unfairness of it all made her want to cry, made her want to scream and rail at fate for tempting her with something she could never have.

"Miranda?" Troy asked, his lips moving against her temple.

"Hmm?" was all she could answer, her legs suddenly weak.

He straightened, tipping her gaze up to his. "Thank you. This was the most perfect dance, the most perfect night. I don't know what made you change your mind, but I'll never forget this, as long as I live."

She shook her head. "Nor I, Troy."

He released her, taking a step back as he shoved his hands into his pockets. "You'd best go now."

Silently, she nodded. Still facing him, she took several steps back, toward the house. Pausing, she took a deep breath, steeling herself to leave him when she wanted so much more.

Unable to stand the temptation a moment longer, she rushed forward, throwing her arms around him as she rose on tiptoe, pressing her lips against his. It wasn't enough, would never be enough.

But it would have to do—for now, at least.

Before she had the chance to change her mind, she released him, forcing her mouth to retreat. "Good night," she whispered, then dashed off toward the house as fast as her feet would carry her, knowing full well that she wouldn't be able to run from him forever.

Troy glanced up at the sky, surprised to see the gray clouds moving closer, darkening the sky. It looked like rain was headed their way, and fast.

"Miranda?" he called out, setting down his brush. "I've lost the light."

Miranda stuck her head inside the gaping hole that was once a vaulted door. "Then you're done for the day?"

He smiled, his heart swelling at the sight of her. She'd been sitting there nearly three hours, waiting for him. He'd never met anyone so patient, so comfortable in the absence of conversation.

"I suppose I am done for the day," he answered with a nod. "What would you like to do for the rest of the afternoon?"

She shrugged. "Walk down to the river, perhaps? Take off my shoes and wade in the shallows?"

"Why not?" He rose from his stool, balancing the palette on top of it. "We'll have to be quick, though. It looks like rain moving this way."

She tilted her face up to the sky. "No, I think it'll blow right past. It's too far behind us, over by the hills, don't you think?"

"I'll defer to your expertise where Weckham weather is concerned. Let's go, if you'd like." He held out his hand, smiling when she took it without the slightest hesitation. Things had changed perceptibly between them since their dance in the moonlight. There was an effortless companionship that wasn't there before, a sense of trust—even without Caroline by her side, acting as her unspoken chaperone.

Twice he'd even convinced her to come back to his cottage, sneaking in through the back garden gate. They'd done nothing illicit—only had a spot of tea and sat and talked in the comfort of the parlor. He'd shown her the paintings he'd completed thus far, all lined up against the wall. The paintings of the abbey, that is.

He'd hidden away the others, the paintings of her, done entirely from memory, usually late at night when the rest of the village lay cloaked in sleepy silence. These paintings were like nothing he'd ever attempted before. A significant departure from his usual style and method, they were less literal, more abstract. He couldn't wait to show them to François, to gauge his reaction. But for now, they would remain a secret, his guilty pleasure.

"What are you thinking about?" Miranda asked him, drawing him from his thoughts as they crossed the grassy meadow behind the abbey's ruins and headed down toward the riverbank.

"Nothing in particular," he said, releasing her hand and snatching the straw boater from her head. "Why must you always wear this thing? Your hair is so beautiful. I don't understand why you're always covering it."

"Because I don't want my face to brown any more than it already has, that's why," she answered, wrinkling her nose at him.

"Well, why must ladies have such pale faces? I'd like to see you with a freckle or two."

"Do French women have freckled faces?" she asked.

He tried to recall the face of a French woman from his past—no one in particular, but any woman he'd encountered during his time in France—but he drew a maddening blank. "To tell you the truth, I don't recall. Perhaps they did. I don't remember them seeming as pale as Londoners, for certain."

"Just be glad I don't paint my face with enamel."

"Enamel?" He imagined a thick, white shiny paint glopped all over a woman's face. "Whatever it is, it sounds terrible."

"It *is* terrible. Pits the face horribly, you know. That's why I stick to rice powder, or pearl powder for evenings." She turned her face up to the sky and frowned. "Oh, dear. I might have been mistaken about the rain. It's beginning to look like we might get a shower, after all."

"I told you so," he grumbled playfully. "Though I don't suppose we'll melt, will we? I used to love to jump about in a warm summer rain when I was a boy. I remember once stripping down to my underclothes and taking off down the street, splashing through the puddles rather unceremoniously. My mother was not pleased, to say the least." He winced at the memory. His father had taken a strap to him that night, if he remembered correctly.

Miranda looked up at him expectantly, as if she hoped he would say more. He spoke very little of his family, after all. For good reason. "Anyway, don't you ever want to feel the sun on your skin?" he asked, fascinated with the subject. "I mean, look at you, always covered from your ankles to your neck, and all those layers underneath. Don't you ever tire of it?"

"I don't suppose I've ever thought about it, really. It's just the way it is. Would you like to see my ankle?" she teased.

His mouth went suddenly dry, his throat parched with the very notion. "You've *no* idea."

She turned toward him sharply, her eyes round with surprise. "Really, Troy? An ankle? There's nothing all that exciting about an ankle, is there?"

His gaze slid down her skirt, toward the

concealed joint in question. "Then why must you always cover them?"

She shook her head, laughing now. "Must you question everything? Goodness, you must have driven your mother mad as a boy."

"I suppose I did." They'd reached the river-bank, and Troy stopped while Miranda sat to remove her boots, her hat lying in the grass beside her.

"And now I suppose you'll clam up, like you always do when I try and ask you about your childhood, about New York," she said, her fingers flying over the buttons on her kidskin boots.

He shoved his hands deep into his pockets, guilt nagging at his conscience. "That's because there's nothing of interest to say about it."

He needed to tell her the truth, and soon. He knew it was so, and still he hesitated. He'd come so close to breaking down that reserve of hers. If he were to tell her now, before he was sure of her affections, well . . . perhaps he could wait a bit longer. He'd kept the secret this long—what was another week or two?

A fat raindrop splashed onto Troy's arm, then another. "Now I'll say 'I told you so' with much more authority. We're going to get soaked."

"The tower?" she asked, quickly gaining her feet and turning toward the crumbling structure perhaps a hundred yards away.

Several more raindrops fell heavily on his head. "It won't offer much protection."

And then the sky seemed to open up all at

once. He grabbed her hand, and together they dashed off toward the crumbling tower where they cowered inside, her hat and boots abandoned out in the downpour. But it was no use; the driving rain blew in through the cracks, through the yawning gaps of stone. He backed her up toward what was left of one wall, attempting to shield her body from the worst of it with his own.

"It's hopeless," she said, laughing now, her dark hair falling wetly against her shoulders. "At least it's a warm rain. It almost feels good, doesn't it? Refreshing."

"Let's make the most of it, then," he challenged, backing away from her, allowing the rain to sluice down between them. Reaching up, he began to unbutton his shirt, his gaze meeting hers in challenge.

Her eyes widened, her mouth forming an "O" of surprise. And then she nodded, reaching for the buttons on her own blouse. In a minute's time, they'd both stripped down to their undergarments—Miranda had even removed her corset, so that all that remained, protecting her from the rain, was a thin layer of fabric.

With her in her vest and knickers and him in his drawers, they both ran out laughing into the rain. A few yards out, he paused, watching as Miranda turned in slow circles, her arms spread wide, her face turned up toward the sky as the rain continued to soak her, her undergarments clinging wetly to her curves now.

Her hair had fallen completely from its arrangement, dark and wet against her pale, perfect skin. "It's wonderful!" she said, stopping to face him, lifting her arms to the sky like some sort of goddess. His cock stiffened at the sight, and all he could think about was taking her in his arms—this wild, free Miranda. Water ran down her face, dripped from her nose—and yet he'd never seen her more beautiful, more free and alive.

"Catch me," she cried, then dashed off, splashing through the river's shallows just as the rain began to let up, reduced to a drizzle now.

Soaked to the bone, he gave chase, following her through the shallows and back up the grassy slope. He caught her by the arm just as she dashed inside the tower. Tugging her toward him, he pressed her back against the stones, caging her in with his arms.

"What now?" he asked, his breath coming fast from the chase.

She shook her head, sending a spray of droplets flying in every which direction. Her thin cotton undergarments were entirely transparent, her rosy nipples straining against the fabric. His gaze traveled lower, to her knickers, to the dark, tantalizing shadow where her thighs joined.

He had to squeeze his eyes shut against the temptation. "Miranda," he groaned, leaning into her, his erection straining against his drawers, pressing urgently against her belly.

And then he felt her insistent mouth on his, her hands reaching around his neck, drawing him closer.

That was invitation enough. He opened his mouth against hers, his hands traveling down her sides, and then back up again as he kissed her deeply, thoroughly. He cupped her breasts, the pads of his thumbs caressing her already erect nipples.

"Troy," she murmured against his mouth, grinding her pelvis against him, rubbing herself against his cock till he feared he might come, right then and there, like an overeager schoolboy.

His entire body beginning to vibrate with pleasure, he pushed down the straps of her vest, baring her breasts, dropping his head to lick the raindrops from her skin, from the rosy peaks that pebbled further as his tongue skated across them.

God, but she tasted good—clean and earthy, her skin slightly salty, like the rain itself.

What was it about this woman that made him want to possess her so, that made him want to rethink everything that he thought he knew about himself, about what he wanted from life?

What was it about her that made him consider abandoning his life of travel, of adventure; that made him picture a neat little house in the country instead, a passel of dark-headed, brown-eyed children toddling about as he sat at his easel, painting his muse?

All these years he'd considered himself a

progressive thinker where women were concerned, valuing their freedoms, their will, their intellectual worth. Yet now, holding a half-naked Miranda in his arms, it was as if he'd regressed several centuries. Some sort of base male instinct had taken over, entirely unfamiliar and frightening in its power.

Wrenching his mouth from hers, he pressed his forehead against her shoulder, taking a deep, ragged breath, trying his best to rein it in. He was vaguely aware that the rain had let up, that the heavy veil of gray had lifted. Miranda's fingers were still tangled in his hair, her head tipped back against the wet, slick stones as she caught her breath.

"Troy?" she whispered at last. "You didn't have to stop, not this time."

He sucked in a deep, fortifying breath and then exhaled slowly, purposefully. "Yes, I did," he said at last. He drew away from her, trying his damnedest to tamp down the lust, to cool the fire that ran hotly through his veins. "I did have to stop," he repeated, as if he might force himself to believe it if he said it often enough.

He couldn't explain it, couldn't make himself say the words—couldn't tell her that something had irrevocably changed since those days back at the Grandview. She wasn't just an easy fuck. This had proved to be far more than a simple affair. It was so much more than that, and there was no use continuing to pretend otherwise.

He cursed under his breath, thinking that he must have lost his mind. He had a willing woman in his arms, wet with desire and nearly naked, and he was refusing to take what she offered?

"I won't take you like this," he began, his voice strangely thick with emotion. "Up against the stones, with no protection. I *will* show some restraint."

She nodded, her lower lip caught between her teeth. She shivered then, folding her arms across her breasts.

He laid one palm against her cheek. "Are you cold, love?"

Nodding, she turned her face into his hand, pressing a heartbreakingly soft kiss against the center of his palm. "Just a bit."

"How are we going to get you home?" She was soaking wet, and her clothes lay in an equally soaked heap several feet away. "I can't let you cycle home, not like this. You'll take ill for certain. I'll have to drive you."

"What about my bicycle?"

"We can strap it to the back of the motorcar. If anyone asks, we'll simply say you were out riding and got caught in the storm. I happened by and offered you a ride. Will that satisfy them?"

"It will have to," she answered with a shrug. "How am I even going to put these things back on?"

He shook his head. "I'm sorry, Miranda. I shouldn't have encouraged—"

She laid a finger against his lips. "Don't apologize, Troy. Please," she begged. "This was . . . this was lovely."

"It was, wasn't it?" He bent to retrieve his own clothes, wet and slightly muddy. Definitely worth it, he decided, even as he set about the uncomfortable task of pulling on his soaked trousers and shirt.

When he was done, he waited patiently, leaning against the stones as she struggled into layer after wet layer, far more than he had to endure. Even as he watched, he fought against the desire to take her, to strip off every last scrap of clothing, and to pick up right where they left off. But besting that urge was another, stronger one, an entirely unfamiliar one—he wanted to court her, like a gentleman would.

He almost laughed aloud at the irony of it. After all, he'd only recently chastised her for suppressing her physical needs and ignoring her desires. He'd bloody well encouraged her to disregard the rules of society and do exactly as she pleased, where men were concerned.

And now *he* was the one backing down from his desires, suppressing them, wanting to follow the very same social mores that he'd criticized. He shook his head, feeling like the worst sort of hypocrite. Yet at the same time, he felt oddly right about his current course of action.

Weak rays of sun had penetrated the clouds now, casting diagonal beams of light across her as she at last buttoned up her blouse. And then he noticed her rose-colored corset, still lying at her feet.

"You've forgotten something," he said, retrieving

it, fighting the urge to bring it to his nose and inhale it, searching for her scent.

"It's too much trouble. Can you take it? I'll get it from you later. Somehow," she added.

He nodded, tucking it beneath his arm. "Ready?"

"I suppose so," she said with a wince. "I think my hat and boots are ruined, though. Goodness, this feels dreadful."

He offered his hand. "You need to get out of those things and into a hot bath quickly, before you take ill."

"Heavens, Troy, I'm not going to fall ill from a bit of dampness. I've a far sturdier constitution than that."

"Good," he said with a nod. "Because if you did fall ill, I'd never forgive myself."

Chapter 20

With a groan, Miranda sat up in bed. Her head was pounding, her mouth uncomfortably dry. "Sullivan?" she called out hoarsely.

"Right here, miss," Sullivan answered, bustling in and filling a glass with water. "Here, drink this. Slowly, now."

Miranda took the glass from her maid, tipping it toward her mouth and drinking in noisy gulps.

"Not so fast," Sullivan chastised. "It'll just come right back up again."

Lord, she hoped not. But she was terribly thirsty, her body aching all over. "What happened?" she asked, setting aside the glass and lying back against the pillows that Sullivan had plumped behind her. She had vague memories of waking up, feeling terribly ill and almost fainting, of climbing back into bed and thinking she'd best stay there a bit longer. After that, her memories were fuzzy, almost like a dream. The doctor had prodded her, Sullivan had laid a cool cloth on her head, but beyond that, it was all a blur.

"You took a terrible fever, that's what. I don't know what you were thinking, out cycling in the rain. It's a good thing that young painter came across you when he did, or else it might have been far worse. As it was, well . . . let's just say you gave us all a terrible fright. Thank God your fever broke when it did."

Feeling oddly disoriented, she licked her parched lips. "How long has it been? Since I took ill, I mean."

"Four days, miss. Your father was nearly out of his mind."

Four days? *Impossible.* She couldn't even remember the last time she'd been ill, much less confined to her bed for more than a day or two. She raised a hand to her temple, trying to make sense of it all. How could four days have passed without her remembering them?

Sullivan went to the door, pausing with one hand on the brass handle. "I'll go tell your father that you've awakened, and then I'll have Cook prepare you some beef broth and toast. Would you like some tea, too?"

"Yes, thank you, Sullivan." She struggled to sit up again, her stomach grumbling noisily. "I vow, I'm suddenly ravenous."

"Very well. I'll be right back." With a nod, Sullivan bustled out.

Miranda glanced toward the window, where the curtains were drawn against the glass, giving no hint as to the time of day. Curious, she threw back the bedclothes, swinging her legs over the side of the bed. When she did, the entire room began to tilt and spin, a dizzying blur of color. Clutching the mattress, Miranda squeezed shut her eyes, trying to regain her balance.

Goodness, it was no use. She was far too weak. She'd have to wait till Sullivan returned. And so she sat there, unmoving, staring at the window as she gathered the strength to climb back under the bedclothes.

But before she could, a knock sounded on the door, startling her. "Miranda?" a voice called out. "It's Caro. May I come in?"

"Of course," she answered weakly, smiling when the door opened and Caro strode in, looking like a vision in pale blue linen. "You've no idea how glad I am to see you," Miranda said with a sigh.

"You weren't trying to get up, were you?" Caro hurried to her side, her face drawn with worry.

"I only wanted to open the drapes." Her tongue felt thick in her mouth, her voice rusty from disuse. Clearing her throat, she gingerly swung her legs back up onto the mattress and pulled up the soft cotton sheet to cover them.

"Here, let me do it." Caro went to the window, pulling aside the heavy fabric. Miranda blinked as sunlight flooded the room, the sky a bright, cloudless blue beyond the glass.

"There," Caro said, returning to her side and taking a seat in a chintz chair beside the bed.

"Goodness, Miranda, you have no idea how glad I am to see you looking so well today! It's almost like a miracle."

Just then a maid bustled in with a tray, setting it down on the table beside Caro's chair. "Tea, miss," the girl said with a curtsey.

"Here, I'll pour," Caro offered, reaching for the teapot.

The maid left, promising to return with the broth. Miranda watched as Caro spooned in two lumps of sugar and a splash of cream, and then took the steaming cup she offered, cradling it in her hands as she waited for it to cool.

"How do you feel?" Caro asked, eyeing her sharply. "The truth, if you don't mind."

"Dreadful," Miranda answered. "And I barely remember any of it."

"Gertie said that you woke up Tuesday morning, got out of bed, and nearly fainted dead away on the carpet." She shook her head in amazement. "After that, you deteriorated quickly. I came by several times, but you didn't even realize I was here."

Miranda shook her head in amazement. "Really? I vow, I remember almost nothing. I suppose I must have been terribly ill."

"Terribly so," Caro agreed. "You were delirious. Apparently your father was making arrangements to take you to a hospital in London. And then, just like that, your fever broke. Thankfully, Grace sent word to me straightaway, late last night."

Miranda just stared at her dazedly, still unable to make heads or tails out of it all. "I can't believe I gave everyone such a fright."

Caro reached for her hand. "I'll stop by the Rawlings' cottage on my way home and tell Mr. Davenport. Poor man, he's been out of his mind with worry, blaming himself. Something about the rain?" She shook her head, giving Miranda's hand a gentle squeeze. "Anyway, he actually came by Holly's Close the day before yesterday. I don't know what he was thinking."

No. "F-Father," she stammered, barely able to speak. "What did he do?"

"Sent him away, of course. Poor man, he was inconsolable. I felt terrible, watching him go without being able to say a word to comfort him lest Sir William get suspicious. I went out to the abbey yesterday, hoping to find him there."

"He wasn't?"

Caro shook her head. "No. I found him at the cottage, instead. Heaven only knows what the neighbors will say, seeing me come and go, two days in a row. But I must go and give him the news straightaway."

Miranda just nodded, taking a sip of her tea. It felt good against her throat—hot and soothing.

For a moment, Caro just watched her, a curious expression on her face. "Did you know that he's been painting you?" she said at last.

"He's been painting the abbey," she corrected. "I haven't sat for him, not once in all the time he's been here in Weckham."

"Nevertheless, he *is* painting you. I've seen his work. There must be"—she shook her head—"why, a half dozen canvases there at the cottage, all paintings of you. They're exquisite."

"It . . . it doesn't mean anything," Miranda stammered, her cheeks flushing. "I'm just a subject, a model."

Looking somehow amused, Caro leaned toward her. "Miranda, darling, I think he's in love with you."

"Nonsense," she said, though her heart began to race. "Of course he isn't. We're . . . we're friends, is all."

Caro shook her head. "I think you're wrong. "And what's more, I think you know it."

Miranda took a deep breath, carefully considering Caro's words. "But even if—"

She stopped short as the maid bustled back in with another tray, Sullivan close at her heels.

"Your father will be up here shortly to check on you," Sullivan said, helping the maid arrange the lap tray in front of Miranda. As soon as that was finished, she peered down at her with a frown. "Oh, dear," she said, laying the back of one hand against Miranda's forehead. "Look at you, you're flushed. I do hope the fever isn't returning. Let me get a cool cloth, and then I'll summon the doctor. Mrs. Cressfield, I'm afraid that Miss Granger isn't quite up for visitors yet. I can't have her overtaxing herself."

Caro rose, releasing her hand. "Of course. I need to go and deliver a message, anyway. Perhaps I'll read to you tomorrow, Miranda. If you're up to it, that is."

Miranda nodded. "I'd like that."

"Get your rest, then," she said with a smile, leaning down to kiss her on the cheek.

Miranda reached for Caro's wrist, drawing her friend closer so that she could whisper in her ear. "Tell him I said that it . . . it wasn't his fault."

"Of course," she answered, and Miranda could have sworn she saw tears glistening in Caro's eyes. "Now eat your broth and get well."

Silently, Miranda nodded. She planned to do just that.

Fingering the letter she carried concealed in her skirt's deep pocket, Miranda made her way past the tennis court, ducking through the high hedgerow and continuing on toward the worn footpath that led into the dense woods behind Holly's Close. Following the path beneath the drooping branches, she quickened her step, the bent fronds of ferns tickling her ankles as birds fluttered through the treetops, chirruping gaily to one another as they rustled the leaves.

At the fork in the path, Miranda headed toward the left, away from the swimming pond. It was mild today, which meant that children would be sitting on the mossy banks, dipping their toes into the cool, clean water as they skimmed stones, watching them bounce in graceful arcs over the water's glassy surface.

Instead she'd head toward her favorite clearing, deep in the woods, where a fallen tree covered in spongy moss lay parallel to the forest floor, raised just high enough from the ground to make the perfect spot to sit. Above the clearing, rays of yellow sunlight slanted down, penetrating the curved canopy above, providing perfect natural light for reading, even in the waning afternoon sun.

It was Miranda's favorite spot to sit, to savor Helen's letters. And Caro had brought one by Holly's Close just that morning, the missive now tucked into her skirt pocket, just waiting to be read.

Her secret correspondence with Helen was undoubtedly Miranda's greatest pleasure. Two or three letters arrived every year—one on the anniversary of Kurt's birth, the others at random intervals. It had been eight months now since Helen's last letter, and Miranda could barely wait to break open the envelope's seal and savor every word contained therein. It had been far too long.

Minutes later, she stepped into the clearing, turning her face up to the beam of sunlight, allowing it to warm her skin. A colorful butterfly flitted past, almost seeming to lead her over to the fallen tree where she took a seat, tucking her skirts beneath her. With fingers that trembled in anticipation, she drew the letter from her pocket, breaking the seal and drawing out the single sheet of paper filled both front and back with her cousin's elegant hand. She began to read, her eyes hungrily scanning the page.

Dearest Miranda,

I fear I have not been the best correspondent of late; I do hope you'll forgive me. The days just seem to fly by, and I often find myself sitting and wondering just where the time has gone. When I look at Kurt, I can only shake my head in wonder, amazed that he's grown so big, almost a man now.

He continues to keep us busy, pleasantly so. He's such a lively boy, so active and bright. He continues to excel at the violin, and Johan I could not be more pleased with his musical abilities. He brings such joy to this house, such happy noise.

Oh, Miranda, if only you could see him! You'd be so very proud. Is there not any way you could travel here to Lucerne? It's been far too long, and only fair that you're introduced as a favorite cousin. Surely your father—

Hearing a branch crack loudly, Miranda glanced up from the page just in time to see Troy duck beneath a tree, stealthily moving into her little clearing. Quickly, she folded the letter and stuffed it awkwardly into her skirt's pocket as she simultaneously swiped at the tears dampening her cheeks.

"I thought I might find you here," he called out, his mouth curving into a smile.

She'd brought him to her clearing many times now, especially in the past fortnight. She hadn't been quite well enough to cycle out to the abbey, so the edge of the woods behind Holly's Close had become their usual meeting place, instead.

He'd been like a changed man since her illness, far too quiet, almost reverent, treating her like she was made from spun glass. He hadn't tried to kiss her, hadn't done or said the slightest thing provocative. It was almost as if . . . as if he were courting her, the proper way. And if Caro had been correct and he did think himself in love with her, he gave no indication of it.

"You looked so contemplative, I almost hated to disturb you," he said, moving closer. "I hope you don't mind."

She shook her head, hoping beyond hope that he hadn't seen her reading the letter. "I wasn't expecting to see you today, is all. I thought you were going out to the abbey."

"I was, but once I drove out there, I simply wasn't inspired. You look a little pale," he said, his brows drawn now. "Are you feeling well?"

"Well enough," she said with a nod. "A bit tired, is all."

"I should escort you back to Holly's Close, then. What was that you were reading?"

Miranda's heart skipped a beat. "Just a letter," she answered, swallowing the lump that had formed in her throat, trying to force a neutral tone into her voice.

"Oh? From a secret admirer, perhaps?" he teased. "Have I competition for your affections?" He closed the distance between them, so close now that he would surely see that she had been crying.

Almost instinctually, she turned away from him. Her hands began to tremble, her fingers moving guiltily toward her pocket.

"What's wrong, Miranda? Good God, have you been crying?"

She couldn't answer, couldn't force herself to form a single word in reply. There was no point in lying, after all; the evidence was there on her face.

"You *have* been crying," he said, sitting down beside her. He took her hands in his, rubbing them as if to warm them. "Have you had some bad news?"

"No," she managed to choke out. She'd been crying happy tears. Tears of joy, of pride.

"Damn it, Miranda, you must tell me what's happened." He glanced down at her hands, still clasped in his. "You're positively shaking all over. Should I take you back to Holly's Close and summon the doctor?"

An overwhelming desire to tell him, to confess everything, washed over her, stealing away her breath. For a moment she feared she might faint, and she clutched his hands tightly, fighting to regain her composure.

Oh, how she wanted to tell him, wanted to unburden herself, wanted him to know the *true* Miranda, rather than the façade she presented to the world. After all, if he could not accept the truth about her, then she had her answer about him. She could walk away from him without ever looking back.

She closed her eyes, breathing deeply, gathering her courage. "It was a letter from my cousin in Switzerland," she said at last, her voice barely above a whisper. *Heaven help me.* She opened her eyes, meeting his questioning gaze. "A letter about my son."

His face visibly paled. "Your *what?*"

She took another deep, calming breath. "My son. Kurt. He'll be ten in December, just before Christmas, though I have not seen him since the day he was born."

"Your *son?*" he parroted, looking almost dazed. Miranda simply nodded.

"But . . . but how?" he stuttered. "I don't understand."

Speaking quickly lest she lose her nerve, she described the days following the discovery of her pregnancy, of her father's reaction, his plan and her eventual acquiescence. She omitted no details, no matter how ugly, how unflattering a picture they painted of her.

"And that's the end of it," she said, perhaps a quarter hour later. She stood directly in front of him, watching him, gauging his reaction, terrified of what he might say.

For a full minute, silence hung heavily between them. Troy simply sat, his head cradled in his hands, refusing to even look at her. After what felt like an eternity, he dropped his hands into his lap and raised his head.

It was the face of a tortured man that met her gaze, his eyes inexplicably wet with tears. "You let them take your child away from you, Miranda?" he asked, his voice rough. "You gave him up, just like that?"

She struggled to breathe, struggled to find her voice. "What else could I do? Go out on the streets? Allow my child to starve to death? Tell me, what sort of employment do you think I might have found, round with child? Without the slightest training in anything practical?"

As if he could no longer stand to look at her, he squeezed shut his eyes. "There must have been some other way. I cannot believe your father would simply put you out on the streets—"

"Then you don't know my father very well." Miranda shook her head, tears blurring her vision now. "Or men like him. You don't understand the value placed on reputation, on a family's good name. You don't understand what it's like to be a woman, entirely at the mercy of the men in your life. You dare to judge me—"

"Dear God, Miranda, I'm not judging you." Abruptly, he rose, reaching for her and wrapping her in his arms. Inhaling sharply, she pressed her face against his chest, listening to the din of his heart as she fought back tears.

"I didn't mean to judge you," he amended, his lips in her hair now. "I shouldn't have. I had no right. I just . . . I cannot imagine what you must have gone through. The pain . . . the loss. Does anyone know? Caroline, perhaps?"

"No, I've told no one," she answered, her voice muffled against his coat. "There were times I wanted to tell Caro, times I felt certain she would understand. But I couldn't bring myself to do it, couldn't let her know just how far I'd fallen."

He was stroking her hair now, soothing her like one would soothe a child. "How have you borne it, then, with no one to talk to, no one to comfort you all these years since?"

"It has been . . . difficult," she pronounced, knowing the word wasn't nearly strong enough to describe what she'd felt, the emptiness she'd experienced. And yet she knew she deserved it, deserved every ounce of pain, of despair.

"All these years you've been punishing yourself . . ." He let the thought trail off, shaking his head as he tightened his grip around her. "Tell me who it is, the man who did this to you. Give me his name. I vow, I'll find him and put a bullet through his head."

"No, Troy," she choked out. "You'll do nothing of the sort."

"The bastard deserves it, and worse."

"You would deprive his children—his legitimate children—of their father? His devoted wife of her husband? They, at least, are innocent victims," she continued. "Unlike me."

"Damn it, Miranda, I'll take you to Switzerland if you'd like, to see him, your son. To tell him the truth—"

"No." She pulled away from him, shaking her head so hard she felt the ground sway beneath her feet. "Don't you see? Helen and Johan are his parents; they've raised him, loved him like their own flesh and blood. I would never take that away from them, never come between them. I know that Kurt is safe and healthy, happy and well loved. That is enough—will have to be enough. You must say that you understand," she pleaded. "I cannot bear it otherwise."

He reached for her, drawing her back to him. With one hand, he tipped up her chin, forcing her gaze to meet his. "Does my opinion matter so very much to you?"

"I just need *someone* to understand," she cried, feeling as if she were drowning, suffocating beneath a heavy weight of water, unable to struggle to the surface no matter how hard she tried.

"I *do* understand, Miranda," he said softly, gently. "I do."

In the distance, the church bells began to toll—four times, marking the hour. Panic rose in her breast as she stepped away from him.

"How did the hour grow so late? I was supposed to be home a half hour ago! Grace and Gertie will be done with lessons by now, and we were to meet Father for an early tea. He's leaving for London tomorrow and—"

"And we can continue this discussion tomorrow once he's gone, Miranda. We must. There's still so much left to say."

Miranda nodded. "Yes, but it will have to wait till Friday." She'd promised Caro that she'd accompany her to Dorking tomorrow. "Sullivan is taking the girls to be fitted for new gowns Friday morning. I'll meet you by the swimming pond at half past eleven?"

"Very well," Troy agreed, leading her away from the mossy trunk, toward the edge of the footpath that would take her back to Holly's Close.

There, at the edge of the path, he bent to kiss her, his mouth suddenly fierce. He cupped her face with his hands as he kissed her roughly, possessively. Nearly pulled off her feet, she clung to him, wishing she didn't have to run off, wishing they no longer had to hide.

He wrenched his mouth from hers with a groan. "Go," he said.

Nodding, she turned and fled.

Chapter 21

Troy sat before the easel, putting the finishing touches on one of his paintings in the Weckham Abbey series. Though he'd begun the series rather unenthusiastically, the results pleased him, nonetheless.

It certainly wasn't a new concept, painting a structure repeatedly from the same viewpoint but during different times of day and changing weather circumstances—Monet had done so famously with the Rouen Cathedral.

But Troy had never attempted it on such a scale as this. Six paintings were near to completion, and he wanted to do two more, still. His paintings of Miranda had taken priority, of course.

Miranda. He'd barely been able to sleep last night, thinking about her. Friday wouldn't come fast enough, as far as he was concerned. He could barely believe the horrible tale she'd told him—though it explained so much. His heart had broken for her, for the young girl she had been, and the woman she was now.

He'd reacted badly at first. But he'd been stunned—never in all his imaginings had he pictured Miranda going through an ordeal such as the one she described. Forced to give up a child? It was incomprehensible to him. He would give everything he had to shoulder some of that pain, to cleave it in half and assume a portion for himself.

He set down his brush and palette, suddenly unable to continue. Closing his eyes, he squeezed the bridge of his nose, hoping to ease the dull ache in his head. He hadn't been bluffing when he said he'd like to find the bastard and kill him, whoever he was. Even now, rage simmered in his breast, a rage like he'd never experienced before.

All he knew was that his given name was Paul. Him, and a few thousand other Englishmen, which would make it suitably hard to identify him, for fuck's sake. And thanks to *him*—this piece of horseshit named Paul—Miranda would continue to mistrust men, to doubt their motives.

And damn it to hell, the truth was he *deserved* her mistrust. He'd earned it, all on his own. Because she might have decided to trust him with her deepest, darkest secret, but he was still lying to her. About everything. About his name, his identity—about the very essence of himself, no less.

Tell her, then, damn it.

If he wanted any future with her—any at all—he had to tell the truth. He would, tomorrow, when they met at the swimming pond. It was time for her to know the truth. And the truth was, her fortune was only a fraction of his, of the fortune that could be his, should be decide he wanted it.

He didn't, though, and that presented obstacles of its own. He'd left that life behind; he didn't enjoy it, didn't want any part of it. But women like her—like Kate and Diana—they *did* enjoy it.

She'd made it quite clear how she felt about a man with no home, no responsibilities. Was he so vain to think that she would give up her elegant, carefree way of life, her luxuries, for *him*? There was no doubt in his mind that she physically desired him, but beyond that, he hadn't any idea how deep her feelings for him ran. Was it possible that she cared for him the way he cared for her?

After all, desire alone was wont to die. It often did, with time. There were no guarantees, no—

A loud rap sounded on the door, startling him. He wasn't expecting anyone, wasn't feeling up to visitors, besides.

"Who's there?" he shouted, rising from the stool and stalking toward the front door.

"A telegram," came a muffled voice. "For Troy Davenport."

Damn. What now? He opened the door and accepted the slip of paper from the boy. Impatiently, he tore open the envelope and scanned the page, barely able to make sense of the words he found there.

> *Mother dying. Come quickly. Passage arranged on* Lusitania. *Sails 3 Sept. from Southampton.*
> —*Kate*

He looked up from the page in shock. Good God, Mother was dying? No one had even bothered to write him that she was ill. But Kate was anything but an alarmist—if she wrote that their mother was dying, then it was likely imminent.

He glanced back down at the page, trying to make sense of it all. September 3rd? Damn it all, that was the very next day. He'd have to drop everything and leave now, in a matter of hours. There was barely even time to pack a trunk.

Bloody hell. What to do? Despite their differences, he loved his mother. He knew he'd broken her heart, knew that she'd never understood the choices he'd made. He'd always thought he'd have time enough to make it up to her, time enough to make her see that his choices had been the right ones, time enough to make her proud.

Apparently, he was out of time.

But to leave now, with so much left unsettled with Miranda, especially in light of yesterday's revelations . . .

He shook his head, hoping to clear it. Damn it, his mother was dying. And if he didn't make this ship, it might be another week, at least, before the next crossing. His sister had already paid his passage, likely first class and expensive as hell. He hadn't a choice, he decided. He would go.

But not before he went to Holly's Close. Tossing down the telegram, he headed for the stairs, taking two at a time in his haste. A quarter hour later, he had a single trunk packed, already strapped to the back of the motorcar.

When he got to Southampton he'd send a telegram to François and explain what had happened. He'd ask him to come to Weckham and close up the house, to pack up his remaining trunks and canvases—all of them—and take them back to London. After all, he had no idea how long he'd remain in New York.

All that was left to do was stop by Holly's Close and speak to Miranda. But what if she wasn't there? He paused, spying a pen and paper on the desk in the room's far corner. Nodding to himself, he hurried over to the desk and snatched up a sheet of paper.

He would write Miranda a letter, in case she wasn't at home. After all, he wouldn't have time to wait for her, not if he wanted to make it to Southampton by nightfall.

He wrote quickly, uncaring of his penmanship. As soon as he was finished, he blew on the page, willing the ink to dry quickly, then folded it into thirds. Digging through the desk's drawers, he found an envelope and stuffed the letter inside, hastily sealing it before shoving it inside his coat pocket.

Hurrying out, he quickly set about starting the

motorcar's engine. A quick pump of the plunger on the dash, and then he set the throttle before moving around to the front of the car and turning the crank several times. At last the engine coughed to life, bellowing smoke.

Not bothering with goggles or gloves, he sped off down the main road, toward the narrow lane that led to Holly's Close. Minutes later, he motored down the long, tree-lined drive, cutting the engine in front of the gray stone house's front steps. He leapt down to the drive, hurrying up the steps and pausing before the front door, where he took a deep breath for courage.

There was nothing to do but knock, as loath as he was to do it. There was no doubt in his mind that he was not a welcome guest at Holly's Close. Sir William had made that clear a fortnight ago.

Still, he was running out of time. Using the brass knocker, he rapped sharply three times, then took a step back, awaiting his fate.

The dour-faced housekeeper opened the door a minute later. "May I help you?" she asked, gazing down at him quizzically.

"Yes, it's imperative that I speak to Miss Granger at once. Miss Miranda Granger," he clarified.

"I'm sorry, sir, but she's not home at present," was all she offered in reply. Which could mean anything, really.

"Do you . . . that is, might she be somewhere nearby? In the village, perhaps? I only have a brief message to deliver, but it's of an urgent nature."

The housekeeper shook her head. "I'm afraid

she's gone to Dorking for the day. We're not expecting her back until—"

"Mrs. Simms," Sir William's voice boomed behind her, "I don't believe Mr. Davenport requires a full accounting of Miranda's whereabouts."

"If you'll pardon me, sir." Her lips drawn into a tight line, the housekeeper bowed obsequiously and backed away as Miranda's father came to stand in the doorway.

"You listen to me, young man, and listen well," Sir William began, his face growing redder by the second. "I have no idea what you're doing here in Weckham. It seems far too coincidental by half, if you ask me. You've no business with my daughter."

Troy set his jaw, trying to tamp down his anger. "I only came to deliver a message to her, nothing more. If you'd be so kind as to let—"

"I'll allow nothing. I've dealt with your kind before, and I won't tolerate it. My daughter is not some . . . some cash cow," he stuttered. "Her judgment might not be sound, but mine is. I'll ask that you leave these premises at once, or I'll have you charged with trespassing. Have I made myself clear?"

"Perfectly," Troy bit out.

Without another word, Sir William slammed the door in his face. *Damn it to hell.* What now? Almost as if in a daze, he stumbled back from the door, reconsidering his options. Perhaps he could find a child in the village and pay them handsomely to act as his courier.

No. He shook his head. It was far too risky. If the letter ended up in the wrong hands . . . *damn.* Slowly, he made his way back down the steps, to the drive, racking his brain as he went.

As he reached the motorcar and started up the engine, a brilliant solution occurred to him. *Caroline.* Of course! He'd quickly drive over to her family's home and leave the letter in her care. He had no doubt that he could trust her. Relief coursing through him, he gunned the engine and set off, only to see someone waving their arms, flagging him down as he neared the end of the drive. He let off the throttle and rolled to a stop, squinting against the sun to make out the figure.

One of Miranda's sisters, he realized. The eldest of the two—Gertrude. Reaching over the door, he pulled the hand brake, waiting curiously as the girl ran to the side of the motorcar.

Why, perhaps she'd do just as well as Caroline. It would save him a trip to the Denby residence, off in the opposite direction. Surely he could trust her; she was Miranda's sister, after all.

"Mr. Davenport," she called out, raising her voice to be heard over the noisy motor. "Whatever are you doing here?"

"I was looking for your sister," he answered, "hoping to deliver an urgent message in person, but your housekeeper says she's not at home." Best not to mention the exchange with Sir William, he decided.

"No, she's gone off to Dorking with Caroline

Cressfield for the day. I hope it's nothing *too* urgent."

And there was his answer. Caroline wasn't at home, either. It was Gertrude, or no one. "I'm afraid it *is* quite urgent. I must leave immediately for New York, quite unexpectedly. I'd hoped to speak with her before I left." He reached inside his coat pocket, fingering the letter.

Damn it, what other choice did he have? Time was running out, and Miranda's sister was a far better hedge than some random child from the village. She, at least, had reason to protect Miranda's reputation.

With a resigned sigh, he withdrew the letter. "Might I trust you to get this letter to her? It's, ahem, of a somewhat personal nature and your discretion would be most appreciated. Even where the rest of your family is concerned."

"Why, of course, Mr. Davenport," she said earnestly, her blue eyes bright in her flushed face. "I understand completely. I'll see that she gets it the moment she returns home. You have my word."

With a nod, he handed her the letter. Looking almost solemn, she took it, folding the envelope in half and tucking it into her skirt.

"Thank you, Miss Gertrude. I'm afraid I must be off in a rush, but I do hope we'll meet again soon."

"I'd like that, Mr. Davenport," Gertrude said with a smile.

"Good-bye, then," he said, releasing the hand brake. He waited till Gertrude took several steps away from the motorcar, and then gunned the engine, his tires spinning in the gravel as he sped off toward Southampton with a heavy heart.

He only hoped he'd made the right decision.

Gertie watched as the motorcar took off in a cloud of dust down the lane that led toward the main road. Only when the speck of red disappeared over the rise in the road did she rip open the letter with shaking hands and begin to read.

2 September

My dearest Miranda,

A telegram just brought me unfortunate news— my mother is dying. Therefore, I must hasten to her bedside immediately. My passage has already been booked aboard the Lusitania, *sailing tomorrow from Southampton. I hoped to see you before I set sail and deliver this news in person. If you've received this letter, it means that I was regrettably unable to do so.*

Please know it pains me greatly to leave you without a proper good-bye, and know that I will carry you in my thoughts, anxious to return to you as quickly as possible. Until then,

Yours, T

Gertie glanced up, off toward the road, a slow smile spreading across her face. At last, her opportunity to get back at her sister. She'd suspected all along that something was going on between Miranda and the painter, and this letter proved it. She wasn't quite sure what the information about his travel plans would mean to Miranda, but Mr. Davenport seemed to think it urgent that she know. Thus, Gertie would make sure that Miranda did *not* know.

After all, Miranda had made certain that none of her letters to Edmund were posted. Worse still, she'd tattled on her when she could very well have kept it quiet and saved her their father's wrath.

Well, she wouldn't tell Father about *this* letter. No, she'd tell no one, not even Grace. Instead, she'd say nothing at all. She had a feeling that, in this particular instance, *not* telling would cause far greater damage.

So she would put the letter in the fire, instead. And as far as her little meeting with Mr. Davenport . . . well, she would not breathe a word of it. Crumpling the letter into a ball, she hurried toward the house, humming a happy tune as she skipped along.

Revenge was sweet indeed.

Chapter 22

Miranda paced back and forth before the swimming pond, wondering what was keeping Troy. She glanced at her watch again, surprised to see that a quarter hour had passed since she'd last checked the time.

Where was he? She was sure she'd told him half past eleven, and it was now nearly noon. It wasn't like him to leave her waiting. And after their last conversation, she felt vulnerable, exposed. She'd heard the incredulity in his voice, seen the shock on his face. Perhaps he saw her in a new light now, an unflattering one. *A woman who had abandoned her child.* Is that how he thought of her? And if he did, could she blame him? It was entirely true.

Why had she thought that he'd understand? That he would be the one to help her see past it? Tears burned behind her eyelids, but she would not let them fall, not yet.

Perhaps he'd only been delayed. It wasn't as if

he could easily get a message to her if that were the case. Her father had grown increasingly suspicious of his presence there in Weckham, especially since he'd shown up at Holly's Close when she'd been ill, demanding news of her health. No, Troy could not simply come and rap on the front door again, even with her father off in London. Servants talked.

She stopped her pacing, staring at the pond's smooth surface, watching as the bright yellow sunlight skittered across it. Perhaps he'd simply forgotten. He was probably out at the abbey, painting, and lost track of the time.

Yes, that had to be it, she decided. It was a far less painful possibility than imagining that he'd purposefully left her waiting in vain. She sighed, watching as a pair of sparrows flitted past, calling out gaily to one another. Insects buzzed around her. A crow landed on a low branch not far from where she stood. It cawed—once, twice—then flew away, its wings beating loudly on the breeze.

Ten minutes slowly ticked by. Fifteen.

He wasn't coming, she realized. Unless . . . unless he'd been confused, unless he was sitting in the clearing, waiting for her there, instead. Only, he wasn't there. Nor was he at the abbey, she discovered an hour later when she cycled out there.

And so she'd ridden home through the village, expecting to see his motorcar there beside the cottage, but it wasn't.

He must have been called away. He would

eventually return, and there would be a logical explanation. Of course there would be, she convinced herself. She simply could not accept the alternative.

"Gone?" Caro asked, her blond brows raised in surprise. "What do you mean, he's gone?"

"Exactly that," Miranda answered. "He's gone. From Weckham. The cottage is closed up, all the curtains drawn, and his motorcar has been missing for two days now."

"But . . . but why? I can't believe he would just leave without a word to anyone. It doesn't make any sense, none at all."

Miranda shrugged, unable to meet her friend's eyes. "I think perhaps he wanted to get away from *me*."

"No." Caro shook her head. "No. I don't believe that. I saw him, talked to him when you were ill. He's in love with you, I tell you. He was devastated, worried beyond words. I vow, there's no way he would just leave without telling you."

"Except he's done just that, Caro," Miranda said with an exasperated sigh. "He was supposed to meet me Friday morning at the swimming pond, the day after we went to Dorking, remember? I waited for him for nearly an hour, and he never showed."

"There must be some explanation. Did you ask Grace or Gertie? Perhaps they saw him the day we were in Dorking."

"I did. I made up some silly excuse, said I'd left something in his car the day I'd been caught in the rain." Which was true, now that she thought about it. *Her corset.* "But they said they hadn't seen him."

Caro rose from the bench beneath the pergola. "What about the pub? Perhaps he told someone there where he was going?"

Miranda shook her head, leaning back against a stone column for support. "I'm not asking at the pub, Caro. What would people think? Besides, if he wanted me to know where he was going, he would have told me. Anyway, it's not as if we . . . as if . . ." She couldn't even put it into words.

"Oh, don't give me that," Caro snapped. "Did you have some sort of disagreement? Some reason why he'd be angry with you?"

"No," Miranda said, shaking her head. It wasn't entirely a lie—it hadn't been a disagreement, not really. And she hadn't given him a reason to be angry with her. Disappointed, perhaps. Disgusted, even. Which was far, far worse.

Caro looked miserable. "I just don't understand."

"Nor I, but I suppose there's nothing to be done. I just wanted you to know, that's all." Miranda's heart wrenched painfully in her breast, making her breath catch.

"Oh, Miranda," Caro cried, reaching for her hands. "I'm so very sorry."

Only then did the tears begin to fall, hot and

fierce, tears she'd been holding back for two days now.

Caro led her back to the bench they'd occupied before, wrapping her arms around her and allowing Miranda to sob pitifully against her shoulder for what felt like an interminable time.

"I feel positively dreadful," Caro murmured once Miranda's tears had finally slowed to a sniffle. "If only I hadn't encouraged you, hadn't been so sure—"

"Don't, Caro," Miranda interrupted, wiping her eyes with her sleeve. "Please. I won't stand for you blaming yourself for any of this. I'm a grown woman, after all, and I should have known better."

The breeze stirred, flapping the hem of her skirt against her ankles. Miranda glanced up, beyond the vine-covered pergola, toward the yellowed stone house behind them where the sun was just beginning to set. She was done crying over him, done racking her brain, wondering just what could have happened. She'd been a fool to hope, to think that she and Troy could have any sort of future together. Now it was time to put it all behind her, to look to the future instead of the past.

She rose on unsteady legs. "I should set off for home before it gets dark. Father comes back from London on Wednesday. Perhaps you could join us for dinner then?" Caro's presence would distract him, would keep him from noticing Miranda's melancholy.

Caro rose to stand beside her. "Of course I'll join you. What will you do until then?"

"The usual." Miranda shrugged, thinking of all the days that stretched out before her, one no different from the rest. "If you don't mind risking life and limb, we could play tennis tomorrow while the girls are in lessons."

"I'd like that," Caro said with a smile. "I'm determined to make a sportswoman out of you, if it takes me the rest of our lives to do so." She glanced up at the sky, now streaked with orange. "I suppose you should start back. Would you like me to walk you? Or I could have Peters drive you, if you'd prefer."

Miranda shook her head. "No, I'm perfectly fine walking. You stay; I won't have you making your way home alone in the dark. Don't worry," she added, seeing her friend's anxious expression. "I'm fine now. I just needed to get it all out, that's all."

"You're sure?" Caro didn't look at all convinced.

Miranda sighed deeply, gathering her resolve. "Entirely so," she said at last, attempting a weak smile.

She would be fine—eventually. She'd gotten over a broken heart before; she could certainly do so again. In fact, it would be far easier this time, given the circumstances.

And when she did, she'd put her heart under lock and key. *Permanently.*

"I'll walk you to the gate," Caro offered, and Miranda fell into step beside her.

Thank God I've got Caro, she thought, not for the first time. *At least, until she falls in love and marries again.*

As Miranda paused by the gate, she couldn't help but think of Troy's friend Sébastien Dumas—would he return to Weckham one day and sweep her friend entirely off her feet? And if he did, where would that leave her?

Alone, of course. And perhaps that was all she deserved, she thought sourly.

"I'll see you tomorrow, then," Caro called, waving gaily as Miranda set off down the dusty lane toward Holly's Close, her heart heavy.

Miranda stepped into her father's wood-paneled study. "You wished to see me?"

"Yes. Please, sit down." He gestured toward the chair in front of his desk.

Eyeing him warily, Miranda sat where directed. Her father had been acting strangely—overly formal—since his return from London. It unnerved her, and even more so when he'd sent word that he wanted to see her in his study today after luncheon.

The past fortnight had been painful enough, trying to make sense of Troy's desertion. Every time she'd push him from her thoughts, someone would bring him up again—one of her sisters, perhaps, or Caro. Word had it that

someone had come from London and packed
up his belongings—his trunks, his paintings, his
easels and paints. Everything.

As far as Miranda was concerned, the message
was simple and clear—he was done with her.
There was nothing more to know than that. At
first she'd been numb, too much so to realize
how badly his rejection hurt. It was only after
she'd finally allowed herself to cry that she'd recognized the true depth of her affections. God
help her, but she loved him.

She'd been a fool to convince herself otherwise, to think she could resist the feelings he'd
awakened in her. He'd made her feel alive, for
the first time in nearly a decade. He'd given her
hope, where she'd had none. He'd restored her
belief in herself, in her worth. Slowly but surely,
her heart had unfurled, blossomed again.

Now it was entirely desiccated. Worse still, she
had a terrible feeling about this meeting with her
father, as if whatever he was going to say would
surely scatter those dried, brittle fragments, like
ashes on the wind.

She swallowed hard, forcing herself not to cry.

Her father leaned against the desk and lit his
pipe, taking several puffs before lowering it and
favoring her with a level gaze. "While I was away
in London, I realized that I've erred where
you're concerned, Miranda. I've made you a sitting duck, an easy target."

Her mouth felt dry, parched. "I've no idea
what you mean by that," she said.

"I should not have left your future so uncertain all this time. I should have known that you were vulnerable. To temptation," he added, then took another puff from his pipe. "And vulnerable to those who would take advantage of you. It simply wasn't prudent."

She simply stared at him, unable to comprehend what he was saying.

Shaking his head, he continued on. "After this latest business with that painter of yours, I realized that I should have married you off years ago. He came by here, you know. The day I left for London."

No. "Dear Lord, Father. Please tell me you didn't . . . not again," she stuttered, barely able to form a coherent sentence.

"I told him in no uncertain terms that you were not going to fatten his pockets. That he wasn't getting a farthing—"

"Please say that you didn't," she cried, her throat aching miserably. *Don't let me cry, not now. Not where he can see it.* "You couldn't have."

He stared down at her coldly, a look of disgust on his face. "I'm told he hightailed it out of Weckham that very same day. Does that not prove my point? Since you seem so hell-bent on making yourself an easy target, you've forced my hand. It's time to settle your future. But first I need assurances from you."

"What sort of assurances?" she whispered miserably, barely able to breathe now. It was true, then. The timing was too coincidental to be anything but. Her father had told Troy that he would not see a farthing from her, and Troy had left her—just like that. And unlike Paul, her father hadn't even had to pay Troy off.

"Assurances that we won't have another situation like the one before, that's what. Because, by God, if you've been so stupid and careless as before, this time I *will* put you out. I will not clean up your mess again, Miranda. Do you hear me?"

Wordlessly, she nodded.

"Speak up, girl," he snapped. "Have I your assurances or not?"

"Yes." Thank God it was the truth.

He nodded sharply. "Very good. While in London, I spoke with Thomas Bell, John Bell's eldest son. You met the Bells last year in London, remember?"

Again, she nodded. The Bells ran an import/export business, and were respectable people of means. The younger Mr. Bell sat in the House of Commons, if she remembered correctly.

"Thomas's wife died in childbed, leaving him with two small sons. He's anxious to marry again, to have someone to mother his sons. I thought you might like that."

"To raise another woman's sons in place of my own?" she snapped, her skin flushed with anger. "You thought I might *like* that?"

"Lower your voice," he growled, taking a menacing step toward her, his face a mottled red now. "You're lucky he's agreed to consider you. I didn't tell him of your blight, that you can't seem to keep your skirts down. You can explain that yourself on your wedding night. By then it'll be too late."

She rose so abruptly that the chair nearly toppled over. All these years he'd made her suffer, made her pay for her sins, as if she had not suffered enough. And now . . . now *this*? Why couldn't he just leave her alone, let her sort out her own affairs?

"That's it, then?" she cried, her voice catching on the last syllable. "Just like that? I'm marrying Thomas Bell, and I've no say in the matter?"

"Of course you do. I can't force you to marry him," he said with a shrug. "But it's likely the best offer you'll get, and you'd do well to take that into consideration. *Careful* consideration," he added.

"Is that all?" she asked, her hands balled into fists by her sides.

"That's all. He'll want your answer soon enough. You'd best think on it right away."

She shook her head. "I won't be pushed to decide right away. I need time."

"Very well. I'll give you till Christmastime to make up your mind. If you'd like, we can travel to London next month and you can get better acquainted with young Mr. Bell." He reached up to stroke his whiskers. "I'm not an unreasonable man, Miranda."

She took a deep, calming breath, refusing to let herself fall apart. She stared at the window, where driving rain pelted the glass, rattling it. She had to think this through, consider her options.

There were far worse men than Mr. Bell. In fact, she remembered him as perfectly innocuous, of average height and looks. He'd seemed rather brisk, perhaps, but affable enough. She had no doubt that her father could do much worse by her, if he took a mind to. And he would, if she refused this match. She had no doubt that he would.

Would it be so bad to go to London, to spend some time with the man? After all, she could use some time away from Weckham, away from the memories of Troy that seemed to greet her no matter where she went.

Of course, Troy might very well be in London himself. Actually, it seemed quite likely that he was. He claimed to make his home with his aunt, in Wrotham Road. Still, it was unlikely that their paths would cross. And even if they did, well . . . let him look her in the eye, then, and explain himself. She could listen to his excuses and then tell him to go to the devil.

"Yes," she said coolly, her mind made up. She met her father's steely gaze with her own mutinous one. "We'll go to London. I'll get to know this Mr. Bell, and then I'll make my decision."

Her father's only reply was a triumphant smile.

Chapter 23

Miranda peeked out of the carriage window as the conveyance rolled to a stop in front of a modest residence. She checked the number. Yes, this was it. The home of Agnes Davenport—and the culmination of a plan she'd hatched nearly the moment she'd arrived in London.

She'd been biding her time, waiting for the perfect opportunity to escape her father's hovering presence. Mercifully he'd had a meeting with his solicitor today, and suggested that she venture out to Bond Street to shop while he saw to his own affairs.

And so she'd set off in a hired hack, directing the driver to Wrotham Road. It had been easy enough to find the direction of Mrs. Agnes Davenport. Lady Barclay, of all people, knew the woman. It was pure providence that she'd run into Lady Barclay and her granddaughter at the opera—in the powder room, of all places.

Naturally, Lady Barclay had brought up the

portrait of Miss Soames that Troy had painted, bragging that it now hung above her mantel, and how everyone complimented the incredible likeness. Miranda had expressed her desire to view the portrait herself, and then innocently remarked that she'd heard that Mr. Davenport had an aunt in London, in Wrotham Road. That had been all the prodding Lady Barclay had needed—she'd provided all the information Miranda had needed to locate the woman, and more.

She only hoped she'd find Troy at home today. She deserved answers, blast it, and she *would* get them. She would force him to look her in the eye and admit that he'd played her for a fool. Only then could she move on with her life. Because she'd tried—heaven help her, but she had.

She'd tried to forget him, tried to imagine a future with Thomas Bell, instead. But a nagging doubt had remained in her mind—something wasn't quite right about Troy's disappearance from Weckham. She had to know, had to have the truth, before she could truly put the past under lock and key and leave it there for good.

"I won't be long," she told the driver. "I'll pay you handsomely if you'll wait."

"'Course, miss," he replied with a tip of his hat.

She climbed down to the walk, taking a deep breath before making her way up the stairs and rapping smartly on the door. There was no time to waste.

A young woman about her age opened the door. "May I help you?"

"Yes. I'm Miss Miranda Granger," she said, producing a crisp white calling card. "I'm looking for Mr. Troy Davenport, and I was told that he resides here, with his aunt."

The young woman smiled, then shook her head. "I think there's been a misunderstanding. Mr. Davenport does indeed take up residence here on occasion, but I'm afraid he's away at present. We don't expect him back for quite a while."

"Miss Hart?" a voice called out. "Who's that at the door?"

"If you'll excuse me for one moment," the young woman said, closing the door, leaving Miranda standing there on the front step in confusion.

A minute later, the door swung open again. "Please come in, Miss Granger. Mrs. Davenport would like an audience with you, if you don't mind."

"I'd like that very much," Miranda said with a nod. More than anything, she was curious.

The young woman offered her hand in greeting as she led her inside. "I'm Miss Hart, Mrs. Davenport's companion."

Miranda took her hand. "Pleased to meet you, Miss Hart."

"May I offer you some refreshment? Tea, perhaps? Or a glass of lemonade?"

"Lemonade sounds lovely," Miranda answered, following Miss Hart into a tidy parlor.

A thin woman with steel-gray hair sat on a brocade sofa, watching her approach with curious

eyes that reminded her of Troy's. Indeed, her re-
semblance to her nephew was striking, causing
Miranda's breath to hitch in her chest.

"How good to meet you, Miss Granger," she
said in greeting, laying aside the knitting she'd
held in her lap.

"Likewise, Mrs. Davenport. I've heard so much
about you from your nephew, I feel as if we are already acquainted."

"Only good things, I hope," she answered with
a smile. "Please, sit."

Miranda nodded, taking a seat on the red
velvet-covered chair directly beside the sofa that
the woman had indicated. "Indeed, he speaks
most lovingly about you."

"He's a good boy, my Troy," she said, her eyes
shining with obvious pride. "You met him at the
Grandview?"

Miranda sat forward in her chair. "Actually, we
first met aboard the *Mauretania*."

"Is that so? Well," she huffed, seemingly indig-
nant, "he left out that part of the tale."

Miss Hart returned then, carrying a tray with
two tall glasses balanced on it. "I hope it's not
too tart," she said, placing a glass down on the
table beside Miranda, the other beside Mrs. Davenport.

Miranda took a sip of the pale yellow liquid,
cool and tangy on her tongue. "It's perfect.
Thank you."

"Miss Hart said you expected to find Troy

here," the older woman began. "I'm afraid he's not yet returned from New York."

"New York?"

"Yes, I only wish I could have traveled with him. But I was just getting over a bout of pneumonia, and everyone insisted I wasn't quite up to the journey."

"Yes, Troy said that you had been ill. I . . . you must excuse me, but I had no idea he was traveling to New York."

Her brows drew together. "He didn't tell you?"

Her heart accelerated alarmingly. "Tell me what?"

"Why, that his mother was dying. She was fading fast, poor woman. Lillian was my younger sister, God rest her soul. We weren't close, but still, I should have been there," she said, sounding regretful.

"I'm so sorry," Miranda said, reaching to cover one of Mrs. Davenport's trembling hands with her own.

The old woman nodded, patting Miranda's hand. "Thank you for your kindness, dear. Lillian is at peace now, and I can take comfort in that. Anyway, they sent for him quite urgently. He barely had time to pack a valise before he was due to set sail."

"And Troy . . . did he make it there in time?"

"He did, with time to spare. The doctors think that Troy's presence there at her bedside likely made her linger longer than expected. I'm told that Troy was there with her, holding her hand when she took her final breath."

The old woman paused, her faded eyes filling with tears. "That would have been the end of it," she continued on at last, "but tragedy often begets more tragedy, doesn't it? At Lillian's funeral, Cornelius collapsed—Troy's father," she explained. "His heart, they say."

"Dear Lord, no," Miranda gasped in horror. Not both parents, not one right after the other!

"Oh, Cornelius managed to survive it, iron-willed man that he is. He's as tough as nails, that one. He's recuperating now. His progress has been slow, but steady. We have reason to believe he'll make a full recovery."

Miranda let out her breath in a rush. "Oh, thank God. I can only imagine what a fright that must have been for everyone involved."

"Indeed. And it also meant that Troy couldn't return to London as he'd planned, couldn't leave Gabriel and Kate to deal with it themselves, not with Kate heavy with child and Gabriel's wife suffering from consumption."

Gabriel, Kate . . . Miranda had no idea who these people were. Troy's family, she assumed. Yes, now that she thought about it, she remembered him mentioning a sister named Kate. It sounded as if they'd had more than their share of hardship lately.

"Anyway," Mrs. Davenport continued on, "until Cornelius is back on his feet, Troy is helping Gabriel run the family business," Mrs. Davenport continued on. "I'm sure he hates every minute of it, poor boy. He never wanted anything to do with it, you know—the DeWitt fortune. But in a situation such as this, he hadn't a choice. As I said, Troy's a good boy."

Whatever was she talking about? "What do the DeWitts have to do with Troy?" Miranda asked, shaking her head in confusion. "He's Troy *Davenport*," she stuttered, her mind a muddled mess.

Mrs. Davenport's eyes widened with surprise. One hand rose to her throat. "Oh, dear. I just assumed . . ." She trailed off, looking positively stricken.

Miranda's stomach did a flip-flop in her gut. "You assumed what?"

"That he told you. After all, I've seen all those paintings of you, all those glorious canvases François brought back from Surrey. I only assumed that he must have told you the truth."

Miranda just shook her head, biting her lip.

"Troy isn't a Davenport at all," the woman said, then paused, as if gauging her reaction. "He's a DeWitt."

Oh, dear God. "A DeWitt?" Miranda's voice was a hoarse whisper. "But how can that be?"

"He's Cornelius and Lillian DeWitt's youngest child. He didn't want anyone to know, wanted to make a name for himself. They wouldn't take him seriously, you see, not with a name like that. DeWitts are art collectors, not creators. Surely you understand."

"But . . . but he's poor," she stuttered, trying to make sense of it all.

"My dear, he isn't poor, not really. He chooses to live simply, is all. He's not the slightest bit interested in the trappings of wealth."

Of course. Now it all made sense. All the missing pieces fell into place—his obvious education, his refined speech and manner. He could dance, play tennis. He seemed like a gentleman because he *was* a gentleman, no matter his simple dress, his rough hands. But why hadn't he told her the truth? It would have removed so many doubts on her part, on her father's part.

"I should not have told you, Miss Granger. I fear Troy will be furious with me when he finds out. I must have your word, must have your promise that you won't tell a soul."

"Of course," she said in a daze. She had no reason to expose him, after all.

Still, the full weight of his lie crushed her beneath its weight. He'd allowed her to believe him as poor as the proverbial church mouse. When she thought back to the things she'd said to him, the accusations she'd made . . .

Her cheeks colored at the memory. Why, she'd made a complete and utter fool of herself. And he'd allowed it, allowed her to go on and on. "If you were a rich man, we would not be having this conversation," she'd said to him when he'd first asked to paint her.

"I don't want your money," he'd answered. Of course he hadn't. He had plenty of his own.

Bucketfuls. Far more than she'd ever have, than Sir William ever dreamt of having. The DeWitts were one of the wealthiest families in New York, as High Society as they came. Railroads and banks, and God only knew what else.

And worse, she'd trusted him with her deepest, darkest secret—the one secret she hadn't dared to tell another soul. And in return, he hadn't even bothered to tell her who he really was. She covered her mouth with the back of one hand, feeling suddenly ill. *Damn him to hell!*

She rose on shaky legs. "If you'll excuse me, Mrs. Davenport. I fear I've taken up too much of your time."

"Please don't run off, Miss Granger. Not like this. I don't know what he's told you, what kind of understanding you had with him, but I'm sure—"

"We had no understanding. I was . . . his model, nothing more." It was true, she realized. She'd obviously meant nothing more to him than that. "I really must go. My father will be wondering where I've gone off to."

"Of course, dear. When Troy returns, I'll tell him of your visit. I'm sure he'd like—"

"I'd rather you didn't," she interrupted. "I don't mean to sound rude, but truly, it's best to pretend as if I never came here today."

"Very well," the woman agreed with a nod.

Thank goodness. "It was indeed a pleasure to make your acquaintance, Mrs. Davenport."

"Likewise, Miss Granger. I *am* sorry to have startled you so. I cannot understand why . . ." She trailed off, shaking her head. "Though I suppose it's none of my business. I hope you'll forgive me if Miss Hart sees you out."

"Of course. Good day, Mrs. Davenport," she said with a bow.

The old woman inclined her head politely. "Good day, Miss Granger. I do hope we'll meet again."

Miranda followed Miss Hart to the front door and said good-bye before hurrying down to the curb where the hired hack waited. Feeling entirely numb, she climbed inside, more confused than ever now. Rather than finding the answers she'd hoped for, she'd only found more questions.

"You seem distracted tonight, Miss Granger. Are you well?"

"I'm sorry?" Miranda asked, glancing up from her plate in confusion. "You were saying?"

Setting down his wineglass, Mr. Bell smiled. "Only that you seem rather distracted. I hope you're not unwell."

She glanced over at her father, deep in conversation with the older Mr. Bell. He, at least, seemed entirely oblivious to her discomposure. Which was a blessing, after all, because how could she possibly explain it?

She'd spent the entire evening lost in thought, trying to process everything she'd learned from Mrs. Davenport that same afternoon. Everything was finally falling into place in a way that made sense.

First and foremost, Troy had had a reason to leave Weckham, a reason that had nothing to do with her. By all accounts, he'd left in haste. According to her father, he'd come by Holly's Close while she'd been off in Dorking with Caro, and it was entirely possible that he'd come to tell her that he was leaving, and why.

But if that were the case, then why hadn't he tried to contact her since? And why hadn't he told her the truth about his identity, besides? Which really left her right back where she'd begun—entirely mystified. Abandoned. Forgotten. Nothing else mattered, she told herself. So why couldn't she just forget him, then? Push him entirely from her thoughts and move on?

"Miss Granger?" Mr. Bell prodded, and Miranda glanced up in surprise. How could she keep forgetting his presence there beside her at the dinner table?

She forced her lips to form a smile. "I'm so sorry, Mr. Bell. I know I've been a terrible dinner companion tonight. I . . . I'm afraid I didn't sleep well last night. I'm still unused to the noise of London, I suppose."

He shook his head. "It just gets worse and worse, with all the motorcars on the streets now. Still, I would not trade it for the world. Never quite understood how some chaps could stand spending all their days out in the country."

"It's a different way of life, no doubt," Miranda

murmured, thinking just how well she liked the country. She glanced over at Mr. Bell, studying him closely. His dark hair was parted down the middle, his eyes a deep, chocolate brown. His nose was long and thin above a neat moustache that curled up at the ends. She wouldn't call him handsome, but his looks were not unpleasant, either. He seemed intelligent, perhaps even a bit bookish. All perfectly fine traits in a gentleman.

He would make a good husband. At least she tried to convince herself it was so. He possessed all the necessary qualities, after all, and she had no doubt that he would provide for her well enough. But there was more to marriage than that, she reminded herself. She tried to imagine lying next to him, to imagine him taking off her clothes and touching her intimately. And yet she couldn't, couldn't picture it, no matter how hard she tried.

Still, living under his roof, his rule, might be far less restrictive than living under her father's. At the very least, he wouldn't be thinking her an immoral whore every time he looked at her, like her father did.

She returned her attention back toward Mr. Bell—Thomas, she corrected, trying to adjust herself to the familiarity of his given name. She would give his suit due consideration, but not tonight. Tonight she just wanted to go to bed, to forget the afternoon's revelations.

"Perhaps I *am* feeling a bit unwell," she said at last, the lie slipping far too easily from her tongue.

Mr. Bell nodded, then signaled their waiter. "I'll get the check, then."

"But tomorrow . . . perhaps we could take that drive you mentioned?" She had to give the man a fair chance. After all, he was simply trying his best to be polite.

"I'd like that, Miss Granger," he said with a nod. "Very much." He looked entirely pleased with himself.

And then she felt it—his hand on her thigh, beneath the table. As if he already owned her, bought and paid for. A shudder worked its way down her spine.

"If you'll excuse me," she said, rising so abruptly that she nearly knocked over a wine-glass.

Mr. Bell snatched back his hand, looking entirely nonplussed. Across the table, her father gave her a scathing glare.

She took a deep, steadying breath, forcing her racing heart to slow before she fell to pieces, right there in the Claridge's dining room.

Thank God she had till Christmastime to decide her future—nearly two months' time. And in the meantime, well . . .

Somehow, she'd have to get through it.

Chapter 24

December 1909
The Grandview Hotel, Eastbourne

A sense of déjà vu washed over him as Troy stepped into the hotel's glass-domed lobby, setting down his traveling case as he stopped to admire the view.

It looked exactly the same as it had when he'd seen it last, almost a year ago to the day. An enormous fir, looking much like its predecessor, nearly reached the ceiling, topped with a shiny gold star. Tiny electric lights twinkled, illuminating the glass balls and baubles hanging from each branch.

A fire still crackled in the hearth, the scent of chestnuts filling the air. People still bustled this way and that, humming a carol to themselves as they went about their business, their hearts merry and light.

Yes, the Grandview was exactly as he'd left it.

Only, a full year had come and gone since. He felt like an entirely different man, and not just because he'd aged a year. No, it was so much more than that. In the time since he'd last stood there in the Grandview's lobby, he'd experienced so many joys, and so much loss.

His mother, he thought, as if ticking them off, one by one. They hadn't been close. Still, her loss had affected him far more deeply than he'd anticipated, and nothing had seemed the same since her death. His father, who'd always been a hardy, robust man, now required a wheeled chair to get around, the victim of a weak heart. He seemed a shell of the man Troy remembered, frail and weak. Which made it difficult to remain angry at the man for forcing him to choose, so many years ago, between his family and his passion for art.

His sister, Kate, had her own life now—a husband, a son, and now a new daughter, as well. She was busy all the time, flitting here and there, to luncheons and galas and charity committee meetings, to check on her children, to meet with her housekeeper, to plan her menus.

And Diana . . . he shook his head. He'd barely recognized her. The victim of an unhappy marriage, she'd grown bitter and round, her once beautiful face now jowly and sour. She had four children all under the age of five—including a set of twins—and the one time Troy had seen them in her company, Diana had acted oddly detached, almost as if her children's very existence puzzled her.

Kate had blamed her state on the fact that Diana's husband had made a public mockery of her, flaunting his affair with a young opera singer. Whatever the case, the beautiful Diana Livingston whom he had twirled around his mother's ballroom all those years ago, was gone.

The only one who remained unchanged was his brother, Gabe—steady, reliable Gabe. His brother had picked up the reins of the family business without missing a beat, and Troy could not have been more grateful. Oh, he'd done as best he could to help, but it was Gabe—with the perfect life, the perfect wife and family—who'd kept everything together, the business running smoothly, until their father had been well enough to return to his massive mahogany desk, at least for a few hours each day.

Which had left Troy free to return to England, free to confront even more loss—*Miranda*. How he'd hated leaving her there in Weckham without a good-bye. He'd felt his heart cleave in two the moment he'd driven away, his message safely entrusted to her sister. It was only then that he had realized the full extent of his feelings, the depth of his love.

As soon as he'd reached New York, he'd sent her a letter, declaring his feelings and begging for a reply. When none came, he wrote again. A letter a week, for two months straight. Eight letters in all. Each and every night, he slept with her corset beneath his pillow—the one she'd left in his motorcar after they'd been caught in the rain. It was all he had to remember her by. For the longest time, it held her scent. But then, slowly, inevitably, the scent began to fade.

And then, at last—he'd received a reply. A telegram, actually. Simple and terse, she'd asked that he never again attempt to contact her in any way, shape, or form. And so he hadn't, and that had been the end of it.

He'd only been back in England a fortnight, but he'd been restless, unable to paint, unable to do anything but stare at the canvases immortalizing his love. He had to exorcise himself of her, and the only way he knew to do that was to confront his memories head-on. And so there he was, at the Grandview, where it had all begun.

He'd brought with him a half-dozen blank canvases, and he hoped to fill them all with images notable for their absence of Miranda before he returned to London and decided where to go next. Düsseldorf, perhaps. Marcus had fallen in love with a beautiful fräulein and remained there, living on the banks of the River Rhine.

Perhaps Sébastien, now returned from Greece, would join him on the journey. Once he talked him out of returning to Weckham, that is. Sébastien was consumed with fascination for the widowed Caroline, but Troy had assured him that if he returned to Weckham to pursue the woman, he would have to do it alone. For Troy, it would all end there, at the Grandview.

"Checking in, sir?" a bellboy asked, pausing by his side.

"Yes, thank you." He allowed the boy to take his bag, and he followed him up to the reception desk.

"If you'll sign the register, please," the bespectacled man behind the desk said, handing him a fountain pen.

Troy took the pen and signed his first name with a flourish, pausing before he wrote his surname. He'd almost written DeWitt. Damn it, but he barely knew who he was anymore.

"Thank you, Mr. Davenport," the clerk said, glancing down at the name he'd written. "We're rather full right now, what with it being Christmas Eve. I've only a small single room left in the Garden Wing—no sea view, I'm afraid. I hope that will do."

"That will do nicely." Troy took the key the man handed him and pocketed it.

"Room 214, then, Mr. Davenport. Do you need any help with your bag?"

He shook his head. "No, I can manage."

"Very well." The clerk leaned across the desk, pointing across the lobby. "Down that corridor there, just past the Christmas tree, and follow it to the end."

"Thank you," he murmured, struck by another feeling of déjà vu. Room 214? Amazing. That was the exact same room he'd occupied last year. Perhaps he should ask for another. What if that same

blue chaise remained—the one on which he'd
pleasured Miranda, and then painted her?

Of course it would be there. Very well, then, he
reasoned. He'd paint it again, without Miranda
this time. An empty chaise—just like his heart.

"Let's go join in the caroling, Miranda.
Please?" Grace begged, her eyes bright with excitement.

It was Christmas Eve, after all, and they were
back at the Grandview Hotel. When her father
had first suggested it, she'd balked. There were
too many memories there, things best forgotten.
It was bad enough that every inch of Weckham
reminded her of Troy. But to come back to the
Grandview, at Christmastime, no less?

But eventually she'd conceded. The first step
toward embracing the future was coming to terms
with the past, she realized. She would make new
memories.

So far, the trip had been far different from
their last one. Where last December had been
unseasonably warm and mild, this December was
cold and crisp. Indeed, all day it had looked as if
it might snow. Grace was beside herself with
hopeful anticipation, imagining sleigh rides and
sledding, ice skating on the pond.

And where last year Gertie had been full of
mischief, gaily chasing after young Edmund
Stratmore, this year was a different story altogether. When they'd first arrived at the hotel,

Gertie had been thrilled to learn that Edmund was due to arrive the following day. And so he had, in the company of Mr. and Mrs. Marcus Trent and their beautiful young daughter, Miss Cecily Trent. It was immediately apparent that Edmund and Miss Trent were inseparable. Rumor had it they had an understanding. Gertie had cried inconsolably for two days straight. Now she mostly stayed in her room, staring morosely out the window.

"I'm not going caroling," Gertie snapped.

"I didn't ask you to go," Grace shot back. "I asked Miranda."

Miranda sighed. "Very well, but we can't stay long. It's already late. Will you be all right, Gertie? I hate to leave you here alone. It's Christmas Eve, after all."

Gertie glared at her. "Oh, don't pretend as if you care. You don't care about me at all, about my suffering."

Miranda sighed in exasperation. It had gone on like this for days now. "You know that's not true, Gertrude Granger, and I'll ask you not to use that tone with me."

"I'm sure you're happy to see me so miserable, after all you did to keep me from him. This is your fault, you know. If only you'd allowed me to write to him, then he wouldn't be with that simpering little fool right now. I hope you're happy."

"No," Miranda said, shaking her head. "I'm not happy at all. It gave me no pleasure to follow

Father's orders, you know. But you must own up to your own responsibility in the matter. If you hadn't been so irresponsible, so outrageously improper where Edmund was concerned, then no one would have objected."

"So you're saying I should have kept quiet about my feelings, then? Snuck around like a hypocrite, like you. Is that what you're suggesting, Miranda?"

Miranda felt the blood drain from her face as Gertie's words hit their mark. Still, there was nothing to do but deny the truth. "I have no idea what you mean," she said at last.

Gertie cast Miranda a scathing glare. "Of course you do. I mean your painter, and you know it," she spat.

"Don't, Gertie," Grace warned. "Please, that's enough."

Gertie turned on her. "You've no idea what she's done, have you? Sneaking around, carrying on with the painter right under our noses, all the while refusing to allow me to even *write* to Edmund. Well, I suppose we're even now."

Miranda's heart began to pound. "Whatever do you mean by that?"

Silent now, Gertie turned toward the window, her arms folded across her breasts.

"Gertie, what have you done?" Grace asked, her voice tremulous.

Gertie glanced back over one shoulder, her features hard. "Nothing, and there's your answer. Though I don't suppose you'll ever know for certain, will you?" she taunted, making Miranda's blood run cold.

"Go," Grace whispered near Miranda's ear. "I'll speak with her. I'll try and find out—"

"Oh, do shut up, Grace," Gertie interrupted.

Angry now, Miranda advanced on her. "Don't speak to your sister that way, you little brat! You should be ashamed of yourself, bullying anyone who gets in your way. God knows I'm not perfect, but I've given up so much, devoting my very existence to raising the pair of you. Well, I'm done, do you hear me?"

She took a deep breath before continuing on her tirade, both girls simply goggling at her now. "Perhaps I will marry Mr. Bell, after all. I'd planned to tell him no, but perhaps raising his sons—strangers to me, both—would be far more rewarding than the likes of you."

She turned toward Grace, reaching for her trembling hand. "Please forgive me, Grace. I'm not at all angry with you, and I don't mean to lump the two of you together. You, at least, can be a dear when you want to be. Now if you'll excuse me, I must go get some air."

Without awaiting a response, she turned and stalked out, headed to her own room where she retrieved her heavy woolen coat and hat. A walk in the cold, clean air would do her some good, would help tamp down her anger. If she remained anywhere near Gertie, she'd likely throttle the girl, and it wasn't fair to Grace, besides. Grace, poor girl, had done nothing wrong.

A quarter hour later, she found herself outside, walking aimlessly down the boardwalk as the first snowflakes began to fall. The grounds were mostly empty, everyone having gathered in the lobby or the dining room instead, enjoying late-night refreshments and entertainment. Certainly no one had ventured so close to the shore where the stiff ocean breeze deepened the chill.

She turned her face toward the sky, allowing the cold, wet snow to sting her skin. Sagging against the wooden railing, she let out her breath in a rush. How had Gertie known about Troy? Perhaps she was only bluffing, trying to get under her skin, she reasoned. But then she'd hinted that she'd done something, something to make them even . . .

She shook her head. She'd never know; it was too late, anyway. There was no point in driving herself mad, trying to figure it out. But whatever was she going to do? Carry through with her threat to marry Thomas Bell, just to spite Gertie? Was that reason enough? *Of course not.* But there were other reasons, too—compelling ones.

She'd gone over them all a million times by now, and still she wasn't convinced. She'd promised him an answer by Christmas—the very next day. Why ever had she thought that coming to the Grandview would help her set aside her past and focus on her future? How could it, when every square inch of the property reminded her of *him?*

Looking out at the great lawn only reminded

her of watching him paint Miss Soames. Attending the theater reminded her of Miss DuBois' Titania, of watching him from the corner of her eye throughout the entire performance. The list went on and on—dancing with him in the dining room, sitting with him in the gazebo. She couldn't get away from the memories, no matter how hard she tried.

She stuck out her tongue, catching a snowflake. It tasted clean, nothing like the sooty snow in London where she'd be forced to make her home if she married Mr. Bell. What to do? If only she had some sort of sign—anything—to guide her.

And then, as if she'd somehow conjured it from her imagination, she noticed a star in the sky behind her, twinkling more brightly than the rest. Why, she'd never seen anything like it before! It was almost like . . . like the Christmas star of lore.

Pushing off the boardwalk's railing, she moved toward the star, following the wooden planks till they ended at a sandy path that wound through several wind-gnarled trees. She hurried her step, her face turned toward the inky sky, snowflakes sticking to her eyelashes as she continued to follow where the star led.

It was almost as if she were being pulled, led by some invisible force. Back toward the hotel, past the darkened theater, down the paving-stone path that led through an ornamental garden, now mostly fallow. She continued on, coming around a sharp bend in the path, her eyes still glued to the sky—and then she froze.

Twinkling brightly, the star seemed to hover just in front of her, its tail seeming to point directly down toward the glasshouse below. She blinked once, twice, wondering if the snowflakes clinging to her lashes were obscuring her vision, making her see things that weren't really there.

But no, the star still hung brilliantly in sky, casting a silvery glow on the glasshouse beneath it, illuminating it like some kind of sign from above. But what did it mean?

She remembered the last time she'd been inside the glasshouse. She remembered it far *too* well, and so she'd entirely steered clear of the place this year.

Now she had no choice but to ignore her instincts. She would follow the sign, and see where it led her. She only hoped it wouldn't mean more heartache, for she'd had just about enough of that for a lifetime.

Chapter 25

Troy rose from the bench, shoving his hands into his trousers' pockets as he stared up at the sky, at the bright star visible through the panes of glass above. *What the hell am I doing here?*

What sort of peace had he hoped to find? So far, he'd found none. Indeed, he'd barely left his room since checking in, choosing to have his dinner there rather than venturing out to the dining room.

It was Christmas Eve, and he was alone. Sad, really, though perhaps it was all he deserved. He should be celebrating the telegram he'd just received from a jubilant François, informing him that his *Woman on a Blue Chaise* had been accepted into the Salon D'Automne for its 1910 exhibit.

Indeed, he should be crowing with delight at present, shouting the news from the rooftops as he gleefully drank himself into a stupor. Instead, there was a hollowness to his victory that he hadn't anticipated.

Miranda would never know.

Not that he would ever identify her as his model, neither publicly nor privately. Never would he expose her in that fashion, risk her reputation so casually and callously. Nevertheless, he would have liked her to know what role she had played in his success. She had been his greatest muse, after all.

He would always remain grateful to her—and a bit in love with her, too. There was no denying that fact, even now. She had been everything he'd ever wanted.

He let out his breath in a rush, the air hissing between his teeth as he stared up at the brilliant star above, wondering why the sight of it had drawn him out of his room, down the path away from the hotel, and led him *there*. The goddamned glasshouse, of all places, where he had such vivid memories of her, memories that time would never erase.

Instead of celebrating his success, he'd sat on the same bench he'd shared with her a year ago, and wallowed in his sadness. What kind of fool did that make him?

A masochistic one, he realized.

If only he could make a wish on that star—just one. He wouldn't wish for fame or fortune. He wouldn't wish for success. No, he'd wish for Miranda, for one more chance. He stared up at the bright, twinkling glow, concentrating, focusing hard, picturing her the last time he'd laid eyes on her, dashing down the thickly wooded path toward Holly's Close.

His heart began to race, his hands clenched into fists by his sides as he remembered her touch, her taste, her smell.

And then with a silent curse of frustration, he dropped his gaze, despising his own weakness. Why did he continue to torture himself? It was time to go. Perhaps he'd have that celebratory drink, after all.

As Miranda drew near the glasshouse's entrance, she forced her feet to slow. She stopped a mere yard away, silently cursing her eagerness, her foolishness. Whatever was she expecting to find there?

Just more memories of him, that's all. And yet . . . and yet she wanted to go inside, to face them, to sit on the same bench as before, God help her. She tipped her gaze to the sky once more, surprised to see that the snow had stopped falling.

The breeze stirred, caressing her cheek with damp, cold air, causing a shiver to work its way down her spine. If only the bright star above was the proverbial wishing star! She'd wish for one chance—just one more—to see him, to hear him, to touch him. *To taste him.*

A single tear spilled from her eye, feeling blisteringly hot against her icy cheek. *I'll go inside where it's warm and sit for a spell,* she told herself, nodding resolutely. *I can do this.*

She would make her decision where Thomas Bell was concerned. Once and for all, she would find her way past the memories of Troy, and move on.

Troy retrieved his coat from the back of the bench and shoved his arms through the sleeves. Just as he took a step away from the bench, a sound near the door, barely audible over the gurgling fountain, made him pause, his fingers frozen on one round button.

He could have sworn he heard footsteps, quick and light, coming toward him. Some other poor soul searching for solitude, he decided, his fingers resuming their task on his coat's buttons. Well, the place was all theirs. He was done, finished.

He made his way around the fountain, quickening his pace as he joined the main path that led back toward the entrance. He took perhaps ten steps when he stopped dead in his tracks, all the breath leaving his lungs in a rush.

I must be dreaming.

He blinked several times, sure that he was losing his mind, that his eyes were playing tricks on him. They had to be. Because he could've sworn that there in the path directly ahead of him—as still as a statue and staring back at him with widened eyes, one hand clamped over her mouth—was Miranda Granger.

His heart began to pound furiously, his blood racing through his veins at a dizzying speed. It wasn't possible. It was a mirage, some cruel joke his mind was playing on him. There was no other rational explanation. *Bloody hell and holy fuck.* He was hallucinating!

"Troy?" the vision called out. "Dear God in heaven, it can't be."

"Miranda?" he croaked pitifully, taking a tentative step toward her and then pausing, terrified that the vision would disappear like a wisp of smoke if he got any closer. "Please tell me I'm not imagining this," he begged, squeezing his eyes shut. "Please. I don't think I could bear it."

"If you're imagining it, then I am, too," came her reply. He opened his eyes, but the vision was still there, staring at him as if she were seeing a ghost.

In an instant, he closed the distance between them, gathering her in his arms. He could feel her entire body tremble as he clutched her tightly against his chest, fighting the urge to kiss her senseless.

Just because she was there—miraculously there, as if he'd somehow magically summoned her— didn't mean anything had changed between them, after all. He had to be cautious, careful. He would not risk raising his hopes, just to have them cruelly dashed again.

"I can barely believe it," she murmured, her

voice muffled against his coat. "I asked for a sign, and then I saw the star, up above. I followed it, wishing for you, wanting you the whole time."

Troy couldn't quite grasp what she was saying, couldn't make sense of it. "I'm here," was all he said, boldly pressing his lips against her temple, wanting more than anything to snatch away the damp woolen cap she wore and bury his face in her sweet-smelling hair.

She took a step away from him, clutching the lapels of his coat as she stared up at him pleadingly. "I need to sit down. I . . . I feel faint."

"Of course," he said, taking her by the elbow and leading her back toward the bench he'd occupied only moments ago. "Perhaps you're too warm. Let me take your coat."

Wordlessly, she allowed him to unbutton her coat and slip it from her shoulders. He felt a bead of perspiration slide down his neck, and released her long enough to remove his own coat, laying them both across the back of the bench.

There it was again, that sense of déjà vu.

"Sit," he ordered, taking both her shaking hands in his.

Mute now, she obeyed, her eyes blinking rapidly, as if she were trying to focus them.

"How are you?" he asked, knowing it wasn't sufficient, wasn't half of what he wanted to ask.

"I . . . I'm well," she stammered. "And you?"

"Well enough, I suppose. What in God's name are you doing here at the Grandview?"

"We came to spend Christmas here, my father and sisters and I. Whatever are *you* doing here?"

He ignored her question. After all, what could he say? 'I came here to get over *you?*' "I never expected to see you again," he said instead.

She shook her head. "Nor I you."

"My God, Miranda." He took a deep breath, unable to staunch his curiosity another second. "After your telegram—" He broke off, unable to complete the sentence.

"My telegram?" she asked, her brow knitted. "What telegram?"

"The one you sent to New York—your reply to my letters. I know I was persistent, but damn it, Miranda, after everything—"

"What letters?" she interrupted. "I never received any letters."

It was his turn to be confused. "My letters. I wrote you, over and over again for nearly two months, hoping you'd understand why I had to stay in New York, why my family needed me."

She shook her head. "I didn't even know you were in New York, Troy. Have you any idea what I thought, what I imagined? Why, I'd just confessed my most painful secret to you. And then the very next day you left, without even telling me why."

His heart accelerated in alarm. What the hell was she talking about? "I came by Holly's Close, just before I left, to tell you in person. But since you were out and Sir William would have none of it, I left a letter with your sister—"

"My sister? Dear Lord, no. No," she repeated, shaking her head. "Gertie?"

"Yes, Miss Gertrude promised to see that you got my letter straightaway. It didn't feel right, entrusting it to her, but I hadn't a choice but to leave right then. My sister had already arranged passage on the *Lusitania,* sailing from Southampton the very next day. It could not wait. Just as I said in my letter."

"I never got your letter," she said, her voice a hoarse whisper. "Gertie, she . . . I don't know what she did with it, but I never received it. I waited for you the next day at the swimming pond. And then you were gone, and I hadn't any idea why."

"But . . . but the other letters? How could she have possibly have kept all my letters from you, the ones I posted from New York?"

"I have no idea." She let out her breath in a rush. "Though I did notice that she became eager to collect the post after you left. I just assumed that she was hoping to hear from Edmund."

An enormous weight lifted from his chest. She'd never even gotten his letters, which meant . . . "And the telegram? Devil take it, you didn't send it, did you?"

Tears had gathered in her eyes, clinging to her lashes before she blinked them away. "I hadn't any idea where to find you had I wanted to send a telegram. What did it say?"

"Not to contact you again. Not to write, and

never to return to Weckham. And like a prideful fool, I heeded your request. Damn it, I should have kept trying. I should not have given up so easily. All this time, you had no idea . . ."

She pulled her hands from his grasp, flexing them before clasping them together in her lap. "I went to London in the early fall, with my father," she said, her voice hard now. "I called on your aunt Agnes in Wrotham Road. She told me that you had gone to New York, and told me why you remained there still. She told me about your mother's death, and your father's illness. I'm so very sorry, Troy."

He swallowed hard, nodding silently.

"But there was more, wasn't there?" she continued on. "So much more that I didn't know, that you didn't see fit to tell me."

His heart accelerated alarmingly. Had Agnes told her?

Her gaze met his, her brown eyes seemingly shadowed now, filled with distrust. "You're not the man I thought you were. You lied to me from the moment we met, Troy DeWitt."

He felt it, like a physical blow to the gut. "Surely you must understand why I did," he said. "Why I had to. And you must know I would have told you the truth—"

"When, Troy? When you decided I'd made a big enough fool of myself? When you decided you could trust me? When you finally tired of toying with me? You must tell me when, because I cannot for the life of me—"

"The very next day, damn it." He slammed a fist down on the bench's wooden slats. "I planned to tell you everything the very next day, at the swimming pond. You must believe me. I was so determined to make my own way, to make my own name. No one knows the truth, not Sébastien, not Marcus. Not even François. Only Agnes."

"I would not have exposed you. Surely you knew that. Of course you did," she said with a nod. "And still, you let me go on believing the lie, making a fool of myself in the process."

"I wanted you to care for *me*," he bit out. "The man inside, irrespective of my name, my fortune. Is that so very much to ask? It would seem that you, of all people, should be sympathetic to such a notion as that." He reached for her hand, but she tugged it from his grasp.

"And yet you knew that was the biggest obstacle standing between us, your lack of wealth. You knew that I had to be wary, knew that my father would never accept a penniless painter. And yet you allowed me to continue to believe—"

"Don't you see the double standard, Miranda?" he interrupted angrily. "I shouldn't want you for your money, but you would not have me, penniless."

"I *would* have had you, penniless," she cried out hotly. "I would have told you so, if only you hadn't left. I would have had you no matter what my father or anyone else had to say about it."

Just like that, his anger evaporated. She was

speaking the truth—he would have staked his life on it. He reached for her hand again, and this time she allowed it.

"So there you have it," he said, squeezing her hand, not wanting to ever let her go. "I would have told you the truth, and you would have had me regardless. I suppose all we can do is take the other's word for it. Or not," he added when she didn't respond. Instead, she stared down at their joined hands, blinking rapidly.

"Miranda." He released her hand and grasped her chin, tipping her head up, forcing her gaze to meet his. It was now or never; he had to seize this chance, had to tell her exactly what was in his heart. "Dear God, Miranda, don't you see? I'll be whatever you want, whomever you want. If you want Troy Davenport, then that's who I'll be. I'll continue on just as I am now, making my own way in the world. But if it's Troy DeWitt you want instead, well . . . I can give you that. I can give you that life, if that's what you desire."

He let out his breath in a rush, realizing the truth in his words. He'd go back to that world—willingly—if it was the only way he could have her. "I love you, Miranda. All you have to do is tell me what you want. *Who* you want."

Just have me, he silently added. *Please, just say you'll have me.*

Miranda nearly choked on a sob, her heart swelling with such love that it felt as if it might burst. Everything made sense now, every last bit of it. He *did* love her, and he would have told her the truth—she believed it, with all her heart. And in the end, it really didn't matter, didn't make a bit of difference what his surname was or wasn't.

And if not for Gertie—

She sucked in her breath, refusing to think of her sister's betrayal. She would deal with Gertie later.

"Do you really believe that of me, Troy?" she asked, once she'd finally found her voice again. "That I'd ask you to give up who you are? Give up your pride, and go back to a life that you willingly left behind? No," she said firmly. "No, I want you just as you are. I fell in love with Troy Davenport. I . . . I don't even know Troy DeWitt."

For a moment, he didn't speak. She saw him swallow, saw his Adam's apple bob, saw a flicker of surprise in his green gaze. At last, the most dazzling of smiles spread across his face, lighting it up from within. "Trust me," he said at last, "Troy DeWitt's a stuffy old chap, and not nearly as much fun as Troy Davenport. Though he does dress far more smartly than this, I suppose."

She couldn't help but laugh, wiping tears from her eyes as she did so. "Dear God, but I've missed you."

That mischievous, boyish glint was back in his eyes. "Not half as much as I've missed you. In fact, why don't you come with me, back to my room, and I'll show you just how much."

She just stared at him, her common sense battling with her desire.

Just as quickly, his smile disappeared, replaced

with a serious earnestness now. "Please, Miranda," he begged, his voice low now, almost gruff. "Please come with me and stay the night."

She nodded, entirely uncaring of the consequences. All that mattered was that he was back again—in her life, in her heart.

He rose, tugging her to her feet. "You can't even imagine how I've dreamt of this," he said, pulling her close, his head bent toward hers.

"Oh, I've the idea of it," she answered, rising on tiptoe, desperate to feel his mouth on hers. It had been too long, after all—far too long.

His lips met hers, so tender, so exquisitely gentle. He groaned, pulling her more tightly against him as he opened his mouth against hers— tasting, teasing, nipping.

This was exactly where she wanted to be, she realized, reaching up to twine her fingers in the hair at the nape of his neck, drawing him closer still. Exactly where she belonged.

"My beautiful Miranda," he murmured, tracing her bottom lip with his tongue, sending shivers of delight up her spine, gooseflesh racing across her skin.

"Hey, what's this?" a voice boomed out.

Startled, Miranda nearly leapt away from Troy, her heart beating wildly.

"Eh, just a greenhouse, Ernie," came a second voice, sounding bored. "Let's go, it's almost midnight."

Troy muttered a curse beneath his breath. "I don't believe it. Not again."

"Aw, I just want to take a quick look around," came the first voice, moving closer.

Miranda slapped a hand over her mouth, suppressing a laugh.

"Let's go," Troy whispered, snatching their coats off the bench and reaching for her hand. They took off at a jog, laughing gaily as they ran past the two men standing near the entrance.

"Cripes!" one called out, jumping out of the path in surprise.

"Looks like some lucky chap just got some Christmas cheer," the other replied, his voice laced with amusement.

Out into the cold winter's night they ran. The snow had begun to fall again, swirling around them as they made their way back to the hotel, pausing near the back stairs.

"I'll go on ahead," Troy said, leaning down to whisper in her ear. "Room 214, same as before. Wait a few minutes, and then follow me."

Miranda just nodded, squeezing his hand. He glanced around to make sure no one was about, then kissed her fully on the lips before releasing her hand and dashing inside.

Chapter 26

Miranda waited several more minutes, until she could stand it no longer. Straightening her hat, she hurried inside, schooling her features into a placid mask as she made her way through the lobby, past the Christmas tree, and down the deserted corridor, ever conscious of the click of her heels against the marble-tiled floor.

Please, don't let anyone see me, anyone that I'm acquainted with. Let them all be safely tucked in bed by now, visions of sugarplums dancing in their heads.

When she at last let herself into room 214, Troy was right there to take her into his welcoming arms, resuming their kiss as if they'd never been interrupted.

Only, there was an urgency now that wasn't there before. Troy half stumbled back toward the bed, dragging Miranda with him. As soon as the back of his legs touched the mattress, he stopped, releasing her long enough to shrug out of his overcoat.

Miranda followed suit, removing her coat and hat and tossing them carelessly to the floor. Troy had already begun removing his coat, then waist-coat when she reached up to his necktie, discarding it herself while he stared down at her, his eyes darkened with desire.

"I can't get you out of these clothes fast enough," he murmured.

Miranda smiled at that, taking a step away from him. "Just see to your own, then."

Almost as if in a race, they both began removing their garments, one at a time. Miranda's boots. Troy's oxfords. Troy's white cotton shirt, unbuttoned and discarded. Miranda's belt. Troy's braces. Miranda's blouse. Troy's undershirt.

And then he smiled. "This really isn't fair, is it? I'm down to my trousers, and I'd wager you've still a half dozen layers to go, probably more."

"Likely so," Miranda said with a nod, a flush heating her skin.

"Then perhaps you won't mind if I sit here"—he lowered himself to the bed—"and watch as I wait for you to catch up."

Miranda just shrugged, hurrying to unfasten her skirt and shove it down. She stepped out of it, then tossed it aside before unbuttoning the tiny row of buttons on her camisole and slipping it down her arms.

From the bed, he watched her, his arms folded across his bare chest. He looked so very hand-some, so beautiful, that he nearly took away her breath. Distracted from her task, her gaze swept appreciatively across the planes of his chest, down the thin trail of hair that bisected his abdomen, down to his narrow hips. Forcing her gaze back up to his expectant one, she hurriedly untied the tapes of her waist petticoat and slipped it down, then unhooked her stockings from her garters and removed them, one at a time.

That left her corset and frilly combinations—no more. "Can you?" she murmured, moving to stand directly in front of him, presenting him with her back.

A small gasp parted her lips when he tugged on her corset's lacings. Slowly, the garment loosened, allowing Miranda to fully fill her lungs now. At last, he began to slip it down, over her hips.

She turned, allowing it to fall to the floor with a *thump* before stepping out of it. "I think we're just about even now," she murmured, reaching for him, for his trousers' fastenings.

He rose, helping her, stepping out of his trousers, leaving him in nothing save his own drawers, his erection unmistakable.

"Come here," he said, drawing her toward him, his mouth moving to her shoulder. Shoving aside her combinations' lacy straps, his mouth moved to her collarbone, his breath warm against her skin.

One hand skimmed down her side, over her hip before moving between her thighs, toward the slit in her drawers. His fingers pushed aside the fabric, finding her flesh, parting her folds, slipping inside her.

"Miranda," he groaned, his lips shoving down the fabric covering her breasts, searching for one nipple as he drew his finger out of her slick sex, then slowly slipped it back inside again. He began to stroke her—faster, harder—at the same time tracing her nipple with his tongue, dragging it over the sensitive peak again and again.

With his free hand, he tugged down her vest, fully exposing both breasts now, his mouth moving from one to the other as Miranda stood there trembling, her legs growing weak.

She was suddenly desperate to feel his skin against hers, to feel the tip of him pressing against her entrance. All this time, they'd tantalized one another, touching and stroking, tasting and teasing. She wanted more, wanted to feel him inside her.

"I've thought of this every night since meeting you on the *Mauretania*," she said, her voice husky and low. "I've imagined what you'd feel like, moving inside me."

His mouth left her breasts, moving up to her neck, to the spot below her ear where her pulse leapt. "Mmm," he murmured against her neck. "Did you know I haven't laid a hand on another woman, not once, not since the day I first laid eyes on you?"

Miranda's breath caught in surprise. It had been how long? Well over a year, and they'd been apart more often that not. All those months in New York . . .

"It's been only you, from the moment we met," he continued, trailing kisses across her chin, moving toward her mouth. "There will never be anyone but you, Miranda. Never."

Unable to wait a single second longer, she tugged at his drawers, shoving them down past his hips till the tip of him was exposed—glistening with desire. Nipping at his lower lip with her teeth, she reached into his drawers to wrap her hand around the length of him, silky and smooth, hard and ready.

She stroked him once, twice, imagining him inside her.

"Dear God, Miranda," he said with a groan, his head tipped back, the corded muscles in his neck standing out. "If you keep at that, I'll never last. We've got all night, you know."

Abruptly, he reached his arms around her, pulling her to the bed. Rolling her onto her back, he began to slip down her combinations. She raised her hips off the mattress, allowing him to remove her underclothes fully before he hurriedly stripped off his own drawers and braced himself above her.

A lock of his bronze hair fell across his forehead, and Miranda reached up, shoving it back, caressing his cheek as her hand fell away. His eyes—so startlingly green, so clear and expressive—met hers questioningly.

"I haven't any protection," he murmured. "I

wasn't expecting . . ." He shook his head. "Never in a million years did I think I would find you here, did I expect this to happen."

Miranda's heart began to race, a reminder of her old fears. "It's . . . it should be relatively safe right now." Her monthly courses had only just ended, just days before.

He nodded, the lock of hair falling back across his forehead. "I would say that it doesn't matter, because truly, Miranda, it doesn't. But after what that bastard—" He broke off, wincing.

"Troy," she whispered, reaching up to cup his cheek with her palm. "You're not him. You're so much more, so much better than him."

"Marry me, Miranda," he said abruptly, turning his face into her hand and kissing her palm. "I know you deserve far better than me, but by God, I'll make you happy. I know I haven't done this properly—"

"You've done it perfectly, Troy." Her heart soared, happiness flooding her veins. Never in all her years had she been this happy, this content, this sure of her own path. "Yes, I'll marry you. You," she added. "Troy Davenport. I'll go wherever you go, wherever your muse leads you. We can live like gypsies, for all I care."

He nodded, his gaze holding hers with such intensity that Miranda could barely breathe. "I *will* take care of you. I would never let you want for anything."

Tears welled in her eyes. "Of course you'll take

care of me, Troy. And I'll take equally good care of you."

The smile with which he rewarded her nearly stilled her heart, it was so glorious. So very beautiful, so filled with sincerity, with love.

He nodded, fitting himself between her parted thighs. "Yes?" he asked, pressing against her sex now.

She nodded. "Yes."

With one thrust, he buried himself inside her. "Perfect," he murmured, his lips against her cheek as he began to move inside her. "I should have known you'd be perfect."

Miranda clasped his buttocks, drawing him closer, her nails digging into his flesh as they sought a delicious rhythm. It didn't take long before her breath came faster, till she raised her hips off the mattress to meet his thrusts, till she tossed her head from side to side, biting her lower lip to keep from crying out as she came closer and closer to release.

And then she found it—wave after wave of pleasure washed over her—exquisite, temporarily stealing away her breath as she arched off the mattress, her entire body quivering.

"Miranda," Troy groaned in response, stiffening above her. His eyes never leaving hers, he clutched her tightly as his hot seed spilled inside her.

And then he collapsed against her, his heart thumping against hers as they both sought to catch their breath. A moment later, he rolled off her. Drawing her against his side, he pulled up the bedclothes, tucking them gently about her.

A sated Miranda could no longer staunch her curiosity as he wrapped one arm about her shoulder, pressing his lips against her hair. "Would you think me terribly rude if I asked you your age?" she asked.

He glanced down at her with a smile. "You've already agreed to marry me, you know."

Solemnly, she nodded. "I know."

His eyes positively glowed with amusement. "Be warned, you can't take it back, just because you don't like my answer."

Whatever did he mean by that? She'd always known he was younger than her, though she hadn't supposed the age difference to be vast. What if she'd miscalculated? What if—

"We came to an agreement already, after all," he went on, and her heart sped up in genuine alarm.

She sat up abruptly, clutching the bedsheets to her breasts. "Good God, Troy! Just how young *are* you?"

He laughed, his eyes aglow with mischief. "I'll be twenty-six tomorrow. Well, in a matter of minutes, I suppose. It must be nearly midnight by now."

"Your birthday is on Christmas Day?"

He nodded. "My mother always called me her Christmas miracle—I arrived several weeks early, I'm told. Never been one to follow the rules."

"Twenty-six," she murmured, considering it. That wasn't *so* very young, she supposed. Only three years' difference. Why, if their ages were reversed, if she were the younger part of the equation, no would even think twice about it.

"It doesn't make a bit of difference, you know," he said, tracing an invisible line from her collarbone down to her stomach.

She swallowed a lump in her throat. "Most people would say you're too young to settle down and take a wife. Especially one of . . . of an advanced age."

"Then most people don't know their arse from their elbow. And good God, Miranda—an 'advanced age'? You're not yet thirty."

"Caro told you, I suppose."

He nodded. "Not that it mattered. I'd want you just the same if you were forty. Fifty, even. Let me turn out the lights," he said, rising from the bed.

"Hmmm," was all she said in reply, growing drowsy. Her lashes fluttered shut as she smiled to herself, remembering that she had all night with him—an entire *life* with him. Sighing contentedly, she snuggled deeper beneath the bedclothes.

"Look at that," he said, and Miranda opened her heavy eyes to see him standing at the window, holding back the drapes as he gazed out at the night. "The carolers have moved outside, just beneath the Christmas star. It's still there, as bright as ever."

Miranda sat up, listening closely, barely able to make out the strains of one of her favorite Christmas hymns. She watched as he dropped the drapes back against the glass and strode back to the bed. "That star," she murmured. "It's *our* Christmas miracle."

"I suppose it is. Happy Christmas, Miranda," he said softly, pressing his lips to her temple as he settled himself back on the pillows beside her.

"Happy Christmas, Troy," she replied, snuggling against his chest as the carolers' voices grew louder, raised in joyous song.

> *"Look now! for glad and golden hours*
> *Come swiftly on the wing.*
> *O rest beside the weary road,*
> *And hear the angels sing!"*

Books by Bestselling Author
Fern Michaels

___The Jury	0-8217-7878-1	$6.99US/$9.99CAN
___Sweet Revenge	0-8217-7879-X	$6.99US/$9.99CAN
___Lethal Justice	0-8217-7880-3	$6.99US/$9.99CAN
___Free Fall	0-8217-7881-1	$6.99US/$9.99CAN
___Fool Me Once	0-8217-8071-9	$7.99US/$10.99CAN
___Vegas Rich	0-8217-8112-X	$7.99US/$10.99CAN
___Hide and Seek	1-4201-0184-6	$6.99US/$9.99CAN
___Hokus Pokus	1-4201-0185-4	$6.99US/$9.99CAN
___Fast Track	1-4201-0186-2	$6.99US/$9.99CAN
___Collateral Damage	1-4201-0187-0	$6.99US/$9.99CAN
___Final Justice	1-4201-0188-9	$6.99US/$9.99CAN
___Up Close and Personal	0-8217-7956-7	$7.99US/$9.99CAN
___Under the Radar	1-4201-0683-X	$6.99US/$9.99CAN
___Razor Sharp	1-4201-0684-8	$7.99US/$10.99CAN
___Yesterday	1-4201-1494-8	$5.99US/$6.99CAN
___Vanishing Act	1-4201-0685-6	$7.99US/$10.99CAN
___Sara's Song	1-4201-1493-X	$5.99US/$6.99CAN
___Deadly Deals	1-4201-0686-4	$7.99US/$10.99CAN
___Game Over	1-4201-0687-2	$7.99US/$10.99CAN
___Sins of Omission	1-4201-1153-1	$7.99US/$10.99CAN
___Sins of the Flesh	1-4201-1154-X	$7.99US/$10.99CAN
___Cross Roads	1-4201-1192-2	$7.99US/$10.99CAN

Available Wherever Books Are Sold!
Check out our website at www.kensingtonbooks.com